The COLOR of DUST

CLAIRE ROONEY

Bella
BOOKS
2009

Bella Books, Inc.
P.O. Box 10543
Tallahassee, FL 32302

Printed in the United States of America on acid-free paper
First Edition

Editor: Cindy Cresap
Cover Designer: Linda Callaghan

ISBN 10: 1-59493-144-5
ISBN 13: 978-1-59493-144-4

This book is dedicated to:
The untold millions of beloved partners, companions and spouses
whose names are still not written into the family tree.

Author's note

The town of Columbia on the James is a real place. However, at the time of this writing, my description of it is entirely fictional. If you visit, don't blink, and bring your own lunch.

Acknowledgments

A special thank you to Joe Manning and the Glenmore Hunt Club of Staunton, Virginia, for letting me tag along and to all the wonderful gyps and hounds who let me hear their voices.

To my ever-revolving number of cats who were absolutely no help whatsoever in the writing of this novel, especially whichever one of you clawed your way through the library's copy of *The History of Richmond*. You owe me, fur ball.

To my Forum Family with my apologies for failing to slip a duck in here somewhere.

To Katherine Forrest, Claire McNab, P.J. and all my fellow Lambda Emerging Writer workshop participants. I still love you.

To Cindy Tingen, Connie Duncan and the Gaston Group though our paths don't cross as often as they did.

To my family for not being overly horrified by my first book and especially Sarah for the insider's view of Chicago.

To Anita who loved this story.

To Lesa who didn't.

And not least, to my darling wife—not that I have one, I've just always wanted to say that.

To the indefatigable Mary Thompson who made me run all the way to the top of the freakin' mountain and then told me she was afraid of heights.

About the Author

Claire Rooney lives on the East Coast and divides her time between the mountains and the sea. During the day, she moonlights as an analyst, holding a degree in computer science with a minor in creative writing. At night, she comes home to an ever revolving number of critters and works hard until the wee hours writing and trying to keep cat paws off the keyboard. Claire has been a frequent collaborator and contributor to Sister Speak, a literary journal and was the guest editor in 2007. She is, at this time, far enough over forty for it to be rude for you to ask and 100 percent certain that gravity works. But she's still cute as a button. Check out her Web site for news and events at www. clairesbooks.com.

CHAPTER ONE

The rich cream-colored envelope looked out of place in Carrie's mailbox, tucked in between a bright orange flyer good for one free kung fu lesson and a shiny booklet full of buy-one-get-one-free pizza coupons. She shut and locked the door of the box without pulling any of it out. It had not been a good day. Summer came early this year and it was turning out to be a hot one on the bright streets of Chicago. The glare of the sun off all the mirrored glass kept giving her a headache, and the heat rising from the concrete sucked the rest of the life right out of her. She didn't have the energy to deal with any more crap, especially of the paper variety. It had been a trying day, full of irritations and frustrations, snippy e-mails from her clients and irksome memos from her new boss.

She paused with the mailbox key dangling in her hand. What if it wasn't crap?

Carrie shoved the key back into the lock, opened the door and pulled the letter out. The envelope was thick and stiff with its own importance, an arrogant missive with fancy scrollwork decorating the front. *Bell, Dumfries & Howe, Attorneys at Law* the return address intoned in its fancy, pompous font. Her name was written on the face in a bold flow of curling ink. Miss Carrie J. Bowden, 77 West Erie Street, 908-A, Chicago, IL. The faded pink postmark was from some smeared place in Virginia.

She felt like banging her head against the front panel of the mailboxes. Hard. Repeatedly. But that wouldn't solve anything, and she already had a headache. This hot and ugly June was turning out to be the worst month of her life. At work, she had been stuck with a new hypermasculine, superhomophobic boss. At home, the problem was Megan and the bunny girl and then, insult to injury, she lost the fight over the cat. Now, here was some ominous looking letter sure to be full of fresh disasters. God only knew what it was. Maybe some ex-tourist from Podunk, Virginia, was suing her for bumping into them on the subway or stepping on their toe or poking them in the ass with her umbrella and causing them mental anguish, pain and suffering. Or some such shit.

She didn't have the strength to open the envelope. Carrie tossed the circulars into the trashcan and slipped the letter into her handbag. The top to her ChapStick was missing, and it smeared a gooey line across the tips of her fingers. She almost wiped her hand on her pants before she remembered that she was still in her good clothes. That was a stain she didn't need on top of the coffee she dribbled into her lap that morning. Carrie fumbled around inside her bag trying to find a tissue, but she only came up with loose change and cracker crumbs that stuck to the smears on her fingers.

Fine. Whatever. She would just go upstairs to her dim, drab, mostly empty, very lonely, nearly abandoned apartment, wash her hand, reheat yesterday's Chinese food, eat and then go to bed. Alone. Without Megan and without the cat. She closed the door of her mailbox and locked it again. Maybe tomorrow would be a better day. Or maybe it wouldn't. She shuffled her tired feet over to the elevator and punched the button. Her finger left waxy cracker crumbs on the up arrow, but it didn't light. She punched the button again and then looked up. The sign on the doors said *Closed for Maintenance* and, of course, Carrie lived on the ninth floor.

CHAPTER TWO

The town was just a tiny dot on the map about an inch away from Richmond on an outside bend of the James River, but from her hotel on the outskirts of the city, it had taken Carrie nearly three hours and two wrong turns to get there.

She drove slowly down Fayette Street for the second time in the last two minutes. It was a very small town, about ten city blocks long and only about six blocks deep. Small clapboard sided houses dotted the back streets with scraggly rhododendrons bordering tiny square patches of lawn. The town seemed to have everything it needed. Along Main Street, she had seen a grocery store, a diner, a movie rental place and one fast-food restaurant of some odd variety that she had never heard of before, but they served a decent burger and a generous cup full of crisp, skinny fries with a friendly smile. The street itself was a broad, blacktopped boulevard with bricked sidewalks and antique-looking streetlamps. Small shops lined the road in two rows of three-story cinderblock buildings. The broad front windows of the buildings all had badly painted signs that advertised healthcare items, secondhand clothes or today's luncheon special at Danni's Diner: BLT, chips and a Coke for $3.99. The lawyer's office was not hard to find. It was the only one.

Bell, Dumfries & Howe, Attorneys at Law said the sign painted across the storefront window in letters that arched over a bad rendition of vaguely lopsided scales. The building looked old with white paint peeling off a red brick façade. It had a wooden door at the entrance, brass hinged, with a knocker in the shape of a lion's head. A shiny brass plaque repeated their names in a flourishing script and announced the hours of business: 9:00 a.m. to 5:00 p.m. Monday through Friday.

Carrie slid her car into the space reserved by the front door, shoved the gear into park and unbuckled her seat belt. She pulled the letter out of the glove compartment and read it one more time. The words hadn't changed since she made her decision back in Chicago. Coming to Virginia seemed like a good idea when she was sitting alone in her apartment on the bright square spot of carpet where her couch had once been. Now that she was here, she wasn't as sure. It could be a trick, some elaborate hoax designed to…To do what? What would anybody want from her? She didn't have a lot of money. She didn't have important family. She didn't have any family at all, anymore. She wasn't exceptionally pretty. She was just an average kind of middle-class person of middling height with medium length muddy brown hair. She was not too tall, not too short, not too skinny, not skinny enough. Just an average kind of schmo. Not too bad, but not really very good either. She was not anything anyone would want, particularly.

She thought of Megan and then wished she hadn't. Megan had wanted her, once upon a time, but it had been almost six months since the day their argument turned a different kind of ugly and everything went so very wrong. Carrie touched her fingers to her cheek and felt every second of her nearly thirty years. It seemed, sometimes, that it all happened just yesterday. Sometimes, it seemed like it was a hundred years ago and she could almost feel her old bones crumbling. Thirty wasn't that old, she knew, but she felt old. Megan had made her feel old. Today, she just felt tired and dry. She read the letter through one more time, looking for the trick, the spam, the virus. The paper was thick and bumpy, the printing bold and black. Carrie sighed and folded the letter carefully. She put it back in the envelope and opened the car door to a wave of damp summer heat.

A bell chimed softly when Carrie opened the front door of the law office. A phone rang from somewhere deep inside. An older woman with a short bob of silver gray hair looked up from her computer screen.

"Good afternoon. May I help you?" The woman spoke in a soft lilt of tangled vowels.

Carrie squeezed her purse in tighter against her side. "I have an appointment to see Mr. Dumfries. I'm Carrie Bowden."

The woman looked at her for just a fraction too long before she smiled and got up. She pointed to a plush armchair beside a table piled high with crisp new magazines. "Please have a seat. I'm sure Mr. Dumfries will be with you right away." She disappeared down a dark paneled hallway with a fast swishing of her skirt. Before Carrie picked up her first magazine, the woman came back and ushered her down the same hallway. She showed her into a spacious office full of neatly lined bookshelves and red leather chairs.

Mr. Dumfries sat behind a large ornate desk. He was an older gentleman, his grizzled hair tending mostly to gray, his long face descending into droops and jowls. He stood slowly when she came into the room and limped out from behind the desk with a hand outstretched.

"Miss Bowden." His voice was rumbly without being particularly deep. He shook her hand warmly and studied her with eyes that were bright and clear underneath the tired sag of his upper lids.

"Welcome to Columbia on the James. I can't tell you how glad we were to hear from you so we can finally put this matter to rest. Would you like some tea?" He turned to the open door and yelled at the hallway. "Gillian! Gillian, some tea for Miss Bowden, if you would be so kind." He let go of Carrie's hand and pointed to a chair beside his desk. He sat himself in the opposite chair with a little hitch of his trouser leg and a grimace that slowly turned into a rueful grin. "Old bones just aren't made for sitting and standing," he said. "Summer's not as bad as winter, but I'm still not sure that getting old is worth the trouble." His smile flashed a yellowish set of small flat teeth.

Carrie didn't know what to say to that. People who hadn't had the chance to get old would probably not agree with him, but she wasn't old enough herself to argue the point. Feeling old wasn't the same thing as being old. She nodded at him and that seemed to be a sufficient answer.

Mr. Dumfries turned in his chair and reached across his desk to pick up a sheaf of papers. "I trust you had a pleasant drive. It's about fifteen hours from here to Chicago, isn't it?"

"Only about thirteen." She could have made it in ten if she had pushed the speed limit to the edge and not stopped for meals, but she didn't like driving like that. Drive-through litter made a mess out of her car, and she always managed to squash a packet of ketchup underfoot. It was a pain in the ass trying to get dried ketchup out of the floor mat.

"Ah, yes." Mr. Dumfries laid the papers across his knees. "I forget how fast you youngsters like to fly. Like time is of the essence." His hands tapped thoughtfully on the top sheet of paper, a blue coversheet with tilde lines and small dense type. "I suppose it is, though, I've always wondered why you young people move through the world like your tails are on fire when you have so much time ahead of you, and yet, we old folk move as slow as molasses even though we're fast approaching the finish line." Mr. Dumfries looked at the blue paper. "But I don't suppose you came all this way just to hear an old man philosophizing."

"No, sir." Carrie clutched her purse tighter as she watched his mouth twitch in a little ghost of a smile.

"So then let's get on with this, shall we?" He flipped a few of the pages back and then looked up at her. "You said when we spoke briefly on the phone that you weren't aware you even had a grandmother. Did I understand that correctly?"

"Yes."

"Well, we're not sure if your grandmother knew she had a granddaughter, but that doesn't change anything. Rest assured that we traced you very carefully. For the sake of propriety, please bear with me as I go over the particulars one more time." Mr. Dumfries took a pair of half-moon glasses from his inside jacket pocket and perched them on his nose. He tipped his head back and held the papers out at arm's length. "You are Carrie Jane Bowden, born September 28, 1980, currently residing in Chicago, Illinois." He looked at her expectantly.

"That's correct."

Mr. Dumfries nodded. "I'll need to see some identification at some point, but all in good time." He looked back down at the papers. "And your mother was Jane Burgess Bowden, of our fair town, Columbia, Virginia, born 1935, died 1982." He stopped reading and peered over the rim of his glasses at her. Deep lines creased the sides of his downturned mouth. "I can't tell you how sorry I was to learn of her passing. I knew your mother, if not well, then at least by acquaintance. I remember her fondly. She was a lovely girl."

Carrie's heart seemed to stutter with a slight hitch in its rhythm, a faint faltering in its stride as it tripped over an old pang. "I don't remember her at all, Mr. Dumfries. I was only two when she died. I didn't even know that this town was where she was born." She tried, not too successfully, to keep the guilt out of her voice. There was so much she never knew about her mother. So many things she never thought to ask.

Mr. Dumfries lowered the papers and put them back on his knees. "You were born late in her life, were you not?"

"Yes. Perhaps…" Carrie looked at her hands. "Or perhaps not." That was not a good line of thought to follow, right here, right now, if ever.

The papers rustled under Mr. Dumfries's hands. "Cancer

takes people of all ages, Miss Bowden, and for all sorts of reasons. One can't argue a cause-and-effect relationship in your mother's case. She, herself, was born late to her parents, and her mother suffered no ill effects at all."

Carrie nodded. It was true, what he was saying, and she knew it, but her small sense of guilt was the only piece of her mother that she still had left. She wasn't willing to let it go on the advice of a stranger, even if it was good advice.

A knock on the door jarred her thoughts. Carrie looked up as a woman came into the room carrying a tray with two tall glasses full of softy clinking ice cubes. Thick slices of lemon were wedged onto the rims.

"Ms. Bowden," the woman said, flashing a warm smile at Carrie. "Welcome to Columbia on the James." She set one glass on the table next to Carrie and the other glass next to Mr. Dumfries's elbow. He gave the woman a light pat on the arm.

Carrie tried not to stare, but it had been quite a while since a woman smiled at her so warmly, with such open and friendly eyes. She couldn't recall any smile ever at all from a woman quite so elegant as this one. The woman wasn't beautiful in the traditional sense, her mouth being a little too wide, her chin a bit too flat, her nose a touch too long, and yet she struck Carrie as being very beautiful, indeed. It might have been the way she carried herself or the way she carried the tea or the way she carried the dress she had on, in soft folds of fabric, neat tucks and pleats that curved in and out at all the right places. Her hair, a dark blond twisted up behind her head in an elaborate braid, made her look very lawyer-like. Suave and professional. A tiny bit scary. The woman lifted an eyebrow just a fraction as her cheeks pinked a little.

Carrie was staring. Maybe with her mouth hanging wide open. Probably drooling all over herself. Undoubtedly, with a look on her face that shouldn't be there for a woman who had only just walked into the room. She dropped her eyes to Mr. Dumfries who was smiling broadly.

"This is Gillian. My daughter." He looked at her with proud eyes. "She's not a lawyer, much to my regret, but she likes to help out here in the office now and then."

Carrie looked at her again. The woman was still smiling, warm and broad.

"It's a pleasure to meet you, Ms. Bowden." She held out her hand and Carrie shook it. It was a real handshake, the tight curl of fingers, the firm press of a thumb, the kiss of palms. "If there's anything else I can get for you, please let me know."

"Thank you. I will." Carrie tried not to smile like a fool, hold her hand too tight or look at her in any other way but a casual one. That was hard. She was used to flirting when she felt like flirting. This woman, Gillian, was certainly worth flirting with, but there was no telling what century this town was living in. It wouldn't be a good idea to irritate the lawyer by offending his daughter in the first thirty minutes she was there. It wouldn't be unlike her, though. Circumspection was not Carrie's strong point. She tended to be a bit too direct, a bit too blunt. She would have to be careful while she was here. The woman, Gillian, walked out of the room, but Carrie didn't watch her go. Instead, she picked up her glass and sipped at the tea. Point for her. And it was good tea, too, if a little on the sweet side.

Mr. Dumfries smiled fondly at the door and then resettled his glasses on his nose. "Gillian is about your age. If, while you're here, you find yourself in need of some girl talk, I'm sure she'd be happy to lend an ear."

Carrie wasn't sure what "girl talk" translated into in this part of the country. For her, it meant something close to "pillow talk," the soft, unguarded conversation that two worn-out woman had when the sun was just starting to lighten the sky. She doubted very much that was what Mr. Dumfries had in mind, but she smiled her thanks as politely as she knew how.

"Now, to continue." He rattled the papers again and shuffled them around on his lap. "Your father, Michael Bowden, no middle name, of Colchester, Connecticut, married your mother in 1953 in Chicago. He died in 2002 with you, yourself, being his sole surviving heir. Do I have that right?"

"Yes." She couldn't swear to the dates, but the names and

places were right.

"To whit, that leaves you as the sole heir to the estate of Celia Covington Burgess, your mother being her only offspring and you being a direct descendant. Is it correct that you have never been married, Miss Bowden? I ask only because, Virginia laws being what they are, your being married or divorced would complicate things a bit."

"I've never married," Carrie said dryly. She would have been married if it were legal. But then again, she would also be in midst of an ugly divorce. A nasty settlement dispute. A custody battle over the cat. So maybe there was a bright side after all. For her, at least.

"Very good." Mr. Dumfries reached for a pen and made a tick mark on the blue paper. "So, you don't have any specific ties to Chicago?"

There was a question underneath the question that Carrie could hear but couldn't quite catch. "I was born and raised in Chicago. I think that counts as some sort of a tie, but I have no other family there, if that's what you mean." Not since Megan left her for a barely-into-her-twenties cocktail waitress with a short skirt and a bunny tail. Not since their ten years together disappeared in the twitch of a nose, the swing of a fist. Their apartment was empty now of anything she cared about, which, at this point, meant the cat. She really missed the cat.

"Have you ever thought about moving to Virginia?"

Carrie sat up straighter. It hadn't occurred to her to think about it. Up until the letter arrived, all she knew about Virginia was that it lay somewhere around the middle of the east coast on the wrong side of the Mason-Dixon Line. She had heard of Mount Vernon, Jamestown, Richmond and Robert E. Lee, though she only had a vague notion of where Mount Vernon was and no idea at all of what the E. stood for. Prior to her arriving here, thoughts of Virginia brought to mind small green mountains and screechy fiddle music played by old men with no teeth.

Even after arriving, she didn't have too different a picture. On her way to Richmond, she drove over and through a series of small green mountains, and Carrie met some interesting people on her drive to Columbia, especially during her wrong turns. Virginia surprised her. She had not been prepared to like the small green mountains and the tall trees that covered them, or the old man in the checkered shirt sitting on the front porch of the convenience store who told her a funny story while his wife laughed with her mouth wide open, slapping him on the knee. It stirred something inside her that she hadn't known was there. She couldn't help but wonder if her grandmother had been a woman like that and what she had missed by not knowing her.

Carrie shook her head hesitantly. "I wasn't thinking about moving. The truth of it, Mr. Dumfries, is that I'm not sure why I drove down here. I had the vacation time and I guess I just wanted to see things for myself."

"An admirable sentiment, Miss Bowden, and a wise decision. I suppose I should get on with showing you the things you drove here to see." Mr. Dumfries paused to take a sip of his tea and then put it back down on the old cork coaster. He shuffled through the papers and pulled out a thick stack, grayish white and stapled at the corner. He handed them to her. The papers had the same small dense type covering all the pages, with whereofs, hereins and therefores scattered all across them. Carrie frowned.

Mr. Dumfries chuckled softly at her expression. "This will was written in 1972, before you were born and before every office in town had a computer sitting on every desk." He cast a disparaging eye at the large flat screen sitting on his credenza. "Your grandmother was eighty-two years old when she wrote that will and she never changed a thing." Mr. Dumfries took off his glasses and pinched at the bridge of his nose. "She was one hundred and eight when she died. Short of the record for this county by only six months and for all of Virginia by only six years. Even so, her death was something of a shock." He put his glasses back on and gave her a thin smile. "We all thought she would outlive the mountains." Mr. Dumfries reached inside his jacket pocket and pulled out a small flat box. "Here are a few of the things that go along with the will." He handed it to Carrie.

She put the will on her lap and opened the box. Inside was a large brass colored key, a small gold ring with stylized flowers etched into it and a very old pocket watch. She picked up the watch and looked at Mr. Dumfries.

He shrugged just a little. "I'm afraid I'm only the keeper of the things. I don't know what they mean exactly. The key, I imagine, is to the front door of the house, but I'm not sure because no one has used the front door since 1953. That was the year your mother ran away to marry your father. The rumor of it is that after your grandmother found her note, she closed up the front part of the house and never went in it again. The pocket watch, I believe, belonged to your grandfather, Robert Burgess. Leastways, his initials are on the back. I have no idea who the ring belonged to or why your grandmother thought it was important."

Carrie put the watch back in the box and looked at the key with some surprise. "She left me a house?"

"Yes." Mr. Dumfries shifted in his chair. "Forgive me if I wasn't clear about that on the phone. There's an old house and a little bit of land to go with it, about twenty-five acres or so. It's detailed on page eight of the will."

Carrie touched the key. It was big, for a key, with fancy scrollwork on the turning end but only three plain teeth on the other end. "Twenty-five acres. Is that a lot?"

Mr. Dumfries pursed his lips and wiggled his hand back and forth. "It depends on what you want it for. It'd be a bit much for a front lawn, but it's a right decent size for a horse or five, though not enough for a herd of cattle. A few goats or sheep would be all right."

A picture flashed across Carrie's mind of herself dressed like Little Bo Peep chasing a flock of fuzzy white lambs bouncing across a bright green pasture. She grinned.

Mr. Dumfries gave her an odd look but he didn't ask. "I'll be happy to drive you out there and show you around. Please keep in mind that it's an old house and it's been sitting empty for a while. It needs a bit of work, but it could be nice if someone put some care into it." His eyes shifted down. "It would be good to see it lived in again."

An old house. The Bo Peep image vanished as Carrie thought of moldy drywall and sagging ceilings, swollen doorframes and wallpaper peeling off the walls. She didn't mind doing some repair work. She was handy with a hammer, knew which end of the screwdriver to hold and was passably efficient with a paintbrush. Maybe, instead of taking the historic tour of Richmond, as she had planned, she would stay here for a week or two, throw on a coat of paint, fix the leaky faucets, patch the drywall and tighten the screws. She could do that. She would even enjoy it. It would be good to be busy.

"There aren't many formalities left," Mr. Dumfries said, pushing his glasses further up onto his nose. "I just need for you to sign a few papers. I can file them with the court first thing tomorrow then we can get to work putting everything in your name and paying off the tax man, etcetera."

Carrie hadn't thought about that. Maybe this was the trick. This could be the part where the kindly old lawyer asked her to empty out her bank account and then stuck her with a tax bill that she would be paying on for the rest of her life. She put a hand back on her purse. "Is there enough money in the estate to cover the expenses?" Carrie watched Mr. Dumfries very carefully.

He blinked at her for a second. "Just flip over to the last page of the will. The estate totals are listed there."

She flipped the pages and froze. There were numbers there that hardly made any sense. "I thought you said there were only twenty-five acres?"

"You asked about the house. Twenty-five acres is what surrounds it. The rest of the land is scattered all over the state. If you add together all the various holdings, it's about four thousand acres in all. Most of the land is rented cropland or pastures, but there are a few more lucrative holdings. Those are leased to companies that have buildings on them and they bring in a bit."

A bit? Lucrative? No shit. Even by Chicago standards, it was a respectable income. Almost three times what she was making shuffling papers around her desk and spending the day avoiding her boss. She wouldn't need that job if she didn't want it. There were choices here and decisions to be made but none to be made lightly. She thought of Megan again and her forever questing for things that were bigger, better, younger, stronger. She would have wanted Carrie to sell everything fast and cheap and run with as much as she could stuff in her pockets back to Chicago. She would have insisted, and Carrie would have fought her, if only for the sake of fighting. It was a good thing that Megan wasn't here with her.

The taste of regret lay sour on her tongue as she thought of the many things they had both done wrong. That was the bad thing. The good thing was that she could take her time deciding what to do. This time she would do the right thing instead of doing the impulsive thing.

Mr. Dumfries cleared his throat. "If you'll just sign and date the back page and initial all the rest. I'll need to make a copy of your driver's license, get your tax ID and then we'll be done here. When you're finished with your tea, I'll drive you out to the house. It's not too far."

CHAPTER THREE

They drove back through town in Mr. Dumfries's big box of a car while he pointed out the things she might need to know about if she was planning on staying for any length of time. There was the city municipal building, the post office, one of two grocery stores and, most important, a hardware store that could put her in touch with good local workmen and that also sold things like buckets, brooms and mops.

They drove south over a long narrow bridge with the gray-blue water of the James River sparkling brightly underneath them. They didn't pass any cars once they got over the river, just farms and houses and trees. Mr. Dumfries drove slowly, well under the speed limit, keeping both hands on the wheel and his eyes on the road. Carrie stared out the window at a herd of cows as they passed by them. A big cow with a bright white stripe around its middle stood by the fence licking a little cow's head. The calf stood with its feet splayed far apart teetering under the rough strokes of its mother's tongue. It staggered, shook its head and looked at her forlornly. They rounded a bend in the road and the cows fell out of sight. Yes, Virginia surprised her in all sorts of ways.

They turned off the main highway, away from the afternoon sun. The road thinned as the pavement changed from a dark black to a pebbly gray, the hum of their tires dropped in pitch, and the farmlands faded into the woods. Carrie thought of the small flat box and the key, the watch and the ring inside it.

"Tell me something about my grandmother's house, Mr. Dumfries."

Mr. Dumfries cleared his throat and shifted his hands on the steering wheel. "The house sits on the inside bend of the river only about a half mile from it, as the crow flies, but it's up high on a ridge, so you don't have to worry about flooding. Even during the last hundred year flood, the water never rose that high. It's about five miles from town as the car drives. That puts you pretty close to everything you need while still being out in the country. If you want to stay at the house instead of at a motel in Richmond, rumor has it that it looks habitable. The electricity and the water are still on."

"Even though the house is empty?"

"We thought we'd get things settled, one way or another, a lot sooner than we did, so we never cut anything off. And it wouldn't do to let the pipes freeze in the winter. We had the old groundsman go around once a week and peek in the windows to make sure nothing had burst or caught on fire."

"But nobody went inside?"

Mr. Dumfries paused. "I suppose I should've given you more time to read the will. It said pretty explicitly that no one was to enter the house until the heir took possession. Your grandmother probably thought that would be your mother." His fingers tapped against the steering wheel. "It didn't end up that way, as you know. No one has gone into the house since the day after your grandmother died. That very evening, the head nurse tidied up a bit, locked the doors, turned in the keys and that was that. We clean up storm damage every once in a while, patched a place

17

on the roof once and were going to replace a window that got broken, but Mr. Bell decided to just have his son board it up from the outside."

Carrie thought again of the large brass key resting in the box. "If my grandmother was dead, what did it matter if anyone went into the house or not?"

Mr. Dumfries seemed to think about that for a moment. "Well, I like to think that I'm an honest sort of a lawyer. I believe strongly in following my client's instructions, even if they're dead, since that's what they pay me to do." His fingers stopped tapping and his shoulders hunched a bit. "Besides, Celia Burgess was a formidable woman. She's the last person I'd want haunting me from the grave." Mr. Dumfries flashed her a quick smile and laughed, but the smile was brittle and the laugh faded into an awkward silence.

Carrie didn't smile. She remembered how strange her father's apartment felt just after he died. It seemed like he was always peering over her shoulder approving or disapproving of everything she touched. Almost three months passed before that feeling went away and she could finally pack his things. Not that there had been much to pack once she trashed all the empty bottles, but she never wanted to go through that again and especially not for a woman she'd never met.

"Just how long has this house been empty, Mr. Dumfries?"

He coughed lightly and the tips of his ears turned pink. "About twelve years."

Her eyes widened with surprise. "Twelve years? It took you all that time to find me?"

Mr. Dumfries cut his eyes toward her but he didn't turn his head. "No, Miss Bowden. It didn't. My predecessor, Mr. Bell, chose to interpret the will's instructions in an unusual way. He argued that the will stated the estate was to rest in the executor's hands unless an heir came forward voluntarily. It wasn't until he retired and I had the opportunity to reread the will that I came to understand his error."

And there was the trick. Carrie felt relieved, almost elated.

She knew there had to be one. Good things didn't happen without bad things to balance them. Still, she gave Mr. Dumfries as hard a look as she could muster. "Was this an error in interpretation or an error in judgment?"

"I imagine the latter would be the more correct." Mr. Dumfries leaned back in the seat, his shoulders slumped rather than hunched. "Please understand, Miss Bowden, that Mr. Bell was a close friend of mine, a mentor and a teacher. He was, for the most part, a good man. It was just that he had these aspirations that weren't entirely in keeping with his means." His mouth turned down in a sharp crease. "You can rest assured that it all came to nothing in the end. He's in a nursing home now and a good day is when he can remember his own name." Mr. Dumfries's voice rumbled deeper than usual, dragged down by the weight of grief.

Carrie understood his sadness. Her father had been a good man caught in a tragic circumstance. It had turned out bad. "I guess even good men do bad things sometimes."

Mr. Dumfries nodded his head slowly. "That is most unfortunately true. There's a full accounting of the fees that Mr. Bell subtracted from the estate. At a later time, you and I can sit down and go over a repayment plan. The firm of Bell, Dumfries & Howe is not a rich one, but I do believe in paying our dues. It is, of course, your option to take further action or to retain other counsel if you should so desire."

Carrie considered his words and the downturn of his mouth that made his long face look even longer. She thought of his daughter, her warm smile and the friendly eyes that seemed so genuine and decided there wasn't any point in getting angry over something that no one present was responsible for doing. "I respect your efforts to put things to rights, Mr. Dumfries. Let's take a look at the house first and then we can decide if any further action is necessary."

Mr. Dumfries turned his head to look at her. He smiled, nodded once and then looked back at the road. "Fair enough. But just to warn you, the grounds are a mess. The grass is knee high to an elephant since we only have it mowed once a quarter, and I truly don't know what the inside is like. I only know that it's not flooded or burnt and the heat still comes on in the winter."

"Did you ever go over and visit my grandmother?"

"Me?" Mr. Dumfries asked. "Lord, no. Other people did, or at least they tried. Mr. Bell went over there occasionally, and the Reverend went over at least once a week, but she would never let either of them inside."

Mr. Dumfries took a hand off the steering wheel to rub at his chin. His face was an odd mix of emotions, most of which clashed. Under his hand, Carrie thought that he looked sadly amused and maybe a little angry with a dash of regret thrown in. No doubt, there were parts to the story that he wasn't going to tell her, but she could tell he was thinking about them.

"I have to say that your grandmother's funeral was just about the saddest thing that I ever did see." Mr. Dumfries put his hand back on the wheel. "She was interred in a cemetery one county over. I was there as her legal representative to make sure her wishes were, for the most part, carried out, and also the three Murray boys were there because they dug the grave. But that was all. She specifically said that she didn't want the Reverend or anybody saying prayers over her or any kind of ceremony performed on her behalf." He tapped at the steering wheel with the palm of his hand. "So, there wasn't any of that, just the practicalities of backhoes, shovels and dirt."

Carrie frowned. Her father's funeral hadn't been much more than that. A priest, his latest drinking buddy and her. "Didn't she have any friends?"

Mr. Dumfries wrapped his hand tight around the wheel again. "She wasn't that kind of person."

"What kind of a person doesn't have friends?" Carrie spoke without thinking. Her words brought a blush to her cheeks. She didn't have any friends anymore after Megan had taken them all with her. What kind of person was she?

Mr. Dumfries shrugged one shoulder. "Your grandmother didn't seem to need anybody or even want anybody around. In her latter years, the nurses were the only people allowed inside the house. She was always solitary to some degree, but as she got older, it got worse and worse. In the end, I hear she was right hard to get along with."

"What about my grandfather? Whatever happened to him?"

"He died about five years after your mother was born, in 1940, I believe. They called it stomach ulcers, but it was probably cancer. A lot of people thought it was a broken heart."

"Can you really die of a broken heart?" Carrie hadn't died. She only felt like she was dying, and that's not the same thing at all.

"Well, now, I suppose anything's possible. It was generally supposed that your grandfather had good cause to die of a broken heart, but no one's quite sure what the whole story was. It was common knowledge that he loved your grandmother something fierce. It was also common knowledge that she didn't see him in quite the same way. He didn't like going anywhere without her, and she seemed to wish he would just go away."

"And no one knew what that was all about?"

"Everyone had a theory. The popular one had to do with her father arranging her marriage to Mr. Burgess. People say that she was such a proud woman she never got over not having her own free choice in the matter. I'm not sure about that, myself. Back in her day arranged marriages for women of her station were the rule and not the exception."

"What's your theory?"

Mr. Dumfries tilted his head and looked puzzled, as if no one had ever asked him that question before. "I don't have one, really. There's just not enough evidence to support a conclusion. I can accept that she didn't love her husband as much as he loved her, but that doesn't explain your mother's part in it all."

"Why? What did my mother do?"

"Not a damn thing, and that was the shame of it. She was a pretty little gal without a mean bone in her body. It was only that she was. As I've said, she came very late in their lives, and the rumor among the house staff was that she was begotten rather harshly. Without your grandmother's consent, as they say." Mr. Dumfries shook his head slowly, his drooping jowls jiggling slightly. "I don't know how much truth there is in that. My father was a foreman in your family's cotton mill before it closed, and he worked closely with Dr. Burgess before he died. He respected him very highly."

Carrie looked out the window at the passing trees. They seemed thick and dark in spite of the bright June sun. "Sometimes good men do bad things," Carrie said again, softly, almost to herself.

Mr. Dumfries nodded his head over the steering wheel. "Yes. Sometimes they do. Whatever the case, there's no denying that something was really wrong with that family. Your grandmother seemed to resent her daughter even more than she did her husband. Still, you just couldn't help but feel sorry for them all."

Mr. Dumfries slowed the car almost to a stop. He turned onto a narrow gravel road half hidden by brush. Overgrown shrubbery reached out with thin-fingered branches to scratch at the sides of the car. Tree limbs hung low overhead while large potholes threatened to bounce them out of their seats. Carrie grabbed for the dash. She held her breath and prayed that the house wasn't as messed up as the driveway. If it was, it would be too big of a job for her to tackle alone. She hoped it wouldn't be. In spite of herself, she was getting interested in this family, in her family, even though they were all dead. Carrie frowned. That sounded weird, even to her.

They swung around a sharp bend in the drive. The road widened out suddenly as the gravel turned to cobblestone. From between the trees, she caught a glimpse of white. One more turn and the trees ended. Carrie froze in her seat, her hands still clutching at the dash.

"Holy shit."

Mr. Dumfries smiled softly and shook his head. "You should've seen it in its heyday, how it looked when I was just a boy, all bright white with lights shining in every window. It was a marvelous thing."

It was still a marvelous thing. The house rose up before them, the very picture of a southern plantation house with the obligatory six columns supporting a large gabled roof that hung over a massive front porch. A porch that looked like it was made for warm summer days full of sitting and rocking, mint juleps and gossip. A more delicate veranda with wrought iron railings ringed the second story, and every window she could see was floor to ceiling with rounded sunburst tops. A stained glass rose window decorated the middle of the large main gable.

It was absolutely marvelous, but as they drove closer, Carrie could see how time sat heavily on the house. The windows were dim and dark. The paint, if it had once been bright white, was now dirty and dull where it wasn't peeling and cracking off the brick. Most of the shutters hung askew. Ancient azalea bushes grew tall and scraggly beside the porch, and all around the house, the grass really was knee high to an elephant. Carrie listened to it brush the undercarriage of the car as they drove slowly over the cobbles.

They pulled into a circular drive that wound around a decaying central fountain where sad cupids tipped empty urns into bone-dry basins. Mr. Dumfries stopped the car near the wide steps leading up to the porch. He shifted the gear into park and sat back in his seat, his hands resting in his lap.

"It's huge." Carrie leaned forward to look out the windshield. The house was more than huge. It was imposing. She was almost afraid to get out of the car. "When you said 'old house' I thought you meant a three bedroom ranch with a sagging roof. I didn't think you meant anything like this." She waved her hand at the porch.

Mr. Dumfries opened his door but didn't make any move to get out of his seat. He stared across the drive, at the overgrown field in front of him, his eyes distant and thoughtful. "In this part of the country when we say 'old' we mean at least a hundred years or more. This house is old even as old houses go. It has a deep history if not a glorious one." He glanced briefly at Carrie and then out at the field again. "It sits on the river, you see. Well, you can't see it from here but you can from the second floor. It's just over and down the rise there." He waved his hand toward the horizon. "The central square of the house was built before the Civil War and both sides, North and South, used it as a supply depot. That's probably why neither side burned it down." Mr. Dumfries shifted his stare over toward the river, his fingers scratching absently at a drooping jowl. "There's an interesting story I've heard told. Just before the battle over Richmond, a Yankee gunboat fired on the house. The cannonball hit one of the columns and left a hole in it. Years later, the bees made a hive in there and then every time someone was stung, they blamed it on 'those damn Yankees'. You can still see the patch way up high on the second column from the right if you look closely."

Carrie looked at Mr. Dumfries. He was rambling and still hadn't made a move to get out. Mr. Dumfries, Carrie realized, was nervous. It was clear that there was much more to his story than he was saying. There was always more to any story than what could be told, but usually the teller left out the parts that didn't matter to the hearer. She wasn't sure that was what Mr. Dumfries was doing. She wasn't sure what he was doing.

Mr. Dumfries swung the car door open a little wider and put one foot gingerly on the ground. "This was such a beautiful place, once upon a time." His voice lost its rumble and took on a wistful timbre. "You can't see much of the land now through all the weeds, but there were formal gardens here once, box hedges and bright flower beds." He waved a hand back toward the trees. "There are still some outbuildings standing that date back to the original structure. There are the remains of the old cook house, a horse barn, a tobacco barn, a smoke house, ice house and such, but I don't imagine they're in very good shape after all this time. Shame about that." Mr. Dumfries turned and put his other foot on the ground but then stopped.

Carrie saw that she would have to be the brave one. The house scared her a bit, but it was only its size that made her nervous and not its history. She opened her door and stood. She took the box from her bag, opened it and took out the key. Dead grass and last year's leaves crunched underfoot as she walked around to Mr. Dumfries's side of the car.

She held up the key. "Shall we go and see if this fits the front door, or is there a better way in?"

Mr. Dumfries stood slowly and shut the car door behind him. He drew himself up as straight as his old back would allow. "It is one of the provisions of the will that the heir would go in first by the front door. I don't know what sense that makes or even if that key will work, but I think we should follow the provisions to the best of our ability." He tugged on the hem of his jacket settling it more firmly on his shoulders.

Carrie looked at the key in her hand. It felt heavier than it should have, like it was made of lead instead of brass. She closed her fingers around it. "Was my grandmother crazy?"

"No." Mr. Dumfries shook his head quickly, fast enough to make his cheeks quiver. "No. She wasn't crazy. Eccentric is more the term. She had both feet on the ground, but..." His eyes went distant again.

"But what?"

"It's hard to explain. I was only in my teens when I had anything to do with her. She was a grown woman with cares and concerns a teenage boy wouldn't know anything about. But it seemed to me like she could only take so much of the world. She'd be moving right along and then something would come over her and she would retreat deep inside the house or out to one of the back gardens. Near the end of her life, she never left her room, not because she couldn't, according to the nurses, but because she didn't want to. She wouldn't see anyone or let anyone see her. It was almost as if she wanted to fade away and be forgotten." Mr. Dumfries glanced over his shoulder toward the river and then back again to the house. "Sad to say that's pretty much what happened."

They walked slowly together toward the front porch. They passed the fountain and Carrie peered inside. The smaller basins were dry, but the main basin held a small pond of stagnant green water. A startled frog hopped off the broken wing of one of the cupids and plopped into the water with a splash. The water rippled and the smell of algae and old rotting things wafted into the air. The dead flowers around the fountain rustled in the light breeze.

She turned and saw Mr. Dumfries waiting for her on the porch. Carrie crossed the drive and climbed the steps slowly, conscious of the dirt and debris her feet were stirring. She thought about how things tended to lay where they'd fallen. Dirt and twigs, leaves and people. Broken wings. She wondered how her relatives ended up here in this specific place, what kind of people they had been, what had become of them and how she ended up being the only one left. She didn't much like the thought of being the only one left.

Mr. Dumfries stood by the front door. "If you would so kindly do the honors." He waved a hand at the doorknob but looked dubiously at the door. "Whenever you're ready, Miss Bowden."

"I'm ready." Carrie fit the key into the lock. It went in easily enough, but it wouldn't turn. She jiggled the key and twisted the handle at the same time. Something gave with a snap. The handle turned and the door swung open. She was expecting a rusty, creaking noise from the hinges, but the door swung open silently. Carrie squinted her eyes and peered into the dim interior. Everything inside was quiet and still.

CHAPTER FOUR

Carrie stepped through the door and into the foyer. Behind her, the sun seemed to fade as the dimness fell across her shoulders. She blinked and waited for her eyes to adjust. They didn't adjust. It wasn't her eyes. She stared all around her. The foyer was two stories tall with a pair of great curving staircases that started on opposite sides of the entranceway, bowed outward and upward and met in the middle as the landing for the second floor. It was a very grand staircase, or would have been if it had not been covered in a thick layer of dust, draped by broken banners of lacy spider webs. Carrie walked to the middle of the foyer and turned around in a circle. Her eyes darted back and forth not quite making sense of everything she saw through dust so thick it almost looked like snow. The air tickled her nose and she sneezed.

Mr. Dumfries came in behind her with his face set in a hard expression, distant and remote. He wasn't looking at what was in front of him but at something far away. Something that hurt.

He walked past her, over to a set of large doors framed by the staircases. His footsteps left tracks across the floor. A clear step with his good leg. A slight scuffing of his heel with the other. He paused in front of the doors, then reached out and swung them open. Dust swirled into the air in a whirling cloud of shimmering gray.

He stood in front of the open doors staring into the room, his back stiff, his shoulders set. Slowly, he shook himself out of his reverie and turned around to face Carrie. "This room, Miss Bowden, was always the heart of this house."

Carrie walked over to the doors and Mr. Dumfries stepped aside. He waved her through with a courteous half bow and Carrie stepped into the room.

It was a library, like nothing she'd ever seen before. The room was open the full two stories with a balcony one story above her head running along three of the four walls. Bookshelves lined the balcony, every shelf stuffed with dusty books. On the floor level, tucked into a corner, was a huge antique-looking desk. In another corner sat a thinly cushioned couch with fancy scrollwork curling over the backrest. Two round-backed chairs and a small tea table sat grouped around a large fireplace. The mantel over the fireplace was wide and broad with a huge old mirror hanging over it. The surface of the mirror was spotted and hazy with age. It rippled in places, reflecting the room in foggy distortions. Tall windows covered the back wall of the library. Sunlight came streaming through them with broad beams that fell in slanted square patches across the floor. But, in spite of the bright sun, Carrie couldn't tell what color anything was supposed to be. Everything was a uniform gray, covered in dust and draped in layers of fine webs. She sneezed again and dug for a tissue.

Mr. Dumfries stood in the middle of the room, his arms folded across his chest. "The stories were true then. She really did lock up this part of the house." His mouth looked pinched. "What a waste."

Carrie rubbed her nose with a shred of Kleenex. "Did you think the stories might not be true?"

He ran a finger along the edge of the tea table leaving a furrow in the dust and looked down at its tip. "I hoped they weren't." He blew, and a small puff of gray swirled into the air. "I liked your mother. I hoped her life wasn't as hard as it sounded like it might have been. But maybe it was." He rubbed at the tip of his finger with his thumb. "A damn shame."

Carrie looked around her at the thick layers of gray, undisturbed except by little mouse feet. "If my grandmother locked up this part of the house, where did she sleep?"

"According to the nurses, she stayed in a room in the east wing servant's quarters."

Carrie sniffed and wiped at her nose again. "Can I see her room? Do you know which one it is?"

"We can find it easy enough." Mr. Dumfries gestured to the dust-shrouded furniture. "It won't look like this."

"But will we get lost trying to find it?" Carrie smiled softly. She'd never been in a house this big. To her, a three-bedroom apartment was a luxurious amount of space. This seemed decadent, and she'd only seen a fraction of it.

Mr. Dumfries smiled back at her with understanding. "The house is big, but it's not really that complicated. It's just basically a large central box, facing north toward the river, with two wings running south off each side." He turned and faced the row of windows on the back wall and pointed to them. "This wall faces south, ergo all the windows. The two central windows aren't really windows but they're actually doors that lead out to a patio and the small garden in between the two wings." He raised his right arm and held it out from his side. "The west wing has the family bedrooms on the second floor. Recreation rooms are on the first floor, a billiards room, an informal family room, a gentlemen's smoking parlor and such." He lowered his right arm and raised his left. "The east wing has the servant's quarters on the first floor. The second floor has guest bedrooms. The kitchen, dining room and breakfast nook are all on the east side of the main box." He turned around to face her and pointed to the door they just came through. "When you walk in through the foyer, the doors on your right lead to a formal receiving room, or a parlor if you prefer. Those on your left lead to a formal dining room. You can get to the kitchen through there, and from the kitchen you can get into the servant's quarters in the east wing." He pointed to a spot behind her and to her right. "Over in the corner there's a spiral staircase that leads up to the book balcony. From there, you can get to the master and mistress suites, or you can take the front staircases to reach them. The master rooms are to the west of the foyer, the mistress rooms are to the east. The veranda over the porch that you saw coming into the house is only accessible from the master sitting room."

Carrie squinted her eyes at him. "And you think that's not complicated?"

He smiled again and shrugged. "Well, you get used to it pretty quickly."

"How do you know so much about the layout of this house if you've never been in it?"

"Well, now, I didn't say I'd never been in it. Just not in the last fifty years or so." Mr. Dumfries scratched his chin and looked around him. "My mother was a maid here when I was young. I'd come over after school and help her out a little, doing the heavy lifting and such. Of course, I had an ulterior motive. I hoped to catch a glimpse of your mother, maybe even to talk to her sometime. I never did get the chance before my mother found better paying work at the cotton mill." The wistful expression crossed Mr. Dumfries's face again.

"You loved her," Carrie said. It was a guess, but she didn't think she was wrong.

Mr. Dumfries shook his head. "What does a fourteen-year-old boy know about love?"

Carrie studied his face, the long lines of his frown, the downward droop of his lower lip. "Enough to make an old man sad."

"That's brutally direct, Miss Bowden," Mr. Dumfries said, his frown deepening, "but you may be essentially correct." He looked around the library and then shook his head again. "I think we've both had enough of this old man's follies. I'll show you the east wing servant's quarters and then we'll find out which room your grandmother stayed in."

He led her out through the south facing patio doors and into the garden between the wings. Only it wasn't much of a garden anymore.

"This must have been beautiful, once," Carrie said as they picked their way over the broken stone path. The grass grew thin and tall. An espaliered apple tree leaned against one wall in a dense cluster of dying branches. The few scraggly flowers fighting their way up through the weeds made the whole garden feel forsaken. They picked their way toward a door in the middle of the east wall. Mr. Dumfries dug around in his pocket and pulled out a set of modern-looking keys. He unlocked the door, opened it and they went inside. Carrie stepped into a dim hallway. It was narrow and the ceiling was low, but it was cleaner looking than the library had been. The dust wasn't as thick and the rugs looked newer, but the air felt heavy, more musty and close.

Mr. Dumfries flipped a light switch. One of the four wall sconces lit with a dim flickering glow. "Well, would you look at that," he said staring at the light in amazement.

Carrie glanced at the sconce and then looked around her. Five identical doors were spaced evenly along the inside wall. At the end of the corridor was a door with bright sunlight shining through a row of small glass panes lined across its top.

Mr. Dumfries gestured toward the sunlight at the end of the corridor. "That's one of the service entrances. The other one is in the kitchen. Originally, the only way into the main part of the house from the servant's quarters was through the kitchen. The door we just came through was a fairly recent addition. Relatively speaking, of course."

Carrie glanced back at the door. "That seems a bit stark."

"Yes, I suppose it does," said Mr. Dumfries's jingling the keys in his hand. "I imagine it's a remnant from a time when servants weren't always hired on a voluntary basis. Limiting their access might have seemed more important then."

Carrie looked up and down the hallway, at the plain un-papered walls and the simple square cut trim. "I think that bothers me a little." She had been so interested in the house, she hadn't thought about what it meant for the hands that might have built it or the hands it took to keep it.

"I think it bothered your grandmother a lot." Mr. Dumfries's eyes followed her gaze. "I like to imagine it was one of the reasons she closed the house and chose to live in the servant's quarters as soon as there was no more family to think of. That's just a guess, though. It might have been something else entirely." The keys clinked together softly as he held them out to Carrie. "Here, you should keep these now. They'll open everything in the house but the front door. You already have the key to that."

"Thank you." Carrie took the keys from him solemnly.

Mr. Dumfries gave a quick nod of his head and turned. "Which door do you think we should try first?"

Carrie hefted the keys in her palm. It was a heavy bunch, but they didn't weigh as heavily in her hand as the first one had. "If the door at the end of hall is to the outside, my guess would be that the door on the other end is to the kitchen."

"Close. It's to the butler's pantry which leads into the kitchen."

She closed her fist over the keys and slipped them in her purse. "I think that an older person living by themselves would probably pick the room closest to the kitchen." Carrie pushed her hair out of her eyes. "Let's try that one first."

She walked down the hallway and turned the knob to the first door. It opened into a small empty room with bare wood floors, dingy white walls and two narrow doors. Carrie walked into the room and opened the first narrow door. It was just a closet and there was nothing in it. The second door was to a tiny bathroom, toilet, sink and shower, shared with the next room over. That room was almost the same as the first except that the closet door was missing, shards of glass littered the floor and a baseball sat resting in the corner. The one small window was boarded over with a sheet of plywood.

The next two rooms were also empty. Their curtainless windows filmed over with grime, bare walls and floors, two more empty closets. Carrie put her hand on the knob of the last door. A small slant of light fell against it, a bright square of sun staining the dull wood. She turned the knob and opened the door. The room was almost empty, but it wasn't quite. A narrow cot sat in the corner with a nightstand beside it, a small bureau beside that. A short-beaded and fringed lamp stood on the nightstand with a book lying next to it. Only a very thin layer of dust covered everything, but the room was still colorless. It felt just as bare as the first four rooms with their small dirty windows and empty floors, their two narrow doors. This room had two doors as well, but they weren't narrow.

She opened one of the doors and stepped into a bathroom. It was small and drearily white. Medicine bottles lined the sink, a worn nub of soap sat in a dish, a frayed toothbrush rested in an old whiskey tumbler. The commode was tall with handles at the sides, and there were grab bars in the shower. A thin white bath rug lay bunched against the wall. Carrie straightened it with her foot, spreading it out in front of the shower. Still, the bathroom felt old. It made Carrie feel worn and hollow.

She turned and went back into the bedroom. The other door was, as she expected, a closet. It was a larger closet than the others had been, but it was still nearly empty. A dress, a few skirts, two pairs of work pants, some shirts, all laundered and pressed, hung neatly from wire hangers. At the bottom, she saw a pair of orthopedic shoes, a pair of bedroom slippers, a silver cane with four feet, a forgotten oxygen tank in the far corner, and that was all. Carrie closed the closet door. Her throat felt thick and tight. There wasn't anything left in there that could tell her who her grandmother had been. There wasn't enough stuff left to fill a Goodwill box.

Mr. Dumfries cleared his throat behind her. "There were a whole string of nurses who came in to look after her. She had round-the-clock care. They made sure she ate, bathed, took her medicine, etcetera. They tidied up a bit, too, and read to her a great deal. Your grandmother loved books even after she couldn't read them herself anymore."

Carrie touched the closet door with the tips of her fingers and then turned her back to it. She looked at Mr. Dumfries still standing in the doorway. "Did you ever know my grandmother well?"

He shook his head. "After my mother quit working here, I had no reason to come back. I was at the tail end of my teens the year your mother ran off. Your grandmother fired all the staff that same day and stopped coming into town soon after. Much later, I had the occasion to speak to her a few times over the phone, but it was only about business. She didn't invite casual questions, and I never had the nerve to ask them."

Carrie walked over to the cot. It was small but neatly made with white sheets and a neutral-colored spread. She picked up the book that was lying on the nightstand. It looked like a diary with an empty leather loop for a missing pen. There was a small flower embossed in the lower right-hand corner. She flipped it open and thumbed through it. All the pages were blank. She shut it again and put it back on the table. "What would you have asked her, if you could have asked her anything?"

Mr. Dumfries raised his eyebrows as he thought about the question. "I would want to ask her a lot of things. I hardly know where to begin." His eyebrows scrunched over his nose. "Well, I guess that's not true. I would begin with Jane."

"My mother?"

"Yes. I want to know why, after Jane married your father, she never came home again. She was only eighteen when she left. That's hardly old enough to be out on her own. Certainly not old enough to be making decisions of that magnitude. And then she never came back."

"Do you think something pushed her out?"

He shrugged. "After your grandfather died, this was not a happy home for your mother. It didn't have to be any one thing that pushed her out. It could have been years of small accumulated grievances." Mr. Dumfries looked around the room with eyes that were distant and dim. "This house has not been a happy home for anyone in many sheaves of years." He shook his head sadly, turned and stepped back out into the hall.

Carrie followed him and shut the door gently behind her. "Was this ever a happy home for anyone, Mr. Dumfries?"

He turned to look at her with shining eyes under his drooping lids. "I sincerely hope, Miss Bowden, that this will be a happy home for you."

Mr. Dumfries drove Carrie to the small diner on Main Street where they had a passable dinner of fried chicken and green beans, mashed potatoes, sweet tea and a slice of pecan pie. They spoke of inconsequential things while they ate. Carrie talked about Chicago, museums and baseball, and Mr. Dumfries spoke about history, agriculture and getting old. Mr. Dumfries paid the bill and they walked the two blocks back to her car. Main Street was quiet. Most of the stores had already turned their lights off and flipped their signs to read "Sorry, we're closed." Standing by her car, Mr. Dumfries shook Carrie's hand and then opened her door. He shut it for her as she got in and put her seat belt on. It was a vestige of his upbringing, she thought, perhaps like paying for the meal or calling her miss. He seemed like a nice man. This seemed like a nice town, but she wondered if either of them would be willing to accept someone like her just as she was.

Carrie drove slowly back to Richmond, the setting sun glaring orange and amber in her rearview mirror, staining the trees red and gold. The drive back was much shorter since there were no wrong turns and she almost knew where she was going. She pulled into the parking lot of her motel as the sun dropped below the horizon.

Inside her room, she sat on the side of the bed, its crisp white sheets turned down at the corner. She turned the television on, but it was news and she didn't feel like watching the news. Carrie flipped through the channels, but there had been quite enough drama to fill up the day and she had never liked violence. Then the canned laughter started to get on her nerves. She turned the television off and, in the silence, thought about her options. What was there back in Chicago? A job that she didn't like very much and a homophobic boss that liked her even less, an empty apartment with only the few sticks of cheap furniture that Megan had left, no friends to speak of or that would still speak to her.

She was planning to move anyway as soon as her lease expired. Why not move to a brand-new place altogether? But this was a very new place and she truly didn't know what kind of reception a woman like her was likely to have. How free would she be to live how she wanted? How much would she have to hide, and what would happen if she didn't hide? She wouldn't live her life in the closet. That wasn't an option for her. She didn't even know where the door was, much less how to open it and step inside.

She kicked off her shoes and pulled off her jeans. Well, whatever. It wouldn't hurt to stay a few weeks and work on cleaning the house a little. Wipe the dust off the furniture and clean the windows. She showered, brushed her teeth and climbed into bed. That was a good plan, she thought as she turned the light off and snuggled the sheets up around her ears. Wipe the dust off and clean the windows and then she could see clearly again.

CHAPTER FIVE

Carrie sat slumped in the hard wooden chair, dirty and sore, sticky with sweat. Her head rested uncomfortably against the backrest and her knee bumped against the drawers of the antique desk, but she was too tired to move. She stared at the ceiling high above her and wondered how one went about getting spider webs off a chandelier that hung from the middle of a two-story ceiling. Or changing all the burned out lightbulbs. Or if they made lightbulbs that fit it anymore. A lot of the lights in the house didn't work even after she changed the bulbs. She tried to trace the problems, but after zapping herself twice, she decided that she was just going to have to call an electrician. And buy a very tall ladder.

But she wasn't going to do that right now or even tomorrow. Right now, she was tired, and tomorrow she had to find a place to buy a set of sheets since the ones she took off the bed in the master suite tore to ribbons in the wash. At least the washing machine worked. She hadn't been sure about that when she found it in a closet in the butler's pantry. It was an ancient clunky looking thing, probably the first electric Whirlpool ever built. The dryer was newer, though that might not have been such a good thing. After she finished drying her first load of linens there was nothing left of the pillowcases but an armful of lint and two tags. The bedcover had come out of the dryer in rags. But they were nice smelling rags, so she used them to dust off the books in the library. She still had to vacuum the rugs around the balcony, but after all her hard work she didn't have the energy to lug that heavy old thing up the spiral staircase. Besides, the lights dimmed and flickered when she ran the vacuum. It would probably be a good idea to have the electrician come out and look at the whole setup before she tasked it too heavily.

Carrie blinked over the tired grittiness in her eyes, took a deep breath and then sat up in her chair. She rubbed at the ache between her shoulder blades as she looked at the desk in front of her. It was the most interesting piece in the room and the only thing that still had a thick layer of dust. She had saved it for last, as a reward of sorts, for her Herculean labors of the last few days.

The foyer was now impeccably clean. A beautiful parquet had been hiding underneath the dust. Multihued woods patterned the floor with interlocking blocks of triangles and squares. The banister of the grand staircase had deeply carved scrollwork on the ends and the rails had a shining richness that only came from countless years of polish. She had tackled the kitchen after that and now enough of it was clean to make it useable, but she hadn't had the energy to go through all the cabinets and drawers. And the library called to her, its books and its strange combination of delicate and massive furniture.

Carrie shook out one of the last of her clean rags, still nice smelling. She had cleaned the library from bottom to top. Everything in it was dusted, swept, brushed, vacuumed and polished to a shine, except for the rugs in the balcony that were still on the to do list and the desk she was sitting in front of. Most everything cleaned up wonderfully, even if the materials underneath were a bit faded and worn. Everything except for the surface of the old mirror hanging over the fireplace. That wouldn't come clean no matter how hard she rubbed. It was hazy and spotted, reflecting the room behind her with funny bends and waves. The frame cleaned up nice, though, with its gold gilding and ornate carvings of grapevines, leaves and clusters, which sparkled under her rags.

The mantel under the mirror became, with a swipe of her cloth, intricately swirled green and white marble. The couches and chairs, even the tall row of windows on the south wall were now dust free and as clean as they could be. The windows had been a challenge, but she found a tall stepping stool in the pantry that let her reach the top. The glass was clear and bright, if a bit wavy in spots. From where she sat in her uncomfortable chair, she could see the scraggly garden outside, the short picket fence that marked its boundary and the low hills just beyond, a dark line of woods after that.

Carrie swiveled her chair around in a full circle. The seat rose about an inch. She twirled around the other way and it went back down. The chair wasn't comfortable to sit in, but it was interesting to look at with its clawed feet and swirling armrests. They matched the carved patterns of the desk, the same swirls decorating the trim and the drawer handles. The desk had all kinds of neat little drawers and cubby holes, stuffed with old yellow papers, small account books and pens and pencils of varieties that she had never heard of before. Waterman, Conklin, Pelican and Dickey. There was even a quill pen standing in a pewter inkwell with a sad looking tuft of feather, gray with time and split with age, a coating of ink dried rock hard on the sharpened tip.

Carrie stretched her tired arms high over her head, sat straighter and began to wipe at the leather blotter with her rag. She cleaned the top of the desk and each little knickknack. The inkwell with its quill pen and penknife, the old rotary bakelite telephone with the cloth wrapped cord and no dial tone, the empty cut glass vase. She peered into the cubby holes and found that they were stuffed with bills from the early 1950s, one from a tailor, the green grocer, one from a workman for painting and repairs, two from a boarding school far north of Virginia.

She shook the dust from the papers and put everything back the same way she found it. That seemed important for some reason and, if she wasn't entirely sure why, she didn't question the notion. The drawers she opened held more of the same, but the bills were a bit older, the paper more brittle. Dark stripes of old glue stained the flaps of the envelopes, the papers inside cracked at the folds. The very bottom drawer held a bundle of letters sitting on top of a large old leather bound Bible. The dried remnants of a rubber band stuck around the middle of the bundle. She slipped the top letter out and opened it.

My Dearest Robert, I can't tell you how glad I am to hear through our mutual acquaintances that you have arrived home safe from the wars...

Carrie turned the letter over to see the signature. The name didn't mean anything to her, though there wasn't any reason why it should, and there wasn't a date. What wars was the letter referring to? Her grandfather could have been in any number of wars, the times of his life being what they were. The Spanish-American War? World War I? The Korean War? Carrie couldn't remember when Mr. Dumfries said her grandfather had died. She would have to look it up. She folded the letter carefully and opened the next one.

Dear Sir, Regarding the matter to which we have had some previous correspondence...

That one was, on the whole, a most uninteresting letter, and Carrie wondered why anyone had bothered to keep it. Maybe it wasn't so much keeping it as it was just not throwing it away. She imagined that most of the letters in the bundle would run in the same vein. Carrie opened the last one just to see.

Robert, Please don't neglect to send back a bolt of chenille while you're in Paris. Kindest Regards, Celia.

It was a scrawl of spidery handwriting and a lot of blank white space. Not a love letter, by any means. The things it didn't say struck Carrie as being a very sad thing. Carrie looked at the bundle of letters, a frown pulling at the corners of her mouth. She folded the last letter and put it back into the envelope. Suddenly, she didn't want to look through the desk anymore.

She shut the drawer and stood, stretching onto her tiptoes with her hands pressed against the small of her back. It was time to quit for the day. The sun was starting to set, and there were only two lamps that worked in the entire library. The dim light at night made the place look big and cavernous and just a bit gloomy. She decided to make a sandwich, grab another book from the upper shelves and curl up on the couch with the one comforter that survived the washing machine, even if sleeping on the couch was starting to get old. Once she had brushed and blown the dust off, the couch turned out to have a busy floral print. It still had a deep maroon color showing along the stitches and seams, but it was faded nearly to pink everywhere else. The thinly cushioned seats and carved wood trim weren't very cozy, even with extra padding, but it worked well enough.

She'd go buy sheets tomorrow. Maybe she'd even call Mr. Dumfries's daughter, what's her name, Gillian, and ask her where the best places were to buy such things. Carrie shook out her dust rag and hung it over the arm of the chair. The way it hung in gentle folds reminded her of Gillian, how she had walked into the office, the ice cubes clinking in soft counterpoint to the swishing of her dress, her warm, friendly smile. Yes. Calling Gillian sounded like a good idea. Which meant, as Carrie knew full well, that it probably wasn't.

CHAPTER SIX

Morning came with a new kink in her back and catch in her hip. Carrie stared up from the couch at the cobwebs still hanging off the chandelier. Sheets were definitely on the agenda today. So was cleaning the master suite. Carrie yawned and scratched her head, rolled herself off the couch and headed for the bathroom. She had been using the bathroom in her grandmother's room since the shower mostly worked and the toilet flushed with moderate efficiency, but she hadn't been able to bring herself to sleep on the narrow cot. She didn't know, because she hadn't asked, if her grandmother had died in that bed. But even if she hadn't, the thought of sleeping in a room where an anciently old woman spent her last lonely years gave her a creepy feeling. The couch was more comfortable than that.

The shower worked, but the water was only lukewarm at best. There was another job for the electrician or the plumber or both. She toweled her hair dry, slipped on her terrycloth robe and headed for the kitchen. She stood looking inside the ancient refrigerator at the nearly bare shelves. It hummed and whirred, clanked sometimes and made a funny buzzing sound when the icemaker dumped cubes into the bin, but it stayed cold inside and that was the main thing. She hadn't bought much on her brief excursion into town the other day, only bread, lettuce, a deli package of sliced roast beef, a jar of mustard and one tomato. Nothing she wanted for breakfast. She remembered to buy coffee but forgot the cream, and she couldn't find a coffeepot anyway, though she did find the crusty remnants of what might have been sugar in a pretty tin canister sitting on the counter.

She closed the refrigerator door but didn't bother to open the freezer. There was nothing in there but opaque plastic containers with very old dates written on the top in felt-tip pen. She wasn't brave enough to try something that had been in the freezer for twenty years, but she hadn't thrown it all away either. To Carrie, there was something very personal about freezer food. Someone had once taken the time to box the remnants of a meal, date it and stack it neatly. Looking at the green and pink plastic boxes made Carrie feel like more of a guest than the house's new owner, like the house still belonged to someone else who was absent for the moment and she was just cleaning it a little before they got back. She didn't know what she would ultimately do with the house, stay or sell, rent it out or turn it into a museum, but that wasn't anything she had to decide in a hurry.

What she did decide was to go into town for breakfast to the diner that she and Mr. Dumfries ate supper in a few days ago. He said they served a good, if not fancy, cup of coffee, which was just what a morning full of busy errands needed.

She threw on some jeans and a blouse and tied her hair back in a damp ponytail before her curls had time to turn to frizz. She jumped into her car and drove the five winding miles into town. There wasn't much traffic, one or two cars ahead of her, three or four passing her on the other side, but Carrie suspected that there wasn't ever very much traffic. That made a nice change from the five o'clock gridlock she was use to that routinely kept her four blocks away from home until six. She pulled up to Danni's storefront diner and parked in between two very tall mud-splattered pickup trucks.

She got out of her car and stood for a moment just breathing. The air still had a slight chill clinging to it, but the sun's promise of warmth pressed like a gentle hand against her skin. She could smell the mud on the truck tires, a strong reek of damp earth with a not-so-subtle hint of cow. What she didn't smell was exhaust, or the taco vender's cart, rotting Dumpster trash or unwashed bodies, or the thick miasma of clashing perfumes and colognes. She didn't smell sewage and concrete dust and, for just that moment, she wasn't sure she missed it.

The door of the diner opened with the tinkling of bells, real bells not electronic ones. A middle-aged lady in a powder blue dress with a pink apron tied around her waist glanced up from where she was pouring coffee for a man in a dirty checkered shirt and a ball cap.

"I'm sorry, honey, but we're not hiring right now," she said topping the man's cup with a well practiced dip of her wrist.

Carrie sat at the counter, two seats away from the man and looked around her. She was the only woman sitting. The others had trays of food or coffeepots in their hands, scurrying in between tables. It wasn't a good sign. Carrie felt the beginnings of a headache stirring just between her eyes. Dinner with Mr. Dumfries hadn't been like that, but then she'd had a lot to think about then and hadn't really paid very much attention. She turned back to the woman who was looking at her strangely. "I'm not looking for a job. I just want a cup of coffee and maybe some eggs and bacon."

The woman looked at her for a long second, put her coffeepot down, pulled a notepad from her pocket and flipped it open. She licked her thumb and turned a page over. "Scrambled or fried?" she asked, pencil poised. "We have a Wednesday morning special on dirty eggs and bacon with hash browns. You ever ate dirty eggs before?"

"I don't think so. What are they?"

"Eggs scrambled up with a little bit of everything thrown

44

in, tomato, onion, bell pepper, cheddar cheese, just a touch of jalapeño…all diced up fine and scrambled in together."

Carrie's stomach grumbled. "That sounds good."

"Right." She scribbled on her pad, tore the paper off and clipped it next to the line of other papers hanging behind her in a small window. She leaned into the window and yelled. "Hank, one dirty egg special and make it a good one. It's for the lady out at the Covington place."

"Right-O." The answer came with a rattle of pans, the scraping of a spatula and the hiss of steam.

The lady turned back around, grabbed a cup from off a stack, flipped it right side up and put it in front of Carrie. She reached for the coffee pot and poured into the cup with one hand while putting a small cream pitcher on the counter with her other. Carrie reached for a packet of sugar, shook it and tore it open.

"Anything else? Juice, grapefruit, a slice of pie?" the woman asked flipping her notepad back open.

Carrie stirred cream into her coffee. "How did you know who I was?"

The woman closed the notepad and put it back in her apron pocket. "You came in here with Jack Dumfries the other day. Betty said you talked all northern. She works the dinner crowd."

Carrie took a sip from her cup. It was hot, sweet and strong, just the way early morning coffee should be. "Why did you call the house the Covington place? It seems like it should be called the Burgess house or something."

The woman wiped her hands on her apron and looked at Carrie with a slight squinting of her eyes. "You look a bit like your mother, you know. Like she was when I knew her. Young, I mean."

Carrie set her cup on the counter. The old familiar sadness rolled through her chest making her hand tremble just a little. "Did you know my mother well?"

The lady shrugged. "As well as any, I suppose. Better than most. We were best friends in grade school."

The man in the dirty shirt spluttered into his coffee. "Amy-

45

Lee, you weren't best friends with nobody in grade school."

"You just shut your hole, Chuck." Amy-Lee shot him a wicked glare. "You don't know what you're talking about."

The man huffed into his cup and half turned his face toward Carrie. "You watch it, missy. Amy-Lee's feeding you a line of bullshit. The next thing you know, she'll be hitting you up for a loan."

"I'm not going to do any such a thing. I'm just trying to have a conversation here, and you're butting your big nose in where it don't belong." She turned back to Carrie with a fist placed firmly on a canted hip. "Chuck's just being ugly because I won't go out with him." Her stenciled eyebrows rose into a pointed arch. "Maybe I would if he took a bath and changed his clothes once in a while."

She said that louder than she needed for Carrie to hear. Chuck's face turned red as he scowled into his cup. A bell dinged and a plate slid into the window piled high and steaming.

"Golden dirty's up," a voice yelled through the window. "Stop gabbing, Amy-Lee."

Amy-Lee huffed. She grabbed the plate and slid it in front of Carrie. "Ketchup?"

"No, thanks." Carrie picked up her fork and turned her attention to her plate. Amy-Lee moved down to Chuck's place at the counter where they leaned their heads together and whispered to each other in low furious tones. There had to be a story there, but Carrie wasn't sure she wanted to hear it, so she did her best to tune it out. She ate her eggs, which were surprisingly good, but left the thin pale toast with the soggy spot of butter in the middle. She drank her coffee and listened to the mutter of conversation around her. It was mostly about weather and prices, politics and rumors. No one talked to her again, even as she paid her bill and left.

She was putting on her seat belt when she realized that the woman, Amy-Lee, hadn't answered her question. Why did she call it the Covington place? Carrie decided that since she was already in town, she would go see Mr. Dumfries and ask him.

Maybe Gillian would be there and she could ask her about a good place to shop for linens and things.

Carrie rolled her eyes at herself. Yeah, right.

Mr. Dumfries was sitting at his desk, reading papers with his half-moon glasses perched far down the slope of his nose. He looked up and smiled as the receptionist showed Carrie in.

"Welcome, Miss Bowden," he said gesturing for her to sit. "What brings you into town?"

"Breakfast, Mr. Dumfries." Carrie sat and put her purse on the floor.

"And how was it?"

"The food was good, the coffee was hot, the conversation was a little strange."

"Was Amy-Lee working this morning?"

Carrie nodded. "Yes, she was."

Mr. Dumfries's smile turned into a scowl. "Did she hit you up for a loan?"

"Um, no. She didn't get the chance. She was too busy arguing about something."

"Hmm. I take it that means Chuck was there." Mr. Dumfries shook his head. "Those two have been in love for the last twenty years, but they're both too stubborn to be the first one to admit it." He looked at her over the top of his glasses. "Don't you do that, Miss Bowden. When you find someone you love, latch on to him with both hands and don't ever let go."

"Even if it was someone you didn't approve of?" She thought of Megan for the first time in a few days. Her father hadn't liked Megan. Megan hadn't liked him either, and it made Thanksgiving and Christmas a little uncomfortable.

Mr. Dumfries looked at her with his clear, bright eyes. "Especially if it was someone I didn't approve of. I'm an old man, you remember, and firmly set in my ways. What do I know of love these days?"

"It hasn't changed. Love never does. Only the expression of it changes."

He smiled again and sat back in his chair. "I take your point, Miss Bowden. And I appreciate it. It helps me a little. Now, what can I do to help you today?"

"I'd like to ask you something."

"Of course."

"The lady at the diner, Amy-Lee, called my grandmother's house the Covington place."

"Ah." Mr. Dumfries leaned his elbows on the armrests of his chair and steepled his fingers. "Your grandmother's married name was Burgess. Her maiden name was Covington. Her grandfather built the original portions of the house and it descended to her father when he died, but her father didn't like the place very much, for whatever the reason, and so he gave it to your grandmother and her new husband on the occasion of their wedding. He built himself a smaller house a little ways down the river. That one, alas, did not survive the test of time. I believe it burned down a bit after World War II."

"You're quite the historian, Mr. Dumfries."

He took off his glasses and polished them against his lapel. "Well, the truth of it is, Miss Bowden, that it isn't me. Gillian studied American history in college and did her thesis on our local historical figures. The cotton mill your grandmother's father built was of some importance for reindustrializing this area after the Civil War and the burning of Richmond or some such thing." He put his glasses back on and thumbed through his Rolodex. "Tell you what. Why don't you give Gillian a call and ask her about it? She'll tell you more than you want to know, I'll bet." He took out a card from the holder on his desk and tapped it against the leather blotter. "Just to warn you, she'll probably ask you for a tour. She's been aching to get inside that house for more years than I can remember. She runs a little antique shop the next town over, you see, and is just dead sure that the whole place is crammed full of important things. I think that was why she wanted to be here when you came." He smiled a little enigmatically and handed her the card. "Here you go. She should be there today."

The card said Carriage House Antiques, Goochland, Virginia. There was an engraving of an old carriage in the upper right corner. "Thank you. I was thinking about asking her where to go shopping for bed linens and things."

"I'm sure she'll be able to point you in all the right directions."

Carrie grabbed her purse and stood. Mr. Dumfries stood too. "One last thing, if you don't mind. Amy-Lee said that I look like my mother a bit. Is that true? I don't remember what she looked liked. There was only one picture of her in my father's apartment and it wasn't a very good one."

Mr. Dumfries scratched at his chin. "Well, you do look a bit like her. There's a family resemblance in the shape of your nose. But if you were to ask me, and you did, I'd say that it wasn't so much your mother that you look like but your grandmother. In fact, I'd say that you were the spitting image of her done up a bit more modern. There's a picture of her in the town library. They hung it up when she donated all of her husband's books after he passed. You ought to go take a look."

Carrie looked at the card in her hand. "Thank you. I just might."

Carrie sat in her car with her cell phone in her hand. Her heart was racing and she didn't know why. She wasn't a shy person, usually, but as much as she wanted to talk to Gillian again, she had to admit there was something about her that she found a little frightening. The self-assured poise and the casual elegance was a bit daunting for someone like Carrie. People like Gillian didn't usually look twice at people like her. Gillian shined where Carrie was dull. But she had looked twice or, at least, she had smiled at her nicely. That probably didn't mean the same thing to Gillian that it meant to Carrie, but it did mean that she was willing to be friendly or willing to fake it until she got her tour. Sometimes that was enough.

Carrie took a deep breath and dialed the number on the card. Two rings and a woman with a smoky voice answered the phone.

"Carriage House Antiques. This is Jo."

"Yes, may I speak to Gillian Dumfries?"

"Who's calling, please?" The voice did not sound pleased.

"This is Carrie Bowden. I'm calling about the Covington place. I heard she wanted a tour."

"Oh. Sure. Just one moment. I'll get her." The tone of the voice changed, and the phone clunked on the counter. Carrie listened to the soft undercurrent of classical music clashing with the static buzz of her cell phone. She tried to still her mind, to calm her racing heart so that she wouldn't trip over her tongue and say things that would make her sound like an imbecile.

The phone scraped across the counter. "Hello? Ms. Bowden? What's this I hear about a tour?" The voice was bright and eager, happy to hear from her, or something close enough to it.

Carrie relaxed a little and smiled into her phone. "Your father seemed to think the promise of a tour would make a good bribe."

"And what a scoundrel he is. I can't believe he told you my deepest desire." There was laughter in her voice. "All right, what horrible task do I have to do to get the tour? If you say clean the stables in one day, I'll have to turn you down. I don't do stables."

"Not to worry. I haven't even found the stables yet. It's just that I'd like to know some things, and you seem to be the one to ask. Your father says you know a lot about local history and something about my grandmother's family. I'd like to ask you some questions and I thought, while we were at it, maybe you could give me some advice on how to clean the cobwebs off the chandeliers."

There was a pause on the other end. "There's more than one?"

"There are two, one in the library and one in the foyer."

"He didn't tell me that."

"If you're talking about your father, that's probably because he didn't look up. I only saw the one in the foyer a few days ago

50

after I finished cleaning the parquet floors."

"Oh, please, please, tell me you're not using floor wax to polish the parquet."

"Um, no. I was only wiping the dust off with a damp rag. It was hell on my knees." Carrie rubbed a hand across her knee. They were still a little sore.

Gillian laughed. "I imagine it was, but that's the right way to do it. Is the floor in good shape?"

"Yes, it is, relatively speaking. It's worn in places, particularly by the front door, but I put a small rug over it and you can't really tell. The chandeliers are a mess, though. They're completely draped in spider webs. You can hardly tell what they are, and neither of them actually work, but then half the lights in the house don't work."

"Sounds like you need an electrician."

"And a plumber. All the sinks drain slow, if at all, and the fountain in the front needs some attention."

"Oh, I'd just love to see that fountain working." Carrie heard Gillian's sigh as a soft brush of static. "You know, now that I think about it, I know all the good workmen in the area and all the ones to avoid. How about if part of my horrible task is that I arrange for the electrical and the plumbing work for you?"

Carrie hadn't thought to ask her anything like that. "Thanks. That's very kind of you. I'd appreciate it very much."

"Consider it done. As for my reward, I can't get away today. I have a number of appraisals that I have to do. But if you'll be home tomorrow, I'll drop by in the morning. You can show me around and ask all your questions."

"That sounds terrific."

"Great. It's a date then. I'll see you soon."

The phone went dead in Carrie's hand. Things definitely didn't mean the same thing to Gillian that they did to her. It wouldn't be a date. Not even close, and that was a shame. She had a feeling that she could really get to like Gillian with her quick brain and bright sense of humor, in a way that went beyond drooling over the drape of her dress.

Carrie wondered about the woman with the smoky voice, but she knew that she was just being an idiot. Having a deep voice and a boy's name didn't necessarily mean anything. It might, but then again, it might not. She turned off her phone. It would be so much nicer if gay women had a better way to identify themselves other than stereotypical behaviors that could be so confusing. A special password or a secret handshake would make things so much easier. That way you could know when it was safe to sigh and when it was better to keep your heart locked tight.

But she was still being an idiot. She forgot all about asking where to buy bed linens. Oh, well. She'd just drive to Richmond and go to a mall. She remembered passing one or two on her way to Columbia. With a little luck, she could find one of them again.

CHAPTER SEVEN

Armed with freshly purchased bed linens, a new batch of old rags and a jumbo pack of thick paper towels, Carrie spent the rest of her afternoon cleaning the rooms in the master suite. The bedroom was large and spacious with an adjoining sitting room that had couches and chairs, an old writing desk and a set of glass doors that led out onto the veranda. The veranda stretched the whole length of the front of the house, but it was fairly narrow, just wide enough for a small table and two wicker chairs.

Carrie slung one of the area rugs over the railing and shook it out. Dust billowed off in thick puffs of gray that drifted and danced in the light breeze before scattering over the drive. She left the rug hanging over the wrought iron rail to air and wiped the sweat off her face with the hem of her T-shirt. The breeze felt good against her hot skin as she leaned a hip against the railing.

Carrie could see quite a way from where she stood. She could see where the driveway wound out of the woods, came in toward the house from the side and curled in a large looping circle around the fountain. Not far from that, the ground rose a bit and then sloped gently to the river. The sun was bright overhead and sparkled on the water with little flashes of diamond brilliance. It was easy to imagine someone sitting at the small wicker table, a hundred years ago, sipping their coffee while waiting for a boat to come up the river to take their cotton, cloth or corn back down the river to Richmond.

That would have been a pleasant thought, but then she had to go and think of the hands that plucked the cotton, wove the cloth, shucked the corn, and then it wasn't a pleasant thought at all. She looked at her own hands, roughened from scrubbing, and tried to imagine what they'd look like after a lifetime of hard toil. Not like hers, though her polish was scuffed and her nails chipped. She tried to imagine her hands covered with hard calluses and swollen, gnarled knuckles. Carrie rubbed her palms against her shorts, gave the rug a few more shakes and went back inside.

She took down the gossamer curtains that hung in the windows and also those that hung around the canopy bed and washed them gently by hand. She tried to wash the pillows too, but those came apart in a large mound of soggy feathers that didn't smell at all nice. It was a good thing she had thought to buy a couple of pillows while she was at the mall, nice solid foam rubber pillows. None of this smelly feathery stuff. She wondered what the lumpy mattresses were made of but then decided that it was better not to know. It would still be more comfortable than the couch.

The master suite bathroom was harder to clean than the curtains. The cast iron claw-footed tub had stains that were beyond her expertise. It stood alone in a corner of the room with an old brass hot water tank sitting next to it. A blue plastic curtain hung on a metal halo above it. The curtain was brittle and cracked when she tried to close it around the tub, but she didn't mind. She liked bubble baths well enough.

The floor was easier. It was made of small octagonal black and white tiles that did funny things to her eyes if she stared at them too hard. They cleaned up well except for the two that were cracked. The sink was a disaster, chipped and rusted, the hot water handle wouldn't turn, and the squeaky cold water faucet dripped, not much, but enough to leave stains in the bowl that wouldn't come out. The mirror over the sink was cracked and the medicine chest below it was full of sticky tubes of hair cream and dried out bottles of aftershave. There was a straight razor and a box of rusty blades on the middle shelf. A few crusty bottles of medicine with labels too faded to read sat on the shelf underneath.

Carrie finished wiping the shelves and washed the hair goop off her fingers. She was tired of cleaning. Her back hurt and her hands were raw and red. She rinsed out all her sponges and rags and dried her hands. She crossed the hallway and went through the door that led to the second-floor balcony of the library. She picked a new book off the shelf. It was nothing she'd ever heard of before, but she was an adventurous reader. She sat in the tub soaking her tired bones and read the book. It was about a detective who drank too much, called women skirts and liked to sock the bad guys who very conveniently all had glass jaws. It was almost funny. Almost. Carrie put the book down, washed her hair and rinsed. She was sleepy now that the water had soaked all the soreness out of her. She didn't wait for her hair to dry but shrugged into her pajamas, crawled into the tall canopy bed behind the clean curtains, between the fresh new sheets, and turned out the lamp.

She wasn't sure what woke her. Carrie turned onto her back and stretched her toes under the sheets. The night was warm and wonderful. All the windows of the bedroom were open to the night breezes. Small gusts fluttered the curtains. The sound of the wind in the trees carried in with it the chirping of crickets and the croaking of frogs, the soft hooting of an owl. Carrie heard a rustling from below the balcony, the steps of something walking lightly through dry leaves. She sat up and listened to the steps creeping closer to the house. She got out of bed, went through to the sitting room and stepped quietly out onto the balcony.

The moon brightened the sky from high overhead and glimmered on the dark band of river. A fox was trotting across the drive, heading toward the fountain, its paws shushing softly through the leaves. It stopped suddenly, ears pointed forward and down. The fox jumped high into the air and pounced with its two front paws pounding into the grass. Carrie heard a brief high-pitched squeak and the fox raised its head. A mouse dangled from its jaws. It trotted past the fountain, ears up, head held high, and disappeared into the tall grass.

It was strange to Carrie that the world worked liked that. The mice ate the seeds from the flowers, the fox ate the mice and, no doubt, something would eventually get the fox. It seemed like a sad way to run things, in a system where ultimately nothing would win. Or maybe that was the wrong way to look at it. Maybe life was a balance of winning and losing. Carrie stood quietly for a time listening to the wind flutter through the leaves. She eventually went back to bed, but it was long time before she could bring herself to close her eyes.

She woke to the twittering of birds, the chattering of squirrels, the far-off drone of an airplane. From where she lay, if she tilted her head just so, she could see the newly dawned sun painting the sky pink and the leaves of the trees an autumn red. Carrie yawned and stretched, breathing in deeply the crisp clean air. She put her slippers on and padded down the front stairs, cut through the formal dining room, through the breakfast nook and into the kitchen to make coffee. There was a shorter route. She could go through to the library balcony and down the spiral staircase, through the library and into the kitchen. But she still hadn't gotten tired of the grand staircase. Going up the left side and down the right. She hadn't tried sliding down the banister yet, but she damn well would one of these days, and soon.

The kitchen was still mostly a mess. Almost everything still had a light coating of dust. The only things she'd cleaned were the sink, the stove, the counter in between and the heavy oak kitchen table. It would be a monumental task sorting through all the cabinets and drawers cluttered with more than one lifetime of accumulations. The pots and pans, sets of odd dishes and mismatched silverware, serving trays and wooden spoons, heat-blackened spatulas. It was a task she would leave for a rainy day.

She never did find a coffeepot in all the clutter, but she did find an old French press and a pretty flowered teapot. She boiled water, poured it into the press over the grounds and waited for it to steep. It was kind of neat how the press worked. She pressed the plunger, and the grounds sank to the bottom. Maybe she wouldn't bother with a coffeepot. She poured the coffee into a cup and took her first sip. It was a good-flavored coffee, not in need of rescuing with cream and sugar. That was a good thing, too, because she had forgotten the cream again. She sipped, and her second taste was even better than the first.

She was just about to take her coffee upstairs when she heard the sound of tires crunching along the driveway. A car horn beeped merrily. Carrie looked at the clock on the stove. It was only eight. She wasn't expecting Gillian so early, but maybe "morning" in this part of the country had as different a meaning as "old" and "date." She looked down at herself. At least her pajamas were decent, even if her hair was a wreck after sleeping on it wet. Gillian would just have to excuse her for not being much of a morning person. She took a large swig of her coffee, relishing the burn on her tongue and the jolt to her system.

The sound of tires on the cobbles seemed louder than they should have and echoed strangely through the open windows. Carrie peeked out the window of the breakfast nook. There was more than one car heading down the drive. She pulled the blinds back further. It was a whole herd of vehicles, a long line of cars, trucks and vans winding as far back into the woods as she could see. Carrie watched them as they approached the house, circled the fountain in a random fashion and parked in a scattered mess in the tall grass of the front lawn. People began to pile out, women and men, girls and boys. They were carrying buckets and rags, rakes and pruning shears, tool boxes and belts. One truck said

Zachary's Electrical. Another said Masterworks Plumbing and Septic. And there was Gillian in the lead. Carrie looked at her pajamas with some chagrin as she saw them all heading for the front door. At least the pajamas were new and covered a decent amount of skin. The hair they would just have to forgive. At least, Carrie hoped that they would.

CHAPTER EIGHT

"Surprise!" Gillian said with an expansive wave of her arms as Carrie opened the front door. Carrie looked at Gillian's neatly bunned hair, light linen shirt, freshly ironed slacks and sighed. Gillian's bright smile wobbled a bit as her eyes jumped from Carrie's wild mess of hair to her fuzzy blue bedroom slippers. "Did we wake you? I'm so sorry. I guess I should've called first," she said as her smile returned, twice as bright as before only now there was the glint of amusement sparkling in her eyes. "I'm sorry I didn't think of calling. It's just that everyone is so excited about you fixing this place up again. Evelyn saw you buying cleaning supplies at the hardware store and word got around. Mind if we come in? I achieved my task." She gestured at the vans and trucks. "Zachary's here to do the electrical work, and Mr. Masters to do the plumbing."

Carrie looked out the door at the porch full of people. "What's everyone else here for?"

"They're here to do whatever you need them to do."

59

Gillian's smile was just way too bright and cheery for eight o'clock in the morning. Carrie blinked at her and then at all the people standing there staring at her. She stepped back and opened the door wide. People poured into the foyer with the growing buzz of whispered conversation that turned into chatter and laughter as they looked around wide-eyed and wondering. Gillian again took the lead, herding everyone through the dining room and into the kitchen. Good thing it was a big kitchen.

Carrie brought up the rear and had to squeeze through the kitchen door between a woman who smelled like purple bubble gum and a man in frayed coveralls who smelled like something she wasn't eager to identify. More people were milling around the old oak table in tight clumps, unpacking grocery bags, laying out doughnuts and pastries, biscuits and gravy, tubs of grits and plates of ham. One small elderly lady unpacked a bag of coffee grounds, cream, sugar and a stack of Styrofoam cups.

"I'm sorry," Carrie said to her. "There's no coffeepot. There's a coffee press, but it only makes two cups at a time."

The old lady laughed and her eyes twinkled. She patted Carrie's hand fondly. "Of course there's a coffeepot, dear. There's a thirty cup urn in the butler's pantry. We used to use it for parties back in the day when there used to be parties here. I doubt if anyone's moved it in all these years. Don't you worry about a thing, sweetheart. I'll just make myself right at home." The lady bustled off and disappeared through the swinging door that led to the pantry.

Gillian appeared at her side and took her by the arm. She leaned in close and spoke softly into Carrie's ear. "That was Anna Beth. She used to be the cook here when your mother was a girl." Gillian pulled on her arm and steered her across the kitchen toward a tall wizened old woman who was rummaging through the cabinets taking down pots and pans. "This is Maria. She used to be the chambermaid." Maria nodded and smiled, but before Carrie could say anything, Gillian dragged her in another direction toward a middle-aged man leaning against a wall with his hands in his pockets. "This is Gregory. His father used to be the stableman in charge of the horses, and his uncle Daniel used to be the kennel man, in charge of the hounds."

"Hounds?" Carrie managed to ask before Gillian pulled her away again. They whirled around the kitchen and stopped in front of a thin young man.

"This is Edward." The young man tipped his ball cap to her. "At least one member of his family has been a gardener here from the time this house was first built. It's such a shame he's never been on the grounds before."

Edward gave her a sad smile, and Gillian started to drag her in another direction. Carrie dug her feet in and stopped her. "Slow down a bit, Gillian. I get your point and I won't remember anyone's name if you go so fast."

"What point is that?" Gillian blinked her eyes innocently.

Carrie ignored the look and waved her hand around the kitchen. "You're trying to tell me that this house is an important part of Columbia's history. Everyone here has had something to do with this house in some way. I get that. This house doesn't really belong to me but to all the people who worked hard to make it what it is."

Gillian gave her a quirky half smile. "I'm not sure I would go so far as that. The house really does belong to you. No one disputes that, but you're right about everyone having something to do with the house. And you're also right about it being an important part of Columbia's history."

"Well"—Carrie shrugged—"however you would put it, I don't disagree with you."

"Then you'll let everyone help you clean it up?"

"Yes, but not for free."

Gillian's eyes narrowed. "What's it going to cost them?"

Carrie shook her head. "No. That's not what I mean. What I'm saying is that I'm not going to let them work for free. I'm going to pay Zachary for the electrical work and Mr. Masters for the plumbing and anybody else for anything they do here."

Gillian looked at her closely, studying her face. "You're not a typical Covington."

"I'm not a Covington at all or a Burgess. I'm just Carrie Bowden and nothing else." Carrie gently shook Gillian off her arm. "Now, if you'll excuse me, I'd like to go put some clothes on."

Carrie turned and made her way through the press of people, most of whom stopped her to introduce themselves and shake her hand. She definitely wasn't going to remember everyone's name. Maybe not anyone's. She squeezed out the kitchen door and headed for the stairs. Gillian followed her. It looked to Carrie like she meant to say something else, but Gillian got distracted by the double-sided dental moldings that ran around the ceiling of the dining room and then by the fancy scrollwork on the banister. She followed Carrie absently up the stairs, down the short hallway and into the master suite looking all around her with a dazed expression. She closed the bedroom door and leaned against it as if her knees wouldn't support her anymore.

"Wow," she said in a husky rasp. "I was so right about this place." She looked around the bedroom and her eyes glazed over again.

Carrie suspected that she was in the throes of an intense antique lust. It was kind of cute in a disturbing sort of way. "This is the master suite," she said if only to have something to say while Gillian tried to pull herself back together.

"Oh, yes. I know. It's bigger than the mistress suite and it has the door to the front balcony. Do you mind if I take a look?"

"The door is in the sitting room," Carrie said but Gillian was already on her way.

There was only silence from the other room and then Gillian came back into the bedroom. She sat on the edge of the bed and put her head in her hands.

"The furniture out there is real rattan," Gillian said, as if that was supposed to mean something to Carrie. It didn't, but Gillian didn't seem to notice. "This house is the second oldest building in the whole county," she said from behind her hands. "And everything in here is nearly original. Even the textiles. A little dusty, a little dented, a bit faded and frayed around the edges, but original. I think I'm going to faint."

Carrie couldn't help smiling. "Do you need a glass of water?"

"Yes." Gillian nodded her head vigorously. "Two glasses. Poured straight over my head, but not while I'm sitting on this bed."

"Those sheets are new. The ones that were on it fell apart in the wash."

Gillian gave her a pained look through her parted fingers. "Yes, of course they did. They were sixty years old or more. Promise me you won't wash any more of them?"

"I washed the canopy curtains by hand. They turned out nice."

Gillian looked up and touched the gauzy curtains. "You did a nice job with these."

"The pillows fell apart."

"Feather?" Gillian's mouth twisted.

"Stinky feather." Carrie wrinkled her nose. "I've never smelled anything so awful in all my life."

Gillian groaned and put her head back in her hands. "No more, please."

"Okay." Carrie turned around and dug in a drawer for a T-shirt. She stripped off her pajama top and slipped on a clean bra. She turned back around in time to see Gillian look away. Women could be so funny about other women sometimes, she thought, curious but too scared to just look. Carrie didn't mind other women looking as long as they didn't mind her looking back. She slipped off her pajama bottoms and reached for her jeans.

Gillian stared hard at the clothes press. "This bedroom suite is a matching set. Do you have any idea how rare that is?"

"Not especially." Carrie slipped one leg into her jeans. "I only know that the bed's up awfully high off the floor. I practically have to dive into it."

"Yes, well, back in the day when this bed was built floors tended to be really cold and drafty."

Carrie looked at the floor. "They're not so drafty now." The wood was polished to a high shine, but there were thick carpets covering most of it. Heavy carpets, she knew from hauling them outside to shake the dust off them. Carrie slipped her other leg into her jeans and looked at Gillian who was still staring hard at everything in the room but her. "Gillian, I want you to know how much I appreciate everyone's willingness to help me clean the house today."

"It's not about you."

"Well, damn." Carrie pulled her jeans up, zipped and buttoned them. "I thought everything was about me." That brought a smile to Gillian's lips and a little color into her cheeks.

"I'm sorry to say that it's not this time."

"What do think it's about?"

"Tradition and history. It's about feeling in touch with your place in the world." Gillian ran her hand over the new sheets. "Having some tie to the past makes people feel a little better about their own futures. If they remember something that happened long ago, maybe when they're dead and gone, someone will remember them, too, even if it's only for a small thing, like cleaning spider webs off the chandeliers." Gillian glanced over at Carrie. "Zachary said he wasn't even going to charge you for the electric work if it's not too bad. He said his father helped his grandfather hang the chandelier in the foyer."

Carrie turned to the mirror and twisted her hair up behind her head. "The electric stuff is pretty bad. I took one outlet apart, and the wires looked chewed on. The fuse box in the kitchen has those little glass thingies in it, the kind you have to take out with tongs and thick leather gloves, and there's no main cutoff switch that I could find." Carrie searched across the top of the dresser for an extra hairclip. "It'll be so much work that he'll have to charge me. Besides, I'd like to pay him. I'd like to pay everyone."

"I have an idea of how you can."

Carrie leaned to one side and looked at Gillian in the mirror. "How's that?"

"When everything is all shipshape, you can have a big fancy dress ball. Let everyone dress up in tux and tails or gown and gloves and pretend for just one night that they're different people from a different time."

"I like that. People tell me that I'm very good at pretending." Carrie turned around to look at Gillian. She grinned, even though she knew she shouldn't, but she just couldn't help it. "I bet you'd look really good in a tux and tails."

Gillian looked at her slacks and ran her hands over her knees. "Yes, I think I probably would."

"No. That's not the right answer," Carrie said shaking her head. "You're supposed to tell me that I would look good in a tux and tails, too."

Gillian looked at her critically. "I think I'd rather see you in a ball gown. A light pink satin maybe with lace trim and lots of ribbons."

"Then we'd have to go to the ball together. You in your tux and me in my gown." Carrie was flirting and she shouldn't be, but she couldn't shut herself up.

Gillian turned away from Carrie's smile with a slight frown of her own. She nodded her head toward the clothes press. "That's an amazing piece of furniture, you know. Very well made and well preserved. Do you know what's in it?"

And that was why. She had just made Gillian uncomfortable. "Sweaters."

Gillian nodded again. "Have you been through all the closets?"

"I've been through most of them. This one has old suits with really wide lapels and some of the ugliest ties I've ever seen."

Gillian was still staring at the clothes press. "Did you know that the original floor plan didn't include closets? Back when this house was built, a closet was considered a room and you got charged extra for it on your taxes, so people didn't build them in unless they had to." She waved a hand at the closet doors but still managed to avoid Carrie's eyes. "These closets were added in much later when the bathrooms were installed."

Carrie turned back around to the mirror. She didn't like the way her hair looked. "That seems like a shame to me. I've never been a big fan of closets. Things tend to get lost inside them." She took the hairclips out and shook her hair down. "One day you're looking for a pair of shoes and you pull out some doodad that your best friend gave you for Christmas when you were kids and you say, 'Hey, look at this. I forgot this was in there.' And then you put it right back and forget it again." Her back was to Gillian, but she could still see her in the mirror. "I think it's better to just have things lying around, out in the open where you can see them."

Gillian's frown deepened. "Then everyone else can see them too."

"Exactly. That's the point."

Gillian stood, walked over to the closet door and opened it. She looked inside and then reached out a hand to touch the tie rack. "I don't know if I agree with you about closets, but these really are some ugly ties. What are you going to do with all this?"

Carrie twisted her hair back up again and held it against the back of her head. "I'd like to keep the ties. I'm guessing they were my grandfather's, and I'd like to keep something of him. The suits we can give away if anybody wants them."

"My partner, Jo, is interested in vintage clothing. I'm sure she'd be happy to take them off your hands and give you something for your trouble."

Carrie's fingers slipped and her hair fell again. "Jo? The lady with the deep voice from your antique shop?"

"Yes. She really looks for things from the nineteen-twenties and earlier, but I'm sure she can do something with these." Gillian pointed to the bottom of the closet. "She'd just love those wing tips."

"She can have them if she wants them." Carrie tucked her hair behind her ears. She was both elated and bitterly disappointed and hoped that neither showed on her face. "So, how long have you and Jo been together?"

Gillian closed the closet door. Her cheeks were a burning red. "Jo is my *business* partner. We own the business together, and that's all. I'm not like that."

Carrie felt her own cheeks flame. "Oh. I'm - sorry. I misunderstood. I hope I didn't offend you."

Gillian's blush deepened, but she shook her head. "No, you didn't offend me. I just get tired of being guilty by association. Jo's pretty obvious about her preferences and people tend to assume things that they shouldn't." A muffled thud and loud laughter drifted up through the bedroom floor. Gillian crossed the room and opened the door. The laughter came through clearly. "It sounds like the natives are getting restless. We should probably go give them something to do before they start breaking things." She stepped out into the hallway. "What would you like us to do?"

"I'm not sure." Carrie hesitated as she followed her out into the hall. She was not used to having people do things for her. "I was really just planning to clean the dust off of everything, but I haven't gotten much past the library, the foyer and this suite of rooms. I don't know what to do beyond dusting and polishing. I still don't feel comfortable throwing things away."

Gillian stopped at the head of the stairs. "What about the outside?"

Carrie stood behind Gillian. She could smell the pungent sweetness of baking peaches rising from below. It suited, somehow, to stand behind Gillian and smell peaches. "I guess a good place to start would be trimming the driveway back so it doesn't scratch the paint off everyone's car, and maybe raking the gravel near the road a little more even. I don't know if the grass is too high to be mowed without a tractor."

"What about the stables?" she asked looking at Carrie over her shoulder with an impudent smile.

Carrie smiled back. "I still don't know where they are."

"I do. Would you like me tell you?"

"Yes, please."

"There are two paths leading out from the garden between the wings that lead away from the river. One goes to the stables and the other goes to what I think used to be a formal garden. It's distinct from the garden on the east side of the house, which was only a kitchen garden, meant for small vegetables and herbs."

"I guess I'll have to do the stables myself. How hard do you think it would be to divert the river?"

"Probably more trouble than it's worth." Gillian ran a hand over the scrollwork on the banister. Her eyes went a little bit glassy as her slim fingers slid over the rich patina. "How about if I direct the inside dusting and polishing and you direct the outside mowing and pruning?"

"That sounds like it will work." Carrie watched Gillian's hand caress the banister. "Only, there's one room I don't want you clean."

Gillian's hand stilled. "Which one?"

"The one at the very end of the west wing hallway used to be my mother's room." Carrie looked away from Gillian's hand. "I've been in it, but I haven't been brave enough to go through it yet."

Gillian looked at Carrie and tilted her head a little to one side. "Why not?"

Carrie felt her mouth go dry. She didn't know how to put it into words because she never had before. People who knew her already knew why, and she didn't have to explain, but nobody here knew anything about her life. She touched her mouth and tried to think of some way to put it that would be brief and painless but honest.

"My mother died when I was only two." Carrie lowered her hand and slid it into the front pocket of her jeans. "My father missed her so much that he had a hard time talking about her when I was young. Later, he wasn't often sober enough to talk about anything." As Carrie spoke, she tried not to picture her father in his final years, his loose skin and his staggering walk. He had been a good man, once. "My mother's death destroyed him. I want to know what it was about her that he couldn't let go of, and I guess I wonder what it would have been like for me to grow up knowing her. I thought maybe her room would give me a hint, but it takes a certain kind of courage to walk into a room like that and I haven't been able to gather enough of it yet." Carrie's hand clenched inside her pocket. That wasn't so brief after all, and not at all painless.

Gillian touched Carrie lightly on the arm. Her eyes were soft and sad. "I'm so sorry, Carrie. I can't imagine what that was like for you. My mother died just a few years ago, but she had always been there for me."

Gillian's touch was light but it weighed heavily on Carrie's heart. No one had ever said that they were sorry before. Carrie didn't know how to respond to that. She shrugged. "I didn't know anything different."

"Well"—Gillian rubbed her arm briskly and let her hand drop—"if you're looking for clues to the past, don't forget the attic."

"There's an attic?"

"Yes, and I heard from a reliable, if gossipy, source that it was crammed full of stuff."

"Oh." Carrie looked at the smooth unbroken ceiling. "I wonder how I get up there."

"There's probably a door somewhere. Most houses this old have a set of stairs to the attic. I imagine it looks like a closet door. I'll have the cleaning crew keep an eye out."

"Thank you." Carrie meant her thanks sincerely and she wished she could say more than that, but she knew she wouldn't say it right. Whatever "it" was. Gillian was stirring things inside her. It wasn't lust. Well, not entirely, anyway. And it wasn't longing. Not exactly. It was confusing. There was a kindness to Gillian that she hadn't seen a whole lot of in her life, but there was distance there, too. It made her feel…she didn't know how it made her feel. Weird. Nostalgic. Unsettled. Strangely hopeful.

Gillian turned and started down the stairs. Carrie followed close behind thinking about the soft sadness in Gillian's eyes. They were pretty eyes, almost the same shade of gray as the dust that had covered everything. So, there was one thing that Carrie could be sure of…Gillian had very pretty eyes.

CHAPTER NINE

Carrie looked up at the sound of feet slapping hard against the ground. A boy was running full tilt down the stable path, his arms pumping wildly. Carrie lowered her clippers and pushed her hair back out of her eyes.

"Miss Carrie!" The boy skidded to a stop, his sneaker scraping over the mossy brick. His eyes were wide and his face flushed with excitement. "Hey, Miss Carrie, you need to come take a look at what we found. It's *so* wicked cool, but we're not sure what to do about it. Come on! Come look."

The boy turned and ran off back down the path before she could ask him anything. Carrie looked at the brush she was trimming. She was already two-thirds of the way to the stables and had been looking forward to seeing what was there, but she supposed they could wait a while for something that was *so* wicked cool. The boy had run down the opposite branch of the path, the one that Gillian said led to one of the formal gardens. She tucked her clippers under her arm and followed at a more dignified pace. As she walked down the path she thought of what a nice job the boys had done trimming and weeding. They had cut the bushes back, pulled the weeds from between the bricks and cut the low-hanging branches off the trees. The few flower beds had long since died out, but it was clear that this path had been lovingly attended at one point in time. It must have been a wonderful place for an afternoon stroll. Carrie hoped it would be again.

At the end of the path, she saw a small group of boys drifting around with their hands stuffed in their pockets, scuffing the toes of their sneakers around in the grass.

"What is it, guys? What did you find?" The boys parted to let her see. There was a small patch of cleared brush. Framed by the weeds was a very old wrought iron fence. Inside the fence, overgrown and nearly unrecognizable, was a cemetery. "Wow," she said.

"Do you want us to clean it up?" one of the boys asked nervously.

"We're not scared of it," another boy said. "We just thought that you should know it was here."

"I think it's wicked cool," the first boy said again. "There's real dead people in there."

"Hmmm." Carrie pretended to ponder. "This looks like at least a few days' worth of work. Maybe you'd better let me clean it up." The boys all looked relieved, except for the first boy who scowled and kicked at a rock. "Tell you what. Let's trade. You guys finish trimming up by the stables and I'll work on this. And let me know if you find a horse in there."

The boys looked at each other, then grabbed their trimmers and rakes and ran, racing each other to the stable path. Carrie grinned as she watched them go. She could still remember being that young once. It wasn't really all that long ago. Or maybe it was. The boys disappeared around a bend and Carrie turned back to the fence.

The iron rails were black and pitted with age. Inside the rails, headstones struggled to rise above tall grass and weeds. What little she could see was weathered and worn. There were real dead people in there, probably her ancestors, people she belonged to but knew nothing about. It made her feel strange that she had no sense of these people as family and yet, they were. Carrie gripped her shears and gave them a quick snip. Staring at it wasn't going to get the fence cleared. She waded into the waist high weeds and began clipping.

She worked steadily all afternoon until she had the whole fence cleared of overgrowth. Naturally, she found the gate three feet from where she started but in the opposite direction. She was tired and dirty, pricked and gouged, mosquito bit and itchy. The day felt old and worn and she guessed it was since the sun was starting to sink below the tops of the trees. She leaned a tired hip against the railing. The inside of the cemetery was still a mess, but it could wait until tomorrow. It wouldn't be right, anyway, tripping over headstones in the dark, disturbing the peace, twisting her ankle. She tucked her shears under her arm and started back to the house with the light of day fading fast behind her.

The path really did look nice especially in the twilight as shadows began to spread underneath the trees. Across the meadow, the wildflowers had folded their petals for the night. All except for the four o'clocks, whose small red faces had only just opened. Late as usual. Rounding the corner, where the garden path met the stable path, the house came into view and Carrie had to stop for a moment. The lawn was mowed, the bushes trimmed and the debris cleared. The windows were clean and lit, the shutters washed and straightened. The sun had set just enough that she couldn't see the cracked and peeling paint. The house looked like something out of an old book. She would hardly be surprised to see a woman in a hoopskirt or a man in a top hat come sashaying out the door.

Something rustled through the brush to her right. A fox streaked across the meadow in a blur of red and black and disappeared into the trees. From far off over the rolling hills, she heard the faint cry of a horn and the distant baying of hounds.

Carrie shivered as goose bumps prickled up and down her arms.

She was met at the kitchen door by a stern-faced Anna Beth who made Carrie take her shoes off, brush the dirt from her clothes with a whisk broom and wash her hands and face in the outside faucet before allowing her to come into the house. Inside the kitchen, a large pot of soup was bubbling on the stove. Plates of sandwiches, bags of chips, bowls of potato salad and pie tins of peach cobbler lay out on the kitchen table. Carrie grabbed a bottle of water and drank half of it down before taking a breath. Gillian, still looking annoyingly fresh and neat, smiled at Carrie's wild mess of hair and handed her a mug of some beefy smelling vegetable soup. Carrie took a sip as she looked around her. The kitchen seemed so different, clean and bright, with the smell of good food cooking, the warmth of good people gathered all around her. Gillian didn't let her enjoy it for very long.

"Come look at the rest of the house," she said pulling her by the arm through the kitchen door.

Carrie put her mug on the table and let Gillian drag her into the dining room. She stopped still in the doorway. It took her breath away. The ladies had polished the dining room table to a high gloss and the silver service sparkled against dark rich wood. They had placed a large candelabrum in the center with two many-tiered dessert trays on either side. Gleaming sugar bowls and salt cellars, pepper grinders, and other pieces of tableware that Carrie didn't recognize dotted the centerline. At the far end, there were place settings for three of beautiful white and blue china plates with filigreed braid around the rims. Cut crystal stemware sat above each place glinting under the bright lights.

Carrie walked around to the place settings and touched a neatly folded napkin. "Why is the table set for three?"

Gillian stood beside her and shrugged. "Anna Beth said that's the way the table was always set when the household wasn't entertaining. For as long as she was the cook, there was always an empty place set no matter how many people were dining. A guest plate, maybe, for unexpected visitors. That wouldn't be unusual."

Gillian tugged on her arm. "Come on, you've got to see the rest of the house."

Gillian pulled her into the foyer. Carrie looked up as a grinning Zachary threw the switch for the chandelier. Light filled the foyer with a soft warmth that made her want to hug Gillian and Zachary, too, but she didn't have time before Gillian grabbed her arm again and dragged her into the parlor, all dusted and polished, and down the west wing hallway through to the billiards room, a quick dash inside the smoking room, back through the library, the foyer and then outside and down the porch steps.

Carrie took a moment to catch her breath as they stood in front of the fountain. It was cleaned and scrubbed. The smiling cherubs seemed unaware of their chipped and broken wings as they tipped their urns and poured water into brimming basins, which overflowed into the main bowl. The water ran clear and clean as it gurgled and splashed with a soft pleasing sound. A group of children, wet and dripping, spotted with muck, stood around the fountain grinning at her. Carrie thanked each of the kids specifically, while studiously ignoring the few suspiciously wriggling pockets.

Old Mr. Masters stood with his thumbs hooked in his belt, looking pleased. Carrie shook his hand and thanked him. He blushed and muttered something about going in to get a sandwich. He turned and herded the kids around to the side of the house to hose them off before letting them into the kitchen. Carrie looked again at the fountain as the last few rays of the setting sun brushed the cherubs' cheeks with a tinge of pink.

Gillian looped her arm through Carrie's elbow. "Well, what do you think?"

Carrie glanced at the house, at the newly mown lawn, back again at the fountain. She blinked the sting away from her eyes. "I think it's amazing. I don't know how I'm going to thank everyone."

Gillian squeezed her arm. "Yes, you do. Tux and tails, gown and gloves. Remember?"

Carrie grinned. "I think you're going to have to help me plan it."

"Naturally. If you give me your cell number, I'll call you and we can get together to make the arrangements."

Carrie resisted the urge to pull her closer. "I think I still owe you a tour."

"I got to see pretty much everything while I was overseeing the cleaning, but I'd love to go over it all again. I'll be happy to do an appraisal for you when you're ready for one."

"I'm not sure I want to know how much all this stuff is worth. I'm still not convinced it's actually mine. It still feels like I'm just taking care of this place until my grandmother gets back."

Gillian gave her arm another squeeze. "Speaking of, we found some interesting things while we were cleaning."

"Like what?"

"There was a ladies' watch stuck behind the music box in the library."

"What music box?"

"The one beside the fireplace. It looks like a chest sitting on top of a table. You open the lid, and if it's wound up, the gears start turning. It's got a metal disk inside that plays a tune."

"Oh. I didn't know what that was. What does it play?"

"It's supposed to play 'The Girl I Left Behind' according to the etching on the disk. That's an old Revolutionary War tune that became popular again during the Civil War. You'd know it if you heard it, but I'm afraid we couldn't get the music box to wind up properly. There's probably something stuck inside that needs a little oil."

"Maybe it just needs a good whack," Carrie said, trying not to grin.

Gillian frowned. "Please tell me you're joking."

"Of course, I am." Carrie wanted to laugh. It was so easy to tease her. Much too easy.

"You should never joke about antiques." Gillian gave her a stern glare that still managed to look amused. "I can have someone come out and look at it, but music boxes are very expensive to repair since no one makes them anymore."

"We'll see. What else did you find?" Carrie wasn't sure she cared, but she liked the feeling of Gillian's arm linked through hers. She shouldn't let herself like it or Gillian as much as she thought she could. Gillian wasn't "like that," she said. Falling for her would be like hitting her head against a brick wall. No matter how gently she did it, eventually, it was going to hurt.

"The most interesting thing we found was a letter that was in the trash can in the library. It seemed very old, but it wasn't dated. I read it, I'm afraid. Curiosity always gets the best of me."

"What was in it?"

"It was a poem about a love won and then lost. The usual... Roses are red, violets are blue, you're not here, I'm missing you...That kind of thing. Very romantic."

Carrie made a sour face. "That doesn't sound very romantic. If someone was going to write me a poem, I would hope they wouldn't go with an old saw."

"It wasn't really about roses but more about flowers in general."

"That sounds a little less awful."

"It wasn't at all awful. It was sweet and sad, just the way a poem should be."

In spite of herself, Carrie shifted a little closer to Gillian. "Well then, if I ever write you a poem, I'll make sure to say all kinds of sweetly depressing things."

Gillian gave her arm a squeeze and let it go. She stepped away from Carrie and turned around to face the house. Carrie turned too. The lights blazed in all the windows as darkness filled in the corners of the porch.

Gillian sighed, deep and wistful. "Zachary's boy said that they found all kinds of old harnesses and things in the stables. Maybe when you get settled you could get some horses."

Carrie shook her head. "I don't think so. I don't know a thing about horses except that they're big, they bite and they step on your feet."

"Oh, that's right. I forgot you're a city girl." Gillian crossed the drive, climbed the porch steps and sat near the top. "I was just thinking that it would be good to see the Covington Hunt Club up and running again. The Tuesday morning hunt was a tradition going back nearly two hundred years until your grandmother put a stop to it the year your grandfather died. Since you're restoring things, I thought it would be appropriate to restore that, too."

Carrie followed her over to the porch and stood on the bottom step. She was almost eye to eye with Gillian. "A hunt club is where people on horses with big beagle dogs chase little foxes all around the countryside?"

Gillian laughed. "More or less."

"Who's doing that now?"

"What do you mean?"

"This evening on my way back to the house, I heard a hunting horn and a pack of dogs barking."

"That's hounds, not dogs and they bay, not bark. Some people say they give tongue, but I think that sounds a little crude."

Carrie grinned. "It does sound a bit suggestive."

Gillian looked like she might grin back, but she turned her face away before Carrie could tell. "I can't imagine what you heard. People don't hunt on horses at dusk. There's too much of a chance that a horse would break a leg or the rider's neck."

"I'm pretty sure that's what I heard."

"Well, it wasn't anybody I know of, but I'll ask around if you're curious."

"It's not important. It's just that there's this fox that I've seen twice now. I think it lives around here somewhere."

Gillian turned back around. She definitely wasn't grinning. "They don't hurt the fox, Carrie. They just chase it a little."

"I'm not saying they shouldn't. All I'm saying is that I'd like the fox to have somewhere safe to run to, especially if it lives around here."

Gillian smiled at her then, in a very peculiar way. The tilt of her head, the quirky upturn of her mouth seemed so intimate that it made Carrie's toes tingle. She dropped her eyes before she did something foolish or said something worse.

"I'll ask around for you," Gillian said again. She stood. "In the meantime, we should probably go inside and warm your soup again. I bet you're just famished."

Carrie realized that she was.

Carrie strolled around the house once more with her re-warmed mug of soup in her hands, taking her time in each room, looking at all the things she hadn't had the time to see before on Gillian's whirlwind tour. The parlor was a large room with couches and chairs strewn all around it in small conversational groups. The furniture was faded and worn but, newly dusted and polished, it still looked elegant. In the billiards room, the kids were playing a game that involved the random knocking of balls around the table. It was a strange looking table with a red felt top and dark leather bumpers, pockets made of netted baskets. The balls clunked together with a dull heavy thud. The kids gave a delighted shout as one dropped into the corner basket.

Carrie wandered back out into the hallway and further into the west wing. She opened the door to the smoking room. The cleaning crew had done wonders with their rags and polishes. The dark wood paneling gleamed and the wavy grains of the oak shone through. The heavy red velvet curtains were clean and the cracked leather chairs patched and polished. Carrie thought she could still smell the faint remnants of cigar and pipe tobacco underneath the lemon-scented furniture oil. Her father had smoked cigars but only on Sundays when he tried not to drink. The room made her think of him. She could picture her father sitting in his overstuffed chair, wreathed in smoke, a cup of coffee at his elbow, his fourth or fifth, the *Tribune* open in his hands, the paper trembling slightly.

Carrie stepped back out into the hallway and closed the door softly. She wasn't going to like that room very much. But she didn't have to. There were plenty of other rooms for her to discover. For example, she hadn't seen the guest rooms in the east wing yet. Carrie headed for the stairs.

The rooms looked like guest rooms, all three of them, with generic wallpaper patterns, neutral shaded throw rugs, plain, solid-colored bedspreads, furniture with straight, simple lines. The bedrooms were made up neatly, the sheets and curtains no doubt hand-washed and air-dried under Gillian's supervision, the pillows fluffed, the floors swept and the rugs vacuumed. The rooms looked ready for guests to arrive.

Carrie walked down the hall to the mistress suite. The bedroom and sitting room were a little smaller than in the master suite. The bed had a faded yellow crocheted bedcover that Carrie overhead Gillian talking about. She said it must have taken someone years to make something that intricate and large.

In the sitting room, Carrie sat at the small writing desk, empty of pens and paper, and stared at the boldly flowered wallpaper. She wondered why her grandmother hadn't stayed in this room. If Carrie remembered correctly, her grandmother had been the mistress of the house for most of her life. Surely, it would have been appropriate for her to claim this room as her own. It was much larger than the little room in the east wing and much less stark even in its emptiness. But it was very empty. The closets, the clothes press, the medicine chest in the bathroom were all bare. The bathroom had not a towel, washcloth or lump of soap in it. Only one dresser drawer had an old sachet of dried flowers, but the smell was long gone. The suite was so empty it was almost devoid of character, except for the wallpaper, large blotches of red flowers with smears of green leaves. Carrie thought it was ugly, but someone must have liked it well enough at one time.

Gillian poked her head through the door. "Hey, there you are. Everyone's getting ready to leave."

Carrie looked at Gillian, at her flushed cheeks and bright eyes. She didn't want everyone to leave. "Okay. Thanks." And her soup had gotten cold again.

Gillian walked into the room and took the mug out of her hands. She licked her thumb, rubbed at a smear of dirt on Carrie's chin and then brushed a lock of hair back from her face. A finger lingered on the curve of Carrie's ear. Carrie shuddered and Gillian turned away. She walked quickly over to the bedroom door, stopped and looked back at Carrie. She looked confused, as if she wasn't sure why she had just done that.

Gillian dropped her eyes to the mug in her hand. "I'll…just go put this in the kitchen."

"Okay." Carrie's voice sounded thin and the air around her seemed almost too heavy to breathe. The soup churned uneasily in her stomach. Her ribs felt stiff against her lungs.

Gillian shook herself slightly. She gave Carrie a shaky smile, turned and left.

Carrie glanced at her empty hand. It was clear why her grandmother hadn't stayed here in this suite. The rooms were just too ugly. The wallpaper was the most horrible thing she'd ever seen. The writing desk, the dressing table, the tall canopy bed were the most hideous pieces of furniture ever made. Carrie stood and walked out of the sitting room. She walked through the bedroom without looking at the bed or the clothes press or the dressing table. She couldn't bear to look at them they were so awful. Her throat was so tight it hurt as her heart began to flutter in her chest. She nearly ran out into the hallway and the door shut behind her with a slam.

Carrie stood on the front porch with Gillian standing at her side. The cleaning and clipping crews streamed out of the door in ones and twos. Carrie thanked each of them for their hard work, and each of them thanked Gillian for putting the day together. They all looked tired, but in a happy, satisfied way. Carrie shook hands and Gillian gave hugs. They said goodbye and watched the cars, vans and trucks rumble down the driveway until there was only one car left parked beside the fountain. The night turned quiet and still, broken only by the whir of the cicadas, the soft croaking of frogs. The same frogs, Carrie knew that had been in the kids' pockets, now safely ensconced back in their fountain.

The front door was still open. Light from the foyer poured out onto the porch, breaking the night into patches of light and dark. Gillian yawned and stretched her arms above her head. Carrie tried not to look at the flash of skin where her shirt rode up, at the tight stretch of material across her chest. She tried, but she failed. She dragged her eyes up to Gillian's face just in time to meet her tired smile.

"Well, I guess I'd better go, too. No point in keeping you up half the night."

Carrie shuffled her feet. "I really appreciate what you did for me today."

"It wasn't about you," Gillian said, her eyes sparkling.

"So I understand." Carrie smiled and held out her hand. "Thanks anyway."

Gillian took her hand and pulled her into a half hug. "Thank you," she said softly against Carrie's ear and then let her go. She grabbed her purse off the bench and dug in it for her keys.

Carrie didn't want her to go. The house would seem so barren after being so full of life and laughter just moments ago. But trying to keep her there any longer might seem strange, and Carrie didn't want Gillian to think she was strange. She liked her and if she could be nothing else, she wanted to be her friend. It seemed that Gillian liked her well enough, too, and that wasn't something you threw away for a hopeless craving.

Gillian walked to her car, keys jingling in her hand. She opened the door and got in. The car started, backed up a space and pulled around the fountain. She started down the drive with a little wave of her hand in the rearview mirror. Carrie stood on the porch until the red taillights of the hatchback disappeared into the trees. The night grew still again. A frog made a little chirping sound and Carrie heard it plop into the fountain. She turned around to look at the porch. It was a big porch. Someone had washed the benches, the tea tables and the rocking chairs, swept the dirt and debris from the steps. In the shadows, everything looked almost new. She pushed on the back of a rocking chair and started it moving. Maybe she should have asked Gillian to stay for a while. Offered her a cup of coffee or tea, a piece of cheesecake, a nightcap. She still had all those questions she wanted to ask, that she forgot to ask.

Yeah, right, Carrie chided herself. She was heading for trouble. She could feel it coming. Nothing good ever came out of falling for a straight woman. Nothing good at all. She was sure to make a fool out of herself sooner or later and would probably lose a good friend in the bargain. She looked at the rocking chair. It was still rocking. She stilled it with her hand. If only it were that easy.

She walked back into the bright, clean foyer and turned the chandelier off. The lights in the parlor were still on and also in the billiards room, the smoking room, the library, the dining room and the kitchen. She spent the next half hour walking around the house picking up cups, closing curtains and turning lights off. She realized that the house was starting to feel familiar to her, not quite so big as she first thought. Each room had its own purpose. Each room had a reason, even if the reason no longer existed. Even if there was no maid for the chambers, no butler for the pantry, no horses in the stables, no dogs in the kennel.

Hounds. Gillian had called them hounds, as if the distinction was important. She remembered the sound of them barking... baying, one long, deep note then a couple of yips. It was an old sound, one that matched the rounded shoulders of the hills, the slow shuffling of the river, the creaking voice of the wind in the trees.

Good God, she was getting positively maudlin. And even that word was old, not something typically in her vocabulary. Carrie felt a sudden urge for a beer and a slice of pizza, a fast drive in a sporty car along an interstate, a brainless sitcom on television. Carrie stopped, a tower of stacked plastic cups teetering in her hands. There wasn't a single television in the whole house. She hadn't realized that before with all the books in the library keeping her entertained. She might have to buy one when she ran out of books. Or she could just buy more books. Tough choice.

She threw the cups in the trash and washed the few soup mugs still left in the sink, dried them and put them away. The kitchen did feel lonely now without all the people in it, just like she thought it would. She wiped at a faint smudge on the counter, at a speck left on the surface of the stove. She picked up a crumb from off the floor. The kitchen was as clean as it was possible for a kitchen to be. There wasn't anything else left for her to do. Except take a bath and go to bed. She folded the dishtowel, hung it up and headed for the library to grab a new book.

It was still dark when Carrie woke to a light rain pattering against the ground, drumming gently on the roof. A small gust blew the curtains back with the smell of mud and wet pine. She got up and closed the windows, wiping the damp off the sills with the hem of her pajama top. Back in bed, with the sheet pulled up under her chin, Carrie listened to the muted sound of the rain. It was rhythmic and soothing, almost like music. She imagined each drop as the light tapping of a drum, each puff of wind as the breathy toot of a flute.

Carrie sat up. She did hear music. In between the drops, she heard a soft tinkling sound, a scratchy trilling just on the edge of hearing, faint and far away. She sat as still as she could and listened, her eyes half closed, her head titled to the side. A gust of wind blew against the house, rattling the windows, driving the rain against the panes in a harsh clatter of drops. The wind died down and the other sound was gone. If it had been a sound. Carrie listened for a few more minutes, but she only heard the rain. She lay back down, snuggled into her sheets and clutched the extra pillow tight against her chest.

CHAPTER TEN

Carrie woke earlier than usual. Her eyes were still gritty and heavy, but she got up anyway feeling just as tired of being in bed as she was still just tired. Her dreams had been disturbing, but she couldn't remember what they had been about. She shuffled her tired feet down the front stairs and headed for the kitchen.

As her coffee steeped in the press pot, Carrie stood at the counter and gazed out the kitchen window. The night rain had washed down the trees, and now the outside looked as polished as the inside with the small drops of water sparkling in the bright morning sun. She pushed the press and poured the coffee into her waiting mug of cream and sugar. She was the one who needed the cream and sugar this morning, not the coffee. Dark mingled with light in a blending swirl and came to an earthy balance near the rim of her mug.

She carried her coffee into the library and sat at the desk. The letter that Gillian had told her about was still lying there on the leather blotter. It had been crumpled and then smoothed out again. The handwriting was spidery and thin. It was hard to make sense of the words that flowed over the page where they bunched up at the edges and then dropped to the next line. Carrie squinted her eyes and tilted the paper into the light.

She read it through slowly and then put the paper back on the desk. She had no idea why Gillian thought it was a love poem. The lines spoke of cutting flowers from a garden. The writer put the cut flowers in a vase to decorate her dressing room table and then wrote of how she felt as they withered. That didn't sound much like love to Carrie, but then again, she wasn't much into poetry. She read the paper again as it lay on the desk. No, it definitely wasn't a love poem to her. It was more of a lament. The words made her feel strange. Almost weepy. Sad for the brief life of flowers and for the guilty knife that cut them.

That wasn't like her. Carrie rubbed at her eyes and took a deep sip of her coffee. She picked up the watch. It was a small fob, meant for a chain that might have been gold once, but now it was hard to tell. The numbers on the face were faded, the hands frozen at a quarter to five. Something about that seemed almost as sad as the poem. She put the watch down and shuffled through some of the other papers lying on the desk. There was a bill from the 1930s written in blotched ink in nearly illegible handwriting for a list of miscellaneous items, a sack of flour, two boxes of nails, a crate of peaches, twelve pounds of coffee, a bolt of cloth. Another was for a dress that cost eighty dollars in 1945. She wondered if eighty dollars was a lot of money back then and what the dress was for and where it was now. That reminded her of the attic. Gillian and the cleaning crew must not have found a way into it since no one said anything. She would have to find it herself, but she didn't want to look for it now. The sun was shining so beautifully, glistening on the wet leaves and grass. The breeze coming in through the library windows was warm and inviting.

It was going to be a good day to be outside, and since the kitchen was already clean, finding the attic could wait for that rainy afternoon. She would go look at the stuff the kids found in the stables, go find the kennel, which she hadn't even seen yet, and then finish trimming in the little cemetery. Not that anyone in there was in a hurry, but it would make her feel better, more respectful of those at rest. She stood and stretched her tired muscles, picked up her mug and then headed upstairs to dress.

As Carrie trimmed around the headstones and the little obelisks, she jotted into a small notebook all the names and dates chiseled into the faces and whatever little homily she found carved at the bottom. She found her grandfather's grave in the near corner, a headstone but no footstone, carved with his name, Robert Daniel Burgess, born 1885, died 1940. *Resting in the arms of our Lord.* He had only been fifty-five when he died, her mother only five years old at the time. A child of his later years. Just like she had been. She wondered what Gillian knew about his story. There was an empty place next to his grave. Carrie supposed it was for her grandmother, but her grandmother was in another place in another county. She wondered if her grandmother would have been buried here if anyone had remembered that this cemetery existed. Who knew? Maybe zoning laws had changed or something. Having a cemetery in her backyard did seem kind of creepy, especially when it was so wild and unkempt.

By late afternoon, Carrie was almost finished with the trimming and the clipping. She sat resting on the grass, her back pressed against the trunk of the gnarled willow tree that grew in the clear space in the middle. Its drooping branching offered a green canopied shade from the heat of the day. There was only the far back corner left to be trimmed, and she had saved that for last because it was such a dense cluster of tangled weeds and thorny vines. Milkweed and straw grass grew tall and twisted among wild tea roses with thick stems and small clusters of pink puckered flowers.

Carrie turned a page back in her notebook, reading through the names and dates. The oldest date was 1863. A Mrs. Jebediah Covington had died then and been buried underneath a small round topped stone. The next oldest was 1887, a Mrs. Beauregard

Covington. The one after that was a second Mrs. Beauregard Covington who died just three years after her predecessor in 1890. Either Beauregard was hard on his wives or he had immensely bad luck. Beauregard himself didn't die until 1923. That would be her grandmother's father, her great-grandfather. Carrie thought she remembered someone saying that her grandmother was an only child, but she wasn't so sure about that. There were two very small graves, the closest to the willow tree, both of them also from 1887. Two boys, William and James, ages five and seven, who might have been her grandmother's brothers or maybe half brothers. It was hard to tell.

Carrie closed her notebook, tucked it in her back pocket and looked over at the tangled mess still growing in the far back corner. She didn't have the first idea about how to prune roses. They were fussy little flowers, she knew, being both hardy and fragile, beautiful and cruel. She remembered reading something about clipping off the deadwood and trimming back the offshoots. She picked up her clippers. The blades were still shiny and sharp, even after two days of hard use, but the thorns in the back corner looked even sharper. Carrie stood and slapped the grass clippings off the seat of her shorts. Doing something was better than doing nothing, and nothing was going to get clipped if she didn't start somewhere. She waded into the densest part of the tangle and shoved her clippers in.

Metal scraped across stone. The sound was jarring in the silence of the cemetery, too loud, too harsh for a place so quiet. Carrie cocked her head and rubbed her ear against her shoulder. She stepped back a little ways from the tangle of vines and began to snip more carefully, taking off the dead branches a piece at a time, paring back the live ones inch by inch. The tall straw grass growing between the twisted branches confused the issue. There was only one rose bush, she discovered, but it grew in a cluster of thick stems twisting in and out and over each other. She cut the grass back and brushed the trimmings aside. There was a small stone under the weeds, not quite a foot tall. A marker of some kind, maybe, but there was no name or date on it. Just the carving of a flower cut deep into the face.

A chill prickled at the back of her neck. She wasn't sure why. There was nothing scary about a small headstone, not anything scarier than the big ones. It was only that it was lying in the far back corner of a wild cemetery, lost under the creepers and the weeds. That wasn't scary. That was sad. Or maybe it was so sad that it was scary. Carrie stood and stepped back from the stone. Its rounded top was worn and the face of it was dark with age and blotched with lichen. Of all the sad things she had run across so far, this little stone struck her as being the saddest thing of all. It was something that was meant to be forgotten. And then, it was.

Carrie rubbed at her cheek with the back of her glove. Sweat stained the dark cloth. At least, she was pretty sure it was sweat. It stung her eyes, ran down her face and tickled her under the chin. She squeezed her eyes shut and shook her head. It was just a stone with a flower. That was not something she would cry over. Carrie wiped her face on the sleeve of her T-shirt, leaving a large damp blotch smeared across her bicep. It had to be sweat. Carrie turned abruptly away from the stone. The rest of the cemetery was neatly trimmed, the grass mowed, the weeds pulled. The only thing left to be done was to rake up the debris.

The day had been warm and bright, but the temperature was falling along with the sun. Carrie grabbed the rake and started sweeping. She made neat little piles and then swept the little piles into big ones, finally piling everything into one great big pile over by the gate. It would all get composted later, when she had time to decide where the compost pile was going to be. Carrie stopped to catch her breath and looked at the mound of trimmings. There were flowers in there, from the scraggly limbs of the rose bush, half buried under the grass clippings and the weeds, but still pink and full. Lying there unawares.

That wasn't right. Carrie picked the flowers out of the pile, gathered them in a bunch and took them back to the house with her where she carefully trimmed the stems, filled a vase with water and put the flowers in it. She was not going to put them on her dressing room table. Instead, she put the flowers in the library on the mantel piece next to the mirror where they could watch themselves fade and she wouldn't have to. But maybe that was too cruel. She took the flowers off the mantel and put them on the desk next to the poem where they could be sure that someone appreciated their predicament. That was better, if not ideal.

Carrie sat at the desk and dropped her head into her hands. She must be losing it. Since when did she ever feel sorry for flowers? They were pretty, but they lived and died just like everything else in the world. She should have gone into town to get that pizza and beer. Two pizzas and a case of beer. Tomorrow, she would go for sure. For lunch. An early lunch. She went upstairs, showered, grabbed a book and went to bed.

Carrie sat up. She looked out the window at the pale moonlight shimmering on the tops of the trees. Something woke her, but she didn't know what it was. There was no wind or rain, no clouds. The night was quiet and still. Through the window, she could see that the sky was full of stars. She tilted her head and squeezed her eyes shut, listening hard. What was it that woke her? Her dreams had been full of things she couldn't remember but they left her feeling odd and disjointed. She tilted her head to the other side and then she heard it. Not clearly, but it sounded like the tapping of a drum, the tooting of a flute, the whine of a bow across strings.

Carrie slipped out of bed. She walked quietly out of the bedroom, tiptoed down the hallway and stood at the head of the stairs. The music was clearer there, though still tinny and faint. It sounded like it was coming from right under her feet. That was the library. She shivered and pulled her pajama top tighter around her. The stairs looked steep and narrow in the darkness, but she hugged the railing and went down them one at a time until her bare feet hit the chilly parquet floor.

The library doors were closed. She didn't remember closing them, but she didn't remember them being open either. Carrie put her ear to the door. The music was definitely coming from in there. She could hear it, the tap-tap of a drum, the trilling of a flute, the scrape of a bow. The sound of a woman laughing. Carrie opened the door just a crack. The library was dark and still. She didn't see anybody but she could hear the music playing from somewhere inside. She stepped into the room and turned on a small table lamp.

Dim yellow light threw crooked shadows across the floor. The music box sat beside the fireplace. It was open, the lid raised. A small winding key turned slowly. She didn't remember the lid being open either the last time she passed it. But, then again, she hadn't known what it was the last time she passed it. Carrie walked over to the box and looked inside. Gears and cogs were turning. Long thin pins plucked at spokes on a brass disk making the sounds of a vaguely familiar song.

Carrie slowly closed the lid. The music stuttered and died. Gillian had told her it was stuck. She touched the winding key and then turned it. The key clicked quietly as it rolled easily under her fingers.

Well, whatever had been stuck must have come unstuck. That seemed likely enough, but she thought she'd better have a look around anyway. Carrie walked around the room, peering under couches, behind chairs and curtains without finding so much as a dust bunny. She jiggled the handles of the patio doors. They were locked tight. She wandered back over to the desk. Nothing had been disturbed. The poem still lay there next to the bills, next to the flowers. Fallen petals from the roses lay scattered across the papers. They were small and dark in the dim light, cupped and curled. They looked like large drops of water or maybe something darker.

Carrie cursed and shook the petals into the wastebasket. She was letting the house get to her. It was too big and too empty with just one person in it. She was letting her imagination get the best of her. There had been music, but it was only the box. The petals were only petals. There was nothing to be scared of or nervous about. Dreams were only dreams. They didn't mean anything. They weren't real. Carrie turned off the light and made her way back up the stairs and back into bed. She lay with the sheet pulled up to her chin, looking at the stars still filling the sky, and tried very hard not to think of the woman laughing.

CHAPTER ELEVEN

The doorbell rang, or thunked, rather, as the brass clappers high up on the wall in the foyer still needed a new spring. Carrie looked up from her book. Her eyes were still tired from staying up so long, listening while trying not to hear. Reading had helped, but it was now nine in the morning and she was still reading, still trying to shake off the odd prickly feeling that sat at the base of her spine. The doorbell thunked again followed by a brief staccato knock. Carrie put her book down and went to open the front door.

Gillian stood on the welcome mat in a bright yellow slicker, sparkles of rain dotting her hair. "Hey," she said with a little wave of her hand. "Good morning to you. I hope you don't mind me dropping in like this."

"No. Not at all." Carrie smiled as she opened the door wider. "I wasn't doing anything much. Come on in and have some coffee or something."

"Thanks." Gillian smiled back at her.

It was an odd smile, quirky and amused, as usual, but also just slightly shy with a dash of distracted. She came in, took her raincoat off and hung it in the closet underneath the right most set of stairs. It was a door that Carrie hadn't opened before. There was nothing in it but a set of wooden coat hangers and now Gillian's yellow raincoat. Carrie led the way to the kitchen.

"Coffee?" She asked holding up the press pot. "This is still warm, but I can make you a fresh pot if you want a cup."

Gillian stopped at the kitchen door and leaned against the frame. She shook her head. "Already done my quota for the day, but thanks anyway. I can't stay but a while. I just wanted to drop by real quick to see how things were going."

Carrie shrugged. "They're fine." She stopped herself. That wasn't a very good answer but she was still feeling a little shy of Gillian, especially with her standing the way she was, leaning against the doorframe with such casual elegance, looking so fresh with her rain-spotted hair. She smiled again, maybe more at herself than at Gillian. "Actually, everything is just wonderful. All the lights work, the toilets flush on the first try, the showers are clean and have hot water. What more could anyone ask for?"

"You may be asking for a new furnace, come winter." Gillian came into the kitchen, pulled out a chair and sat at the table. "Zachary took a look at the old one and said that he didn't recommend turning it on before you had someone out to take a look at it. I forgot to tell you that the other day." She smoothed her hands over her hair smearing the raindrops into darker streaks. "In fact, there were a whole lot of things I forgot to tell you, but now that I'm here, I can't remember what they were."

Carrie looked at the pot and then poured herself the last of the coffee. It was her fourth cup, but she still felt tired. "I get like that, too. I'm only thirty, but, God, sometimes I feel so old."

"Makes me wonder how we're going to feel when we really do grow old." Gillian tapped her fingers on the surface of the kitchen table. "Have you made any decisions about this place? I know it's none of my business, but I was just wondering what your plans were." Gillian's eyes shifted around the room. "If you're going to sell the house, I can help you get good prices for the furniture and things." Her fingers kept tapping as her voice trailed off softly into nothing.

And there again was the trick. There always was a trick. Good never happened without bad, but as bad things went, seeing what motivated Gillian wasn't too awful. More disappointing than anything else, but Carrie knew from the beginning that people like Gillian didn't look twice at people like her without a good reason. Potential commission money was always a good reason. It was heartachingly disappointing but not unexpected.

Carrie took a sip from her cup. It had been steeping for far too long. The coffee tasted bitter and burnt. "I take it you think I should sell the house and move back to Chicago." After all, what did she know about small towns and old houses? Or antique dealers for that matter?

Gillian's fingers stilled. She flattened her hands and moved them back and forth across the tabletop, her fingers bumping over a knot in the wood. "Actually, no. I was hoping to talk you out of it if that's what you had decided."

Carrie stared at her as she took another tentative sip of her coffee. Maybe it didn't taste all that bad. "That's not exactly what I would have expected from you."

"Oh, I know." Gillian flashed a wry smile at her. "I don't understand it myself. Just look at me. I'm practically salivating over this table, but I don't think I could stand to see it anywhere else but right here." Gillian's hands stilled. "I think you should stay, too."

Carrie watched Gillian's hands pressed against the tabletop, fingers parallel to the grain, palms flat, and discovered that it was possible to feel jealous of a slab of wood. She cleared her throat lightly. "I have been thinking about it some. I don't know what I'm going to do, ultimately, but I think I'll stay here for at least a while. There's still so much that needs to be done before I can make any final decisions."

Gillian's hands curled as she looked at Carrie. "Do you miss your friends in Chicago?"

Carrie heard the subtext of that question clearly. Gillian wasn't asking if she missed her friends but if she had any friends and what kind of friends were they?

"Yes, I do miss my friends, but I would be missing them even if I was still in Chicago." Carrie leaned against the kitchen counter, both hands wrapped tightly around her coffee cup. "I was at the ass end of an ugly breakup before I came here. It got a little physical there at the end and I lost most of my friends because of that. And all of the good furniture."

"I'm sorry." Gillian took her hands off the table and put them in her lap. "I went through something like that, once. It's hard to watch your friends walk away from you. I'm sure you miss everyone terribly."

"Actually, I miss the cat most of all."

Gillian laughed and then shook her head. "Lord knows, he must have been a real sorry bastard to take your friends, the furniture and the cat, too."

Carrie took a deep breath, inhaling the faint scent of coffee, wet hair and Gillian's perfume. What did she have to lose, besides another friend? "She was. A complete and utter bastard. Although, I have to say that it's still hard for me to think about it very rationally. Megan had a way of pushing every last button I owned."

"Oh." Gillian looked at the hands in her lap, her brow creased with a frown.

That wasn't the reaction Carrie was hoping to get but, again, she wasn't surprised, only a little disappointed. "If that makes you uncomfortable, you don't have to stay."

"No, it's not that." Gillian looked up. "I'm not uncomfortable. I was just trying to remember what I said about Jo the other day and if I said anything that might offend you."

Carrie shrugged. "If you did, I don't remember it."

But, in spite of what Gillian said, she did look uncomfortable with her spine stiff and straight, her hands buried in her lap. There wasn't much Carrie could do about it. She was already standing a respectful distance away from her and with a kitchen table in between, her posture as casually non-threatening as she knew how to make it.

Carrie looked into her mug. The coffee wasn't that bad, but it had a sour aftertaste. "I still can't tell you how much I appreciate you putting together that cleaning party. It's amazing how people are willing to come together to help a stranger."

"It really wasn't for you." Gillian spoke down at the table.

"You keep saying that."

"It's true." Gillian smiled softly. "Did you find the poem?"

"Yes." Carrie gave up on her coffee and put it on the counter. She folded her arms across her chest. "I thought it was strangely moving."

"I thought so, too." Gillian looked up, caught Carrie's eyes and then looked down again.

There was a spark of something in that glance that was hard for Carrie to identify, nervousness or fear or a fierce flash of... something. She couldn't tell.

"Do you know what else I found?" Carrie asked. "In the little graveyard out past the south meadow, there's this marker way in the far back corner. It's very small with no name or date. There's only a flower carved on it. I was wondering if it could have been someone's pet."

Gillian's expression turned thoughtful. "It could be a pet, but that would be unusual. In the past, people didn't tend to personify their animals as much as we do today." She glanced over toward the kitchen window. "Maybe when it stops raining I can come back over and take a look at it."

The coffee stirred in Carrie's stomach, not in an entirely unpleasant way. She folded her arms tighter against her chest. "Thanks. That'd be great." It would be something to look forward to, anyway. She felt a large stupid grin slowly spreading across her face, but she couldn't stop it. "Thank you," she said again. "Now, if only we could find the attic I'd feel like all the bases were covered."

"Oh," Gillian said as her eyes lit up, "we did find it. That was one of the things I forgot that I forgot to tell you. It's in the back of the linen closet upstairs in the east hallway. Very hidden, but that's not unusual for a house this age."

"Really? What was up there?"

"We didn't go up because it was dark and we didn't have a flashlight handy. Would you like me to show you where it is?"

"Sure."

Carrie followed Gillian out of the kitchen, up the stairs and down the east hallway. She hadn't looked through this wing very much, only a quick glance at the guest rooms, a light rummage through their empty closets and drawers. Gillian stopped in front of a plain looking door and opened it. Behind the door was a large, deep closet with old sheets and towels, blankets, comforters and crocheted throws piled on shelves built into one side. On the other side was another door. Gillian stepped inside the closet and pulled at a small latch. The door opened and revealed a wide, steep staircase. The stairs were dark and dusty. Gillian stepped out of the way and Carrie went up a few steps. She could see from the spill of the hallway light an empty light socket and a chain hanging down.

"It looks like there's a light at the top of the stairs but it doesn't have a bulb in it."

"I know where the lightbulbs are. Should I run and get one?"

"Yes, thanks."

Gillian disappeared and Carrie walked up a few more steps. The air was hot, dusty and dry. It tickled her nose. Her eyes began to adjust to the darkness and she could just make out squat square shapes and tall thin shapes. Gillian came back and stepped carefully up the stairs. She handed Carrie a lightbulb. Carrie reached up and screwed it into the socket. She pulled the chain.

Gillian shrieked and Carrie nearly jumped out of her skin. A woman in a formal dress was standing right beside them. A wide hat and frizzy hair framed an empty face.

Gillian began to laugh.

"It's only a mannequin," Carrie said.

"It's a dress form...not quite a mannequin."

Carrie was holding Gillian's hand. She wasn't sure when that had happened, but she had probably better let it go. She didn't want to, but she made her fingers relax and Gillian's hand fell away from hers. Gillian was staring at the dress with wide eyes. It was very beautiful in an old-fashioned way, with puffy crinoline and a tiny waist, lace and pearl trimming at the neck and wrists, fancy embroidery around a hem that swept the floor. It was too dusty to tell what color it had been.

"Wow," Gillian said and stepped away from her. She walked around the dress, reaching out a hand but then letting it fall back again before her fingers brushed the fabric. "This is just so amazing."

Carrie was staring, too, not at the dress but at Gillian, at the flush of her cheeks, the cling of her shirt, the slope of her shoulders, the drape of her slacks. It wasn't anything special. The shirt was cotton, her shoulders were thin, the slacks were just a pair of chinos. But taken all together, each part in its place, it was extraordinary. Carrie had never seen anyone more stunning than Gillian was when she was lusting after some dusty old antique thing.

Carrie shook herself mentally. She was being stupid again. With a stubborn willfulness, she turned her back to Gillian and the dress and looked around the rest of the attic. It was a large space running the length of the east wing and it was stacked with old broken furniture, boxes, trunks and crates. There was a lot of stuff. Too much stuff. Certainly, it was more stuff than any one family needed to have and far too much stuff for just her. She looked back at Gillian still gawking at the dress. What would Gillian look like wearing a dress like that? The thought made Carrie weak in the knees.

Gillian finally tore herself away from the dress and looked around at the rest of the attic. Her eyes began to sparkle in a way that made Carrie's chest feel fluttery. "We definitely need to do an inventory."

"Should I go get some paper?"

Gillian looked at her watch and then shook her head slowly,

reluctantly. "I don't have time today. Damn it. I have to get back to the shop."

"How about tomorrow? We could do the inventory and then I could take you out to dinner or something." The words came out of Carrie's mouth before her brain registered what she was saying. She felt her face flame but didn't try to take back her words.

Gillian frowned. "That almost sounds like you're asking me out on a date."

Carrie looked away with a sigh. She hated these conversations. She'd had them before and they never went well. Anything she said would be wrong. She pushed her hair back from her face with a quick brush of her fingers. "You said you weren't like that, Gillian, and I'm not interested in chasing phantoms."

Gillian folded her arms across her chest and then unfolded them. She put a hand in her pocket and then took it out again. "I said—" She closed her mouth and looked at the attic floorboards. Her hands were clenched into fists, her lips pressed in a tight line, but she didn't look angry. She looked scared. "I said I'm not like Jo."

Carrie watched Gillian for a moment. She didn't know what her words meant or understand why saying them would scare her so much. "So, what's Jo like?"

"She cuts her hair short and wears men's clothes. I don't do that."

"Yes, I can tell." No, that was the wrong thing to say. Carrie frowned as Gillian's arms wrapped around her middle. "But I don't see anything wrong with Jo wearing whatever clothes make her feel comfortable."

Gillian shook her head. "I didn't mean to say that there was."

"Then I don't think I understand what you're trying to say."

"I'm just saying that I like being a woman."

"There's nothing wrong with that either."

Gillian shook her head sharply. Her shoulders hunched as her arms tightened around her stomach. "You're going to make

99

me say it, aren't you?"

Ah. She understood now. Carrie smiled gently even as her heart started racing. "Have you ever said it before?"

A flush spread over Gillian's skin. "Not out loud."

"Then you should try it. Just this once. If it comes out all wrong, I won't tell anyone. I promise."

Gillian took a breath, her chest rising and falling. "I'm not like Jo, but I am…I mean, I have…" She turned her back. "No, I can't say it. I'm sorry, Carrie. I can't. It's such an ugly word."

All of Carrie's tiredness slipped back into her bones. She sat heavily on the flat top of a steel trunk. "It's not an ugly word, Gills. People say ugly things about it, attach ugly ideas to it, but the word itself isn't ugly. Gillian, you're not an ugly person, no matter who you find attractive."

Gillian turned halfway back toward Carrie, her profile emphasizing her long, straight nose. "You're not ugly either."

"Thanks," Carrie said dryly.

Gillian let her arms fall to her sides. "I mean to say that I think you're really quite attractive."

"That almost sounds like you're asking me out on a date."

Gillian looked at the floorboards again. "There isn't anywhere around here where two women can go out on a date. You have to drive to Richmond for places like that."

"Don't friends go out to dinner sometimes? Can't they meet for pecan pie and coffee at the diner?"

"Not in this town. It's too small and everyone's in everyone else's business. Friends have to be very careful if they don't want people to know they're…friends."

"What would happen if everyone knew they were friends?"

"They would end up like Jo, a pariah, an outcast that everyone talks about and no one talks to. She has no friends here other than me. Her family doesn't even acknowledge her anymore."

Carrie rubbed at her eyes. "I'm sorry to hear that."

"I've always been sorry about that too, but you can't change the way people are."

Carrie nodded her head slowly. "Especially if you don't try."

Gillian turned with an angry spark in her eyes, hands planted on her hips. Her eyes met Carrie's steady gaze and the spark faded. She let her hands fall back to her sides. "It's not as simple as that, but I hear what you're saying." Carrie smiled at her and Gillian smile back, tentative and shy. She looked at her watch again and the smile faded. "I really do have to get on with my day. Places to go, people to see and all that. I'm already late for my first appointment."

"Will you come over tomorrow to do the inventory? We can argue about dinner and dates after we count things."

Gillian laughed softly, almost too softly for Carrie to hear. She touched the face of her watch and then covered it with her hand. "Yes. I'd like that."

Carrie's smile turned into a huge grin as she got up off the trunk. It probably made her look like a fool, but she didn't care. She was going to go on a date with the most elegant woman she'd ever met.

Carrie could almost feel the pieces of her heart snapping back together.

CHAPTER TWELVE

Carrie sat in the library in one of the thinly cushioned chairs that flanked the fireplace with her feet propped up on the ottoman, crossed at the ankles, as she tried to read the oldest copy of *The Scarlet Pimpernel* she'd ever seen. A 1905 edition with yellow pages that crackled under her fingers. She hated the story just as much as she did the first time she read it, but it was still strangely fascinating in an "*oh my god I can't believe she wrote that*" kind of a way. The late afternoon was gray and gloomy with the rain starting and stopping, pretty much as it had been ever since Gillian left that morning.

The only lamp on in the room was the small fringed table lamp beside her chair, but the light it shed was soft and warm. It made Carrie's eyes feel heavy. She turned the page gently and settled deeper into the chair. The words seemed fluid and hard to catch. She read about an inn by the sea, a fancy ball in London, an angry crowd in Paris and a mysterious someone who always signed his notes with a flower. The flower meant something that her mind only half grasped, but pimpernel was such a crazy name for a flower. Other flowers had better names like iris or rose, lily, violet, daisy, holly, laurel…Carrie's eyes closed.

The book fell to the floor with a thud and Carrie started awake. She rubbed her eyes and then at the crick in her neck as she looked at her watch. It was five thirty in the morning. Her back and legs were sore. Her knees and hips were creaking stiff, and she had to move slowly to get her feet onto the floor. She turned in her chair and looked out the patio doors. The sun should have just been starting to rise, but it was still mostly dark. A deep gray fog pressed close against the windows. All the plants in the little garden in between the wings looked steel gray through the mist. The color of Gillian's eyes. The air was quiet and chill. She rubbed her neck again, rotated her shoulders in a circle, bent her knees and wiggled her toes. Her left foot was still half asleep, the other half had pins and needles poking and scratching.

The clear note of a horn blew through the fog and then came a faint baying of hounds. Carrie looked at her watch again. It was still five thirty. The hunters were out very early. She couldn't imagine what the difference was between breaking your neck at dawn and breaking your neck at dusk. Whoever they were, they must be half-baked to risk horse and neck for a chase on a morning like this. She wondered if they were riding across her land. It was okay if they were, though they should have asked first. She didn't mind too much. It was only that she hoped the fox really was as clever as its reputation.

Carrie yawned and stretched. She picked the book up off the floor, closed it and put it on the table beside the chair. She turned the lamp off. A nap before breakfast wouldn't hurt, or a quick brush for her fuzzy teeth. She headed for the stairs. Her foot was on the first step when she heard the music, the tinny plinking of metal tines against brass spokes, the odd harmonics of short, sharp notes brushing up against one another. The library doors were still open and the steel gray dawn made the room beyond look black and white.

Carrie walked slowly back into the library. Over by the fireplace, the lid to the music box was open. The winding key turned slowly. It hadn't been open. She knew it hadn't, and the song seemed more familiar to her this time than it did before. Carrie shivered as a chill washed over her skin. The shade of a memory fluttered through her mind. Soldiers with ghastly wounds playing an oddly cheery tune on fife and drum, a tattered flag hanging limp in the wet heat of a summer afternoon. Words flowed into her head, onto her tongue…

In hurried words, her name I blest
I breathed the vows that bind me
And to my heart in anguish pressed
The girl I left behind me…

…and then they were gone again. She couldn't remember the words she'd just sung.

Carrie slammed the lid shut and the music died abruptly. She closed her eyes tight and thought hard of pizza and beer. Right. Pepperoni pizza and pasteurized beer. Something specifically of her time and not of another. Not of foxes and hounds or soldiers and flags, but pizza, fresh and hot from the oven and buckets of cold beer chilled in the ice house. Carrie shook her head sharply. No, not buckets, not the ice house. Bottles in the refrigerator. Beer came in bottles and went in the refrigerator. That's right. And later today, Gillian would come over and she would take her out for pizza and beer, drive to Richmond if they must, in her car, on the interstate, very fast. Pizza and beer.

She took a deep breath and opened her eyes slowly. The lid was still down on the music box. The key was not moving. The library was silent as the fog. Her eyes rose to the mirror. And she froze. A lady was standing behind her. Her image was wavy and faint. She smiled at Carrie from underneath a wide-brimmed hat and lifted a gloved hand out to her.

Carrie spun around. There was nobody in the room. She looked back into the mirror and saw only her own pale face, her own eyes wide and bright. She looked back at the room again. It was still empty but for the faint smell of flowers and the tea roses still slowly wilting in their vase.

Carrie was bleary-eyed when Gillian came back over to help her with the inventory. She was showered and changed, but she opened the door yawning.

Gillian laughed as she came through the door. "It's ten o'clock. Were you still asleep?"

"No," Carrie said but she couldn't bring herself to smile back. "I woke up early."

"Is something wrong?" Gillian asked with the smile slowly fading from her face. "You look a little, I don't know, frayed around the edges."

Carrie looked down at herself, sneakers and blue jeans again. "Gosh, I'm sorry. I showered and everything. I can change into something nicer if you want me to."

"No, I don't mean that you look bad, just really worn."

Carrie opened her mouth to tell her about the music box and about the lady in the mirror, but she closed it again. She really liked Gillian and didn't want her to think she was crazy. Even if she might be going a little crazy.

Gillian touched her arm. "You're sure you're okay?"

Her touch seemed to clear Carrie's head, ground her a little more firmly. She managed a weak smile. "I'm okay. Just a little tired." Carrie closed the front door and Gillian followed her deeper into the foyer. "I didn't sleep well. It was the rain, I think. It made funny sounds on the roof and gave me strange dreams or something. But I'm fine. Really."

Gillian looked like she didn't believe her. "You weren't dreaming of me, I take it."

Carrie blushed. She'd been dreaming of another woman, but it hadn't been that kind of dream. Not exactly. "I've been thinking of you. All day yesterday. All this morning."

Gillian laughed. "Good recovery. I'll accept that." She looked at the stairs. "Shall we get started on the attic?"

"Sure." Carrie headed for the steps. "I put bulbs in all the sockets yesterday, so it lights up really bright, and I stashed pen and paper up there too, so we wouldn't have to search around for some this morning."

"Excellent. It's always nice to work with someone who's prepared," Gillian said from behind her.

At the top of the stairs, Gillian passed her and led the way down the east hallway. She opened the door to the linen closet and flipped the latch to the attic stairs. Carrie followed her as she went up the stairs and pulled the string on the first light. They both looked at the dress form and then grinned at each other. Gillian turned in a slow circle, looking around the attic.

"Well, where should we start?" Carrie asked.

"Let's start with an overview. We'll just open boxes and trunks to see what kind of things are in them, make a note of it and then do a detailed list of the more interesting ones."

Carrie pulled the strings on two more lights. "What if everything is interesting?"

Gillian pointed a toe at a box marked "Christmas Decorations." "If that's not more than a hundred years old, it won't be very interesting." She knelt, opened it and pulled out a tattered green garland.

Carrie peered over her shoulder and at the boxes of thick-wired cords strung with large-bulbed lights and tangled ropes of bright-colored beads. "I see what you mean."

Gillian rummaged around in the box a little and then closed it back up. She shoved it to one side. Her eyes fell on the steamer trunk Carrie had been sitting on yesterday. She pointed to it. "Let's open that. If it's not locked."

Carrie reached for the latch and flipped it up. "It's not locked." She opened it.

"What's in it?" Gillian asked reaching for paper and pen.

"It looks like clothes." Carrie picked up a blouse with a big puffy bow at the neck and an outrageous pattern of swirls and stripes running every which way across the fabric. "Ick."

"You can say ick all you want, but retro is very much in fashion right now. Somebody will want that blouse." Gillian leaned over the trunk and shifted some of the clothes around. "Nothing too interesting here."

Gillian jotted a note on her pad. She moved over to a smaller trunk sitting beside the large one, and Carrie moved to open one on the other side. Carrie's trunk was again full of clothes, but these were much older. Thickly woven coats, ankle-length skirts and high-collared jackets. Carrie looked over at Gillian who was sitting still as statue, staring into her trunk, her mouth hanging open. "What do you have over there?"

Gillian looked up. Her eyes were glazed and her face flushed. "Beaded purses and old hats." She gently picked up a hatbox and tilted it so Carrie could see inside. It was a small round hat that looked like it was made out of thousands of tiny black feathers.

"Aw, poor little bird," Carrie said, looking into the box.

"Birds," Gillian corrected her. "Many poor little birds. This is an extremely valuable hat. Very old. Very rare."

"Very gross." Carrie turned back to her trunk. "I like the stuff in here much better."

"What is it?" Gillian put the lid back on the hatbox and put it back carefully. She pulled a small packet of sticky notes out of her pocket, wrote something on one and stuck it on the lid of the trunk. She turned to watch Carrie rummaging. "What do you have in there?"

"It's mostly old clothes, but they're old enough to be interesting. And then there's this at the very bottom." Carrie pulled out a long flat case of wood and cracked leather.

Gillian looked like she was going to faint. "Oh my God." She put a hand to her head. "Open it."

Carrie opened it. The inside was gray felt. Nestled in the felt was a sword. Carrie laid the case on top of the steamer trunk and put a hand on Gillian's arm to steady her.

"Easy, Gills. It's just a sword."

"It's not just a sword. It's an exquisite sword." Gillian reached for the case and tilted it up to catch the light. The blade gleamed under the bare bulbs. "It's Civil War era. See the C.S.A. on the pommel? And look at the etching on the blade. Oh, hell, just look at the blade. There's not a spot of rust on it. It looks almost brand-new. I've never seen one in such pristine condition."

"What does the etching say?" Carrie had to ask because Gillian was hovering over the case, blocking her view.

"It reads, Lieutenant Beauregard J. Covington, C.S. Artillery, Eighth Battalion A.N.V. Valor under fire. Fredericksburg, December 1862."

"I know that name. He's buried in the cemetery out back under one of the bigger obelisks. Only I think it said Colonel on the stone."

"That was your great-grandfather, if I remember correctly. He served in the Army of Northern Virginia for almost the whole four years, mostly under General Lee. Men were promoted quickly back then if they were reasonably competent and lucky at staying alive."

Carrie looked over Gillian's shoulder at the sword shining in the attic light. "Is it worth anything?"

"Quite a bit I'd say, historically and monetarily." Gillian closed the case and ran her hands gently over the wood and old leather. "I'll need to bring an oil cloth the next time I come over and wipe that down properly. I recommend that you don't handle the sword or even open the case if you can stand not to."

Carrie shrugged. She wasn't much interested in bright swords and old wars. "Wonder why it was in this trunk? You'd think there would be uniforms or something to go along with it."

"What else is in there?"

"Dresses and pointy-toed shoes. Nothing as fancy as the dress on the form, but there are still a lot of puffy sleeves." She held up a shirtwaist with flowing bishop sleeves and a high, stiff collar.

I don't understand how anybody got any work done wearing clothes like this. Of course, I don't imagine that people who wore clothes like this had much work to do."

"That depends on how you look at it and what you consider to be work." Gillian fingered the material. "Women who wore clothes like these didn't plow fields or pick cotton, but they were expected to bear children, whether they wanted to or not, and then they raised them all pretty much on their own. Running a household of this size wasn't easy either. They had to manage the household finances, organize supply and delivery of raw materials to meet the needs of both family and staff. Even a wealthy woman had to know how to cook, clean, wash, darn, knit, crochet and all that stuff. I'd bet that your grandmother or even her mother made some of those throws in the closet." Gillian took the top from Carrie and held it against her chest.

Carrie shook her head. "Too brown. It's not your color. Maybe something in gray or a pale pink."

Gillian frowned at the shirtwaist. "Some woman made this. Some woman sat with a needle and thread, or a simple foot-powered sewing machine if she were lucky, cut the cloth and stitched this together. The thing that gets me riled is that they didn't have a choice. They had to live how society demanded that they live, within their expected roles, or they became an outcast."

Carrie gave her a sideways look. "A bit like your friend, Jo?"

Gillian's head tilted to one side as she thought about that. She started to nod, but it changed into a shake. "Jo has choices now that women back then never had. She has the freedom to cut her hair short and dress like a man if she wants to, and if no one will talk to her, at least no one's burning her at the stake. She does work that she loves and is not bound to the work that society deems proper for a woman to do."

Carrie took the shirtwaist from Gillian's hands, folded it and put it back in the trunk. "I guess things have changed quite a bit since then."

Gillian looked over her shoulder at the dress on the form, at its tiny waist and sweeping skirts brushing the floor. "Yes. Things have changed but not nearly enough." She turned to Carrie with an embarrassed half smile. "Don't let me get started, or I'll rant and bore you to tears. Studying history can make you mad sometimes. So many things were so unfair."

Carrie smiled and shrugged. "You can rant if you want to, but you'll be preaching to the choir."

Gillian laughed. She stood and slapped the dust off the knees of her pants. "What should we open next?"

"I tripped over an interesting box yesterday when I was putting in the lightbulbs. I thought it was different because it had funny little flowers painted all over it. It looked like a child had painted them, and I wondered if it was a toy box, but I didn't open it because I wanted to wait until you could see it, too."

"Where is it?"

Carrie got up and pointed. "Over there in the back."

"Let's take a look."

Carrie threaded her way between boxes and crates, broken chairs and sheet-draped shapes to the back of the attic. The light was not as bright there, but she knew what was she was looking for. She knelt and shifted a cardboard box out of her way. "Here it is."

Gillian knelt and looked at it. "This is strange."

"Why?"

"It's a travel trunk, not a storage trunk."

Carrie knelt beside her. "It doesn't look like much. It was only the flowers that caught my eye."

"It's not much. This was the kind of thing a poor person would pack all their things in if they were moving." Gillian pointed at the edges. "Look. You can tell it's homemade. The dovetailing is a little off, and here are some chisel marks still on the corner. There's no metal banding around it either."

"Open it."

The clasp was wooden with only a little dowel on a string to keep it closed. Gillian pulled it out gently and opened the trunk. An old newspaper was lying on top of folded bundles of clothes. She picked it up and tilted the sheets into the light. "This is a really old newspaper. *The Richmond Dispatch* from...good God."

"What?"

"It's from August 1920. Look at this little article right here. It says that the nineteenth amendment has been ratified. That's the one that gave women the right to vote. I wonder why it's not a banner headline?"

"Maybe because it's Richmond."

"Maybe so." Gillian laid the newspaper aside carefully. "I'll have to look at that more closely. Let's see what else is in here." Gillian dug through the trunk. She frowned into it. The further she dug the more her frown deepened. "I don't understand this."

Carrie shifted closer as she peered into the little trunk. "What are those?"

"Underwear." Gillian pulled out a pair of light shin-length cotton drawers and a chemise. "This is what women of the time wore under their clothes. It's pre-brassiere. Most bust support was built into the dress and not the underwear." She put the underwear back into the trunk and pulled out a shirt and a skirt, both made of the same thin brown cloth. "This is strange."

"Why? It looks more comfortable than the things in the other trunks."

"Yes, it would be. These are things I would expect a servant to wear, a maid or a char woman. Someone who was expected to do hard physical labor."

"Why is that strange?"

Gillian looked at the frayed shirt cuffs. "Everything else up here is from your family. It's all top-quality-machine-milled fabrics. This looks almost homespun. It didn't belong to a Covington. This was from someone not of the same class. It's strange that it's up here along with all the family stuff. Why keep the maid's things up here in the attic?"

"Why keep them at all?"

"Yes, exactly."

"What's that at the bottom?" Carrie reached over Gillian's arm to pick up something shiny from the bottom of the trunk. She held up a locket that glittered gold in the bare attic lights. It hung on a tarnished silver chain. A chill prickled at her arms. "There's that flower again."

"What flower?" Gillian leaned in closer to look at the locket.

"It looks like the same one that's carved on the little headstone out back." Carrie touched the flower with the tip of a finger and then looked at the crudely painted flowers decorating the trunk. "Do you think that the little grave could be for a person and not a pet?"

Gillian tilted her head a little to one side. "Like a beloved nurse, maybe? One honored by being included in the family cemetery?"

"Something like that. But, then, why no name?"

Gillian thought and then shook her head. "I don't know. Maybe there's a picture inside."

She cradled Carrie's hand in hers and pressed something on the side of the locket. The locket opened. There was no picture, only a small plait of hair wrapped into a loop with a thin ribbon tied around it. The chill crept all the way up Carrie's arms and danced with icy feet across the back of her neck. She shivered and her ears started to ring with a crazy hum that made her feel a little sick. The attic lights dimmed. The floor began to waver and tilt.

"Carrie, are you all right?"

Gillian's voice buzzed. It sounded thin and distant, echoing strangely inside her head. She felt herself starting to fall. The mouth of the trunk opened wide into a great yawning blackness eager to swallow her. The world jittered and swayed and swam out of focus.

Carrie's fist closed hard around the locket and it snapped shut. She squeezed it tight. Sharp edges dug into her palm, but the pain was good. It was real and present. She focused on it and her head began to clear. Gillian's arms were around her, holding her up.

"Carrie?"

Carrie lifted her head. "I'm all right." Her voice twanged oddly. The sound made her shudder, and Gillian held her tighter.

Carrie looked into her concerned face. Her eyes were deep and dark. Her face was too close to hers. Carrie's gaze fell to Gillian's mouth and there were her lips, full and berry ripe, open slightly, the bottom one jutting out just a bit. Carrie stared at the little dent in her upper lip and thought of how she would love to trace it with the tip of her tongue.

She needed to move away or she was going to kiss this woman. She desperately wanted to kiss this woman. Carrie tried to turn her head, but it wouldn't respond. The eyes and the lips held her. She leaned, but it was the wrong way. She meant to lean away from Gillian, but she had leaned into her instead.

Gillian's gaze fluttered to Carrie's mouth. Her arms tightened around her and then she dipped her head. Carrie felt the brush of her lips, the warmth of her breath against her cheek, and she wanted her, all of her, in a fierce rush of need. She leaned in harder to feel the push of breast against her shoulder as Gillian nibbled at her mouth. Carrie's hands trembled, wanting to rip her shirt away, to feel the touch of her skin, the weight of her breast resting in her palm. Gillian's mouth opened over hers and Carrie forgot about the breast, forgot about the press of her arms, about the locket and the attic. She forgot everything but the soft caress of lip and tongue that warmed her mouth and set her body on fire.

Gillian made a soft sound in the back of her throat and then lifted her head. Carrie had to fight not to follow. Gillian slid her arms from around her waist and leaned back. Carrie opened her hand and the locket dropped back into the trunk.

"I didn't mean to do that," Gillian said softly. She looked at her hands resting in her lap.

Carrie's breath seemed stuck in her throat. "I'm not sorry you did." Her words came out in a harsh whisper.

"I didn't want to stop." A delicate blush pinked the tips of Gillian's ears.

"I didn't want you to stop either." Carrie reached to touch Gillian's knee. "I still don't want you to stop."

Gillian slipped her hand into Carrie's. Their fingers twined and the sharp bite of the locket faded against the soft press of palms. Gillian looked at her with a shy, worried expression. "I'm not sure what to do next."

"Stay the night. That's what usually comes next."

Gillian smiled. "That's a little too fast for me, big city girl." She squeezed their fingers together. "I think we should talk some first. Find out a little more about each other."

"What do you want to know?"

"It's more about what I want you to know."

Carrie shifted closer and leaned against her, pressing their shoulders together. "I'm listening."

"My father doesn't know about me." Gillian stroked the back of Carrie's hand. "This town doesn't know."

"Are you sure?" Carrie asked. "You're thirty years old, not married and not dating." She raised an eyebrow slightly. "That's a bit of a clue, don't you think?"

"I'm thirty-three and no. It's not much of a clue in this part of the world. If things move slower here sometimes, nobody really thinks it's so strange. We have an ancient and venerable tradition of old maids and crazy Aunt Betsys. Nobody thinks much of it."

Carrie rubbed her thumb over the back of Gillian's knuckles. "So, what are you saying? That if we decide to see each other, you'll want to sneak around to do it?"

"No. I'm not saying that. Not exactly. I would just like for us to be a little circumspect."

Carrie's thumb stilled. "I'm not sure I know what that word means."

Gillian rolled her eyes as her shoulders slumped. "Why does that not surprise me?"

"Gillian." Carrie touched her chin and turned her eyes back to meet hers. "If we have to sneak, I'll think you're ashamed of me. If you *are* ashamed of me or of yourself, then that's something we need to work out right now. I'm not ashamed of who I am, and I won't live my life pretending to be something I'm not. I won't deny myself and I won't ever deny you."

Gillian shook her head. "Nobody said anything about denying. I just don't want to jump all around waving a red flag or run a pink triangle up the flagpole."

Carrie grinned. "Would you consider getting a pink triangle tattooed on your butt?"

Gillian laughed and then the laughter faded. She looked into Carrie's lap. A quick flare of heat darkened her eyes. "Do you have a pink triangle on your butt?"

"Would you like to find out?"

Gillian's grip tightened on Carrie's hand. "Yes. I would."

Carrie squeezed their hands together. "How would you like to go about it?"

Gillian looked at Carrie. Her eyes were still dark and deep. "I think we should go on a date, maybe drive into Richmond for the day. I can show you the historical sites and all the important antique shops. And then we'll see what happens from there."

Carrie looked at the little travel trunk, at the old homespun skirts and the one pair of button-up shoes, at the glitter of the locket as it lay on top of a rumpled chemise. A faint buzz still hummed behind her ears. "Can we drive to Richmond on the interstate and then stop somewhere for pizza and beer?"

"Of course we can. If that's what you'd like."

"I would like that." Carrie let go of Gillian's hand. She reached up to touch her cheek. "What would you like?"

Gillian's arm circled back around her waist. "I'd like to kiss you again."

Carrie nodded her head slowly and let her finger brush lightly over the line of Gillian's jaw. "I'd like that, too."

Gillian pulled her closer, dipped her head and kissed her. With the touch of her lips, the buzz in Carrie's head faded and died.

Carrie knew she was asleep. She was dreaming about the hounds, large spotted dogs with friendly faces and big floppy ears, bounding over the grass to come and sniff at her hands, leaning their weight against her legs with tails wagging. She knew these dogs, knew each of their names, the notes of their bay. Barley and Skipper, Jealous and Nellie, Warrior and Hobo, Sultan and Spot, and then there was Captain with his strong, deep voice. A horn blew a single note, loud and bright, and the dogs disappeared.

She was standing outside in a fog-drenched dawn at the top

of a hill, straining her eyes trying to see through the mist to the top of the next hill. A man on horseback crested the ridge and stood silhouetted against the gray sky. The horse snorted, tossed its head and pawed at the ground. The rider raised the horn to his lips and blew. The hounds came running over the ridge, milled around the horse and rider and then, at a gesture, took off again, noses to the ground, tails held high, whipping back and forth. Captain cried out, his deep voice bounding off the hills, and the rest took it up. The rider blew again one sharp, short blast and took off at a gallop, up and over the top of the hill, and disappeared into the mist.

Carrie turned at a soft rustling sound behind her. A woman stepped out of the woods. She had burning red hair and bright beautiful eyes that looked at Carrie with a hunger so raw it made her heart jitter and skip. Carrie saw herself reaching out to her, her hands sheathed in long white gloves, but the woman began to melt. She shrank down and twisted into red fur and a bottle brush tail, a sharp muzzle and big pointed ears. The fox turned its head and winked at her. It jumped and ran past her, close enough for its tail to brush her skirt.

Carrie heard the hounds coming closer, the baying of so many voices, excited and eager. Eager for what? To nip at her heels, to bite her, shred muscle, crunch bones, taste blood. Suddenly, she was afraid. She turned and ran for the trees. She ran as fast as she could through brambles and bracken, around tall trees and over fallen logs, but the hounds drew closer with every step. Her breath came short and fast, rasping in her throat. She stumbled. Her skirts tangled between her legs and she fell to her knees. There was a howling right behind her, a snarling in her ears. Hot breath burned the back of her neck.

Carrie woke with a start, the blankets twisted around her legs, her knees stiff and sore. Chilly air nipped at her cheeks as a brisk breeze billowed the curtains, stretched them out full and then let them fall back again. She touched the back of her neck. It was hot and damp with sweat. She threw the sheets back, crawled out of bed with a shiver and closed all the windows. The curtains fell and laid still. Carrie got back into bed and tucked the covers close around her ears.

She heard a sound and lifted her head. There it was again. Music, tinny and distant. Underneath it, just at the edge of hearing, the woman was laughing. She didn't want to hear it, not on the heels of that dream. Carrie put the pillow over her head and squeezed her eyes shut. She listened hard to the sound of her own heart beating, to the rush of her breath underneath the pillow, in and then out again, a beat and a thud, a whistle and a rush, until her eyes grew heavy.

Eventually, she fell into a restless sleep and dreamt of bloodied and bandaged soldiers standing in the middle of a ballroom, playing and drumming, while women in stiff formal dresses and men in dark tailed coats danced all around them.

CHAPTER THIRTEEN

Carrie sat still in the bright noon sun. The neatly trimmed grass of the little cemetery was still tall enough to tickle the backs of her legs. The warmth of the sun pressed with a comforting hand against the tired sag of her shoulders. It had been more nights than she wanted to count since she'd slept all the way through. Her dreams were not nightmares, but they were gently disturbing, enough to make her not want to close her eyes. She scratched absently at her calf as she watched a ladybug crawl up the face of the little headstone. The ladybug stood still for a moment in the middle of the etched flower then it opened its wings and flew away.

She touched the stone where the ladybug had been, traced the deeply etched lines with her outstretched pinky finger. The ring with the twining flowers, from the box that Mr. Dumfries had given her, was on that finger. The ring was very small. It would only fit on the pinky of her left hand and then only just barely. The locket from the small trunk was resting in the palm of her other hand. She looked at it glittering in the sunshine. It was heavy for its size, still bright and shiny underneath the scratches and scuffs. The flowers etched on the front looked almost the same as the flowers that twisted around the ring. The flowers on the locket looked exactly the same as the flower carved on the headstone. Exactly the same.

That had to mean something. Carrie looked at the woods just a little ways off to one side, the rolling meadow off to the other side, at the iron fence, the worn brick path, the head and foot stones and the old willow tree with its weeping branches standing in the middle of it all. The stone with the flower sat apart from all the others, in the far corner, farthest away from the gate, more plainly styled, more cheaply made. Just like the trunk in the attic and the clothes that were in it. It meant something. It had to. But what?

It was a puzzle and there were pieces missing, but she wasn't really sure if she wanted to find all the rest of the pieces. The ones she had in her hands were troubling enough. Carrie touched the locket. It meant something, of course it did, but she didn't think it would turn out to mean anything good. She closed her eyes and listened. There was nothing to hear but the chattering of squirrels, the twittering of birds, the sad, whispery voice of the wind in the trees.

Carrie got to her feet and dusted the grass off her shorts. Weariness pulled at her arms and legs. But there was still so much left to do, trimming and sorting, scraping and painting, raking and polishing. Mooning around wasn't going to get any of it done. There was still her mother's old room to go through, but she wasn't going to do that today. She didn't have the strength. She wasn't going to go back into the attic either. It was too exhausting and she was already two winks beyond tired. And tired of being tired. The iron latch of the gate closed behind her with a click. Carrie walked down the broken brick path heading back to the house, her feet feeling heavy in her shoes.

Carrie tried polishing the silver tea service. It didn't really need it that badly, but it was something she could do sitting in the kitchen surrounded by modern appliances. It made her feel more anchored, somehow, to listen to the hum of the old refrigerator, to see the clock blinking zeros on the microwave she just bought. She held the sugar spoon up to the light to check for spots. Something red flashed in the bowl. She turned around. The kitchen door was closed, but the swinging door to the butler's pantry was moving just a little. Carrie put the spoon back on the tray and laid her head on the kitchen table. She was a mile beyond tired. She was so far beyond tired that she was starting to dream sitting up in a chair.

The doorbell clunked noisily from the foyer. She lifted her head and then got up slowly to look out of the window in the breakfast nook. Gillian's car was sitting by the fountain. Carrie breathed a sigh of relief. She just didn't have the energy to be polite to strangers.

"Come on in, Gillian," she yelled out the window. "I'm in the kitchen." Carrie went to the sink and washed the silver polish off her hands. She was drying them on a dishtowel when the kitchen door opened.

Gillian smiled and then frowned. "You look terrible."

Carrie draped the dishtowel over the side of the sink. "That's not quite the greeting I was hoping for."

Gillian walked over to Carrie and kissed her, soft and slow, cradling her cheek in the palm of her hand. She drew back and looked at her critically. "Well, that helped. You do look a little better now but still a bit rough around the edges." Gillian smiled suddenly. "Do you think that if I kissed you for long enough you would turn into a handsome princess?"

Carrie leaned her face deeper into Gillian's hand. "Are you implying that I currently look like a frog?"

"More like a raccoon." She stroked her face and frowned again. "Can you tell me what's wrong? You look a little worse every time I see you."

Carrie looked at the door to the butler's pantry. She looked back at Gillian and shook her head a little. "I'm still not sleeping very well."

"Why not? What's bothering you?"

Carrie shrugged one shoulder. "Maybe it's because this is such a big house." And that wasn't any sort of a lie. It was a big house. The kitchen alone was bigger than her old living room, and sometimes she forgot there even was an east and west wing. "I used to think that a three bedroom apartment was big. But this," Carrie waved her hand around the kitchen. "I'm just not used to all this space, and I'm really not used to the noise."

"What noise? I'd think that a house in the country would have much less noise than an apartment in the city."

"Then you'd be wrong. It's not less noise. It's just different. I can't believe how loud the wind in the trees can be."

"So loud that it keeps you awake at night?"

Carrie opened her mouth to say something flippant, but she closed it again with only a sigh. No matter what she said, she didn't think Gillian was going to let it go this time. "It's not the wind. It's the noises the house makes that keeps me awake."

"Like what? Popping and creaking and things?"

Carrie closed her eyes. If they were going to start dating, it would be better to start it on honest footing. Her father used to say that to begin something with a lie usually meant that it would end with one. She liked Gillian enough to tell her the truth. Maybe she even owed Gillian the truth, no matter the consequences. And anyway, she was already in for a penny.

She opened her eyes again and looked at Gillian. "The house does pop and creak, especially when the wind blows, but the part that bothers me is the strange music I keep hearing and the woman laughing. I hear this hunting horn blowing at all hours and then the hounds answering it, and I'm never quite sure if it's real or if I'm dreaming. But the thing that bothers me the most is the mirror in the library. Sometimes I see things in it that shouldn't be there."

Gillian took half a step back, her face full of alarm. She looked around the kitchen and then back again at Carrie, her eyes wide.

Carrie slumped against the kitchen counter. "I shouldn't

121

have told you. Now you probably think I'm nuts." Her shoulders sagged and she covered her eyes with her hands. "The thing of it is, Gills, is that I just may be going a little nuts. God, I'm so tired, but every time I go to sleep I have these dreams and I think they mean something but I can't figure it out and then I don't want to sleep anymore but I'm so tired that I'm afraid I'm starting to dream standing up." Carrie's hands slid down to cover her face. She felt like she was going to cry, but she didn't want Gillian to see that. It was ugly and she was already making such a mess out of everything.

Carrie felt Gillian's arms slide around her shoulders. She let out half a sob and leaned into her, buried her face in the crook of her neck. Gillian's hands were on her hair, stroking softly.

"I don't think you're nuts, Carrie. The universe is a really big place. There's room in it for all kinds of strange things." She lifted Carrie's face from her shoulder, fingers underneath her chin, her thumb stroking at her cheek. Gillian looked at her closely. "I want you to tell me about it, okay? I don't want you to think that I won't listen to anything you have to say, however strange it might seem. Can you do that?"

Carrie nodded and stood straighter. "If you really want me to."

"I do."

The warm circle of Gillian's arms was very comforting to Carrie, but she stepped out of her embrace. That was better than having to feel Gillian run from her. She rubbed her nose and took a breath. "I keep having these dreams about people I've never met before, but it feels like I should know them if only I could remember who they were. And then there's the music box. I close the lid, but then I come back into the room and it's open. It plays sometimes, all by itself, this song that I don't know, but then I find myself singing the words. As soon as I realize what I'm doing, I can't remember them anymore." Carrie looked at her hands. "Last night I dreamt about this woman with red hair who turned into a fox and then I heard the dogs coming, but they weren't chasing her, they were after me and then I fell and they

122

were almost on me. I woke up and everything was still as death except for the music playing and the woman laughing. I can't remember why she's laughing, and that makes me so sad that I just want to cry."

Gillian took her hands and held them. "Carrie, maybe you don't need to be here in this house."

Carrie squeezed her fingers, grateful for the touch, but she shook her head emphatically. "No, I should be here. I have to fix things, put them back to rights. I can't explain it, but I know that I'm supposed to be here."

"Not if it's killing you, you aren't."

"It's not. I mean, she doesn't mean to hurt me."

"She who? The laughing girl or the house?"

Carrie gripped her hands tighter. "I don't know. I can't put all the pieces together. There's still something missing." Gillian looked at her with a deep frown creasing her face. Carrie dropped her hands and looked away. "You don't believe me."

Gillian turned her face back to hers. "I do believe you. The music box thing is a little weird, but I do believe that you believe everything you're telling me."

Carrie glanced at the tea service sitting on the kitchen table. Pieces of her and Gillian reflected back at her but nothing red. "Do you think I'm going nuts?"

"I think you're under a great deal of stress." Gillian stepped closer, slipping her hands across Carrie's shoulders, squeezing them gently. "It might help if you didn't stay here by yourself."

Carrie leaned in closer to her, resting her own hands on the soft swell of Gillian's hips. "Should I rent a room out or something?"

Gillian kissed her softly. Once, then twice. "You could do that, or you could just ask me to stay."

Carrie drew back and blinked at her. "But people will talk. You remember, jumping all around with red flags? Pink triangles?"

Gillian smiled and touched Carrie's cheeks with the tips of her fingers. "That does concern me but, at this point, I'm a little more concerned about you." Her fingers brushed lightly under the hollows of Carrie's eyes. "You really do look like a raccoon."

Carrie's skin tingled where Gillian touched her face. Her fingers seemed to brush the tiredness off her skin. "I would love for you to stay, but we haven't had our first date yet."

Gillian's eyes sparkled. "Let's have it now."

Carrie felt herself grin. "I don't suppose there's a pizza place in town that delivers."

"No, I don't suppose there is."

"I guess I could make you a sandwich, turn the lights down low and light a few candles."

"That would be very romantic," Gillian said with a mischievous smile, "if only the sun weren't still shining."

Carrie glanced out the kitchen window at the bright afternoon. "Right." She rubbed her hands in slow circles over Gillian's hips, feeling the gentle slopes and curves. "Well then, I would ply you with wine instead, but I haven't got any."

Gillian gave her a peculiar look. "What about the wine that's in the cellar?"

Carrie's hands stilled. "I didn't know there was a cellar."

"In a house like this? Of course there's a cellar. The stairs are in the butler's pantry." She stepped away from Carrie and tugged at her hand. "Come on. I'll show you."

Carrie looked at the swinging door that led to the pantry. It had only moved just a little bit. It could have been a breeze. The house was old and drafty. Gillian pulled her toward the door and held it open for her. Carrie walked through it and it was, after all, just a door. Just like the door to the cellar was just a door even if it didn't look like a door but a piece of paneling on the wall.

"It was meant to be hidden," Gillian explained as she fumbled with the tiny latch. "Every great house had a place to hide the silver and the whiskey if the need arose. And it surely did. That silver tea service wouldn't have survived the war if it hadn't been hidden well."

The door opened and they looked on a dark set of cold stone stairs. Gillian pulled at Carrie's hand and led the way down. At the bottom, she pulled the chain on a bare lightbulb. It lit up a small space with hewn rock walls, dirt and cobble floors, spider webs and dust, boxes and crates.

The entire far wall was an old stone wine rack full of bottles, but Carrie stared at the bulb. "I can't believe that still works."

"Oh, it didn't. I changed it when I came down here on cleaning day. I'd heard stories about the cellar and I wanted to see it."

"Did you find anything down here?"

Gillian waved her hand at the back wall. "Wine." She grinned. "Some very curious wines."

Carrie smiled and shook her head as she walked over to the rack. She began to look at all the bottles, one by one, twirling them in their beds, trying to read the faded labels. "Clos de L'archevêch, Rouge de Cathan, La Burthe Briazae, Madeira Justinos Boal…" Gillian laughed as she garbled names and mispronounced words. It made Carrie's heart feel lighter to hear her laugh even if she was laughing at her.

"And this last one." Carrie knelt to wipe the fine white dust off the label. "La Malque. Hey, look at the date on this. It says 1862. I wonder if old wine tastes any different from new wine." Gillian leaned over her shoulder, her face flushed with laughter. Carrie looked at her, and the distance between them, though only an inch or so, seemed too far. "Which one do you want?" Carrie asked. "I don't know anything about wine like this."

Gillian laid a hand on Carrie's shoulder. "I don't think it matters. It's either all magnificent or it's all vinegar. We won't know until we open one."

"How about this one?" Carrie tapped at the neck of a funny-shaped bottle in the middle of the rack. "Madeira's a nice name."

"That's port, not wine. And the one next to it is cognac."

"Isn't port just like wine?"

"No. Not at all. It's more potent and much sweeter. It's an after dinner drink, not a with dinner drink."

"You pick one then."

"Let's try the one in the skinny blue bottle. That's bound to be interesting." Gillian reached around Carrie for the bottle.

She screamed. The bottle hit the ground and rolled. Carrie stood and reached for her.

"What? What is it?" Carrie's heart was pounding hard. She looked around the cellar half expecting to see a woman floating down the stairs or a fox among the bottles. But there wasn't anything. She pulled Gillian close and held her. "Talk to me, Gills."

Gillian was shivering. "It was a spider."

"A spider?" Carrie's arms relaxed. "Damn, Gillian."

Gillian squeezed her tighter. "It was a *big* spider. With long fuzzy legs, and it crawled on my hand." She shuddered. "I hate spiders. Not the little ones, they're okay, but the big furry ones are just awful. You can see their googely eyes and their wiggly mouths and everything."

Carrie spread her hands against the flat of Gillian's back and pressed her closer. "Gills, please don't scare me like that again, okay? If you're going to scream, make sure it's a ghost or something so I can scream too."

Gillian leaned harder into her. "I can't make any promises where spiders are concerned. But if I see a ghost, you can be assured that I will scream so you can scream too."

Carrie laughed and it felt good. She realized it was the first time in more months than she could remember that she'd laughed out loud. It felt very good and so did Gillian, pressed tight against her. She mouthed a silent thank you to the spider. "Are we done picking the wine, or do you want to pick a different bottle?"

"That one will be fine, but I think you should pick it up off the floor."

"What if the spider's still on it?"

"Then you can just brush it off. You're not afraid of spiders, are you?"

"No. I'm afraid of wasps, but I don't think there are any down here." Carrie let go of Gillian, slowly and somewhat reluctantly. She walked over to the corner and picked up the bottle with two fingers, holding it out in front of her. "I don't see the spider. You must have scared it away when you screamed. Are you sure this is the one you want?"

"I'm not about to reach in for another one."

"Good point," Carrie said looking at the bottle. "I hope it goes well with turkey and Swiss."

"Let's open it and find out." Gillian headed for the stairs almost at a run and Carrie was right behind her.

The wine was a ruby red, smoky and very strong. It didn't go at all well with turkey and Swiss. Carrie wrapped the sandwiches and put them back in the refrigerator while Gillian carried the wine upstairs to the veranda off the master suite. They slid the two wicker chairs close together and sat with arms and fingers twined, sipping slowly from their long-stemmed glasses. The sun, halfway down among the trees, stained the sky pink and purple, shading the river orange to black. The air was warm and smelled like green leaves and growing things. Carrie took a deep sip of her wine, savored the bite of it across her tongue, the warm curl of it inside her stomach and the pleasant buzz growing behind her ears.

Gillian leaned in closer to her, pressing their shoulders tight together. "This is wonderful, Carrie. I think it's the best date I've ever been on, excepting the spider, of course."

Carrie smiled. She was content with it, too, including the spider. She sipped her wine and breathed in deeply of the night air and of Gillian's peachy pale perfume. Sitting on the veranda with the buzz of the wine drowning out the evening noises, her feet propped up on the iron railing, her thumb making small circles on the back of Gillian's hand, she was almost happy. Almost. There was still something unfinished that nagged and scratched at the back of her mind, like a rock in her shoe or sand in her socks that even the wine couldn't dull.

Carrie's thumb stilled. "Gills, how much do you know about this house and about my family?"

"Quite a bit." Gillian swirled her glass and watched the wine slosh against the sides. "I used your family as a case study for my thesis paper on postbellum southern Reconstruction. The house was an integral part of your family's history."

"Postbellum. That means after the war, right?"

"Right. Like antebellum means before the war. This house was built in the antebellum classical Greek revival style of the mid-eighteen hundreds. Your great-great-grandfather, Jebediah Covington, built the central portion in eighteen fifty-three from the money he made in cotton distribution. I'm not sure how he got the land. His father's name was Ezekiel, but there's no record of where he came from or what happened to him. Your great-grandfather, Beauregard, built the wings and then modernized a bit around nineteen or so. He added the indoor plumbing, an attached kitchen, a telephone and eventually electricity. He was a very progressive technologist for his time. Probably because his life was so full of tragedy."

"Tragedy? How was that?"

Gillian twirled the stem of the glass between her fingers. "Beauregard was only twenty-two when the war broke out."

"The Civil War?"

Gillian smiled. "Yes. Here in the south, when we say *The War*, we always mean the Civil War, much unlike you northerners who think *The War* means World War II."

Carrie shifted her feet on the railing. *The War* didn't have any particular meaning to her at all, unless it was the threat of some future war, but she didn't care to think too much about that. "Why was the Civil War tragic for Beauregard? He survived it, didn't he?"

Gillian looked at her and squeezed her hand as if acknowledging the thoughts Carrie left unsaid. "The war itself wasn't particularly tragic for him. He survived it without serious wounds or capture and he served with distinction, but he never went back to finish his college education. I doubt it was an option while the north occupied Virginia. After that, I doubt he had time. His father, Jebediah, survived the war only to be killed in a duel a few years after. God only knows what it was over, probably some point of honor that we wouldn't understand today. Beauregard took the remains of his father's cotton distribution business and used the equity to build a cotton mill."

Gillian sipped from her glass as she stared out over the railing. "That was both good and bad. The mill helped to reindustrialize this area and gave people, black and white, much needed jobs. But he took full advantage of the hardness of the times. The workday was often ten hours or more and the conditions were difficult and dangerous. The pay was barely sufficient for a grown white man. He paid black men half of that and women got only a third. Children were paid a pittance even though they did some of the most dangerous work.

"Beauregard made a great deal of money from the mill, but it didn't buy him any happiness. He married in eighteen seventy-nine, a few years after his father's death, and had two sons, but both his sons and his first wife died in a flu epidemic in eighteen eighty-seven."

Carrie nodded. "William and James. Their graves are in the cemetery out back."

"Right. Beauregard married again about a year later, but his second wife died in childbirth leaving only a daughter as his heir."

"That was my grandmother."

"Celia. Yes. He never married again, and Beauregard must have been painfully aware that the Covington line was going to die with him. I can't imagine your grandmother's childhood was all that ideal." Gillian looked out at the river, her face was just a little sad. "I don't know anything at all about her mother. Women weren't considered very important back then, and so when things were written down, they weren't included except in the most cursory way. I've never even found out what her first name was. She was just Mrs. Covington or Mrs. Beauregard Covington, as if her husband's existence was the sole justification for her own."

"That makes you sad." It wasn't a question. Carrie could see it plainly.

"Of course it does." Gillian took a small sip of her wine. "It makes me angry, too, and it scares me because we're not all that far away from it now. Farther than we were, but not nearly far enough. Women are still judged by the men they keep company with, and if they don't keep company at all then that's an even harsher judgment." She took a large swallow, drinking about half of what was left in her glass. As Gillian stared out at the river, Carrie could see the blush of wine rise to her cheeks even in the failing light.

"I wish I could be whatever I wanted to be," Gillian said softly, "without worrying that I'm going to end up like Jo, ostracized and outcast with my family not speaking to me. I'm not asking anyone to change their beliefs to accommodate me. I just want to be allowed to hold my own beliefs without everyone in town telling me that what I believe is wrong." Gillian shook her head slowly from side to side. "I honestly don't understand why people care what other people do when the door is closed."

Carrie took her feet off the rail and set them on the floor. "I don't think I ever thought it out like that. It never occurred to me to hide what I felt from my father or my friends. I was what I was and if some people didn't like me for it, there were plenty of other people who didn't care."

Gillian nodded. "Things are always different in a city. When you pack people in close together, you have to be more tolerant to survive. It's better in some ways and worse in others."

Carrie looked into her glass, a deeper burgundy now that the light was fading. "You always think such deep thoughts?"

Gillian looked at her, worry pulling at her mouth. "Yes. Is that going to be a problem?"

"That depends. I doubt I'll be able to match you thought for thought. Do you mind if I just sit back and say 'wow' every now and then?"

Gillian smiled and squeezed her hand. "I love it when you say 'wow.'"

"Wow."

Gillian put her glass on the table and turned in her chair. "I'd like to ask you something, Carrie."

"Sure. You can ask me anything."

Gillian's gaze dropped to Carrie's mouth. "When are you

going to kiss me again?"

Carrie felt her cheeks grow warm. "I was trying not to move too fast for you."

"I think that you should think about moving a little faster."

"Are you sure? I want you to be sure because I don't want to scare you."

Gillian leaned over the arm of her chair and unbuttoned the top two buttons of Carrie's shirt. She slipped her hand inside. "Is this too fast for you, big city girl?"

"No. It's okay. I'm mean, it's good." Carrie caught her breath when Gillian's hand slid over the cup of her bra. "I'm guessing that wine makes you frisky."

Gillian leaned over farther and bit Carrie's earlobe. "It's not the wine."

The words whispered in her ear made Carrie's skin prickle into goose bumps. "What is it?"

"It's you," Gillian said, sliding her hand inside Carrie's bra, cupping her breast in the palm of her hand.

"Really?" The word ended in a squeak as Gillian trapped her nipple between finger and thumb, but she still managed a shaky smile. "Is it my stunning good looks or my witty repartee?"

Gillian squeezed gently, smiling at Carrie's soft groan. "Neither." She kissed lightly down her cheek. "You're just so real. You don't pretend to be anything but what you are."

Carrie turned her head and let Gillian kiss her lips. "I don't know how to be anything but what I am."

"I know." Gillian pulled away from her suddenly. She stood and tugged at Carrie's hand. "That's what makes me frisky."

Carrie stood with her. She put her glass on the table. Her heart was pounding in her chest as she let Gillian pull her inside through the glass doors.

Carrie woke with a start. She turned her head to see moonlight staining the sky outside her window with a brilliant shimmery silver. Gillian stirred softly in her sleep and Carrie leaned over to kiss her bare shoulder. She froze with her lips hovering just over her skin.

It was the music. Carrie cocked her head to listen. It was different this time, less tinny and more like real music, and under it she could hear people talking. It sounded like a party going on in some distant place. She slipped quietly out of bed, moving carefully so as not to disturb Gillian, and followed the sound out into the hallway and then down the stairs. A bright patch of moonlight shone in through the foyer window staining the floor a silver gray. Carrie stopped to listen again. The music was not coming from the library this time but from the parlor, though she could hear voices in the library. People were talking, not in the hushed whispers of thieves but in a faint conversational tone.

She leaned her head around the corner of the parlor. She could hear a piano and a fiddle and something with strings, but the sound was faint and far. The room, dimly gray where the moon shone in, was empty.

Carrie went over to the library doors and opened them. It was dark inside and everything was still, but the voices were there, a little louder than the music in the parlor but still sounding faint and far away. She stepped into the library and slowly walked the circumference trying to find out where the voices were coming from, trying to hear the words they were saying, but it stayed just on the wrong side of decipherable. They were loudest by the fireplace. She stood still in front of it, straining to hear. There was a woman's voice, she could tell, soft and lilting, but she couldn't understand the words.

Carrie caught movement out of the corner of her eye. She turned toward the old mirror. In it, she could see the fuzzy reflection of the library, but the room was different, not as dark as it should be, the furniture brighter than she remembered. A dim glimmer of sun seemed to shine through the reflected windows. Carrie stepped closer to the mirror. The desk was in a different place, there were more knickknacks lying around, the telephone was a tall thin stick. Her own face looked thinner, younger, more pinched. Behind her, a lady sat on the couch in a long plain dress, her hat tilted at a jaunty angle, her hands gloved

132

up to the elbows. Her eyes were bright, her expression amused. Carrie remembered that face. It was familiar to her. She knew that expression. The lady's name was on the tip of her tongue, in the back of her mind, scratching at her brain. Carrie wanted to turn around, but she couldn't seem to move.

The lady took off her hat and laid it on the couch next to her. Her hair was red. She smiled, and Carrie felt her heart stutter and skip. She knew this woman, had known her for ages and ages, forever maybe, if only she could remember. Carrie opened her mouth, to speak or to scream, she wasn't sure which, but no sound came out. The lady rose from the couch with a graceful swish of skirts and walked toward her. The face was pale underneath the bright red hair with a splattering of freckles across her nose, or that might have been the spots from the mirror. The mirror's images grew hazier and then sharper. It wavered, stilled and then wavered again in a way that made Carrie feel slightly nauseous. The lady stood peering over Carrie's shoulder. A mischievous half-smile curled on her lip. Her eyes were laughing. A gloved hand reached out to touch her shoulder. Cold trickled down Carrie's spine.

The lights in the library came on, full and bright. Carrie squinted against the glare. She turned to see Gillian standing in the doorway, her hand on the switch. Carrie looked over her shoulder in the other direction, but there was nothing there. She looked back into the mirror. It was only her face and the brightly lit library, the furniture dull with time-faded colors. The phone on the desk was squat and square.

She turned back to Gillian. "Did you hear the music?"

Gillian frowned and shook her head. "I thought I heard you talking to someone." Gillian looked very concerned and close to frightened. "Did you hear music?" Her eyes cut to the music box. The lid was closed and the key was still.

"It was different this time. It was coming from the parlor. It sounded like real instruments."

Gillian's eyes searched her face. Carrie didn't know what she was looking for but, apparently, she was satisfied with what she saw in it. Her expression softened but her concern deepened. "I think you might be sleepwalking. Have you ever done that before?"

Carrie shook her head. "I don't think I was asleep. I woke up and then I heard noises. It was dark and I didn't see anything in the parlor, but in the mirror..." Carrie looked at the mirror with its hazy distortions and black tarnish spots. She touched the frame. It was cold, but it was just a frame. The reflections were wavy and indistinct, but they were just reflections. "Maybe it was a dream." Carrie rubbed at her eyes. They were sleepy and gritty. She looked over at Gillian and saw her clearly for the first time. "I must still be asleep. I'm dreaming right now that you're standing naked in the doorway."

Gillian grinned. "What a wonderful dream that must be."

"Oh, yes." Carrie's grin never made it to her lips. "It most certainly is."

Gillian took a deep and deliberate breath. "What do think is going to happen next in this dream?"

"I think I'm going to take you upstairs before you catch a cold and tuck you back into bed."

"What about you? You realize, I'm sure, that you're naked, too."

Carrie hadn't realized it, and the parquet suddenly felt cold against her feet. Gillian held out her hand. Carrie walked over to her and took it. Her hand was warm, and when Carrie pressed it to her cheek, she could feel her heart beating through her palm. "I'm sorry I woke you."

"I'm not." Gillian pressed hard against her, warm and soft, her hips fitting flat against Carrie's as she kissed her, deep and slow, pushing into her with hips and tongue.

Carrie slid her hands down Gillian's spine, fingers trailing. She cupped her butt in her palms and pulled her in tight. Gillian made a sound, both harsh and helpless. Carrie doubted they would make it all the way back upstairs.

134

CHAPTER FOURTEEN

Carrie took a swig from her mug. The coffee was cold while the late afternoon sun beating down on her head was hot. She and Gillian had slept the morning away, waking on the library floor tangled around each other with the sun slanting in on their faces, both of them feeling lazy and sore. A slow breakfast on the patio took them past lunch. Slow kisses in the old claw-footed bathtub took them past all remembering. Carrie savored her coffee as she remembered the feel of Gillian's soapy skin, slick and slipping against her, Gillian's hands sliding down, touching all her bumps and curves, her mouth, agile lips and inquisitive tongue, stroking and caressing as elegant fingers dipped inside her again and again until she was thick with wet and swollen to bursting. She thought of her own hands meeting the thrust of Gillian's hips, her mouth sucking the beads of water off her breasts, licking down the line of her stomach, touching and tasting the warm wetness, the musky scent of her and then Gillian exploding all around her. Carrie shuddered as the echo of her cries tickled across her skin.

"What's wrong?" Gillian reached out and touched her thigh.

Carrie wanted to get up, throw her down and pin her to the bricks. If only she had the strength. "I was just remembering."

Gillian grinned. "Oh. A nice memory, was it? Or were you shuddering with horror?"

Carrie felt a slow smile spread across her face. "Nice. Very nice. Thank you."

Gillian's fingers curled around to the inside of her thigh. "My pleasure."

"Really?" Carrie asked seriously.

Gillian's fingers tightened to a pinch and then relaxed. "Yes, really."

Carrie looked at the tanned hand resting against her pale leg. "I want to make love to you again right now, but I don't think I can move."

"It's too hot out here to move around much," Gillian agreed patting her leg. "You want to go inside?"

Gillian sat up and turned in her chair. "Do you know what I really want to do?"

"No. What?"

"I want to inventory the books in the library."

Carrie looked at her with a cocked eyebrow. "I have no clue why that strikes you as a really exciting thing to do, but if that's what you want, that's what we'll do."

Gillian leaned over the arm of her chair and kissed Carrie on the cheek. "I'll tell you why if you want to know."

"Tell away," Carrie said with a loose wave of her hand.

Gillian shifted her chair a quarter turn and propped her feet up on Carrie's legs. She leaned back and steepled her fingers. Carrie tried hard not to smile as Gillian adopted a professorial expression. She was guessing that Gillian loved to lecture.

"I'm sure you've realized that both your grandfather and your grandmother were voracious readers. What you may not realize is that all those books in the library were purchased as they came out. Each one is a first edition, the best sellers of their day, hot off the press and, I would guess, in more or less pristine condition."

"How do you figure that?" Carrie put her hand on Gillian's leg and began circling an ankle with her thumb. Gillian paused. Her eyes got a distant, dreamy expression. Her mouth opened and then closed. Carrie tapped her on the big toe. "Best sellers of the day?"

Gillian blinked. "Oh. Right. Well, when your grandfather died, your grandmother donated all his books to the library. They were mostly war books, memoirs and remembrances and such. Things, I guess, she wasn't very interested in. I had the opportunity to go through them. There were eight hundred books, and they were all first editions ranging from eighteen eighty to nineteen forty. I nearly fell out when I saw them. Maria always said that books were the one thing that the Burgesses spent money on without a thought, and I guess that was true for the Covingtons too. I never thought much of it until I saw the books for myself and realized what they were."

"And why is that so exciting?" Carrie rubbed a finger back and forth across the top of her shin.

Gillian smiled but she didn't pause. "There couldn't be a more perfect opportunity to really understand what moved people in the past than by examining an unbroken chain of the books they read. Your grandfather's books stopped at nineteen. The year he died. I'm betting that the books in the library don't stop until nineteen ninety-eight."

Carrie rubbed her palm over the top of her knee. "You'll lose your money if you make that bet."

"What makes you say that?"

Carrie's hand did a slow slide back to her ankle. "I've dusted every book in the library, and I haven't found a single one older than nineteen fifty-three. There's *The Robe, Battle Cry, From Here to Eternity, Desiree, The Silver Chalice*, all best sellers from ninteen fifty-three, but not *This I Believe, Angel Unaware, A Man Called Peter* or the Kinsey Report, all best sellers from nineteen and fifty-four. And also…What?" Gillian was staring at her like she'd just sprouted an extra head.

"You remember all that just from dusting the books?"

"No, of course not, silly." Carrie pinched her big toe. "I've read all of them, so I know what's missing."

Gillian's eyes got wider. "You've read every book in that library in the few weeks that you've been here?"

"More or less. Well, not all of them. Not yet. To be honest, I'm skipping the ones that I've already read, and that's most of them." Carrie met Gillian's flabbergasted look with a confused look of her own. "Why are you staring at me like that?"

"You've read almost every book in that library?" Gillian asked again, her feet sliding off Carrie's knees. She leaned forward in her chair and pointed to the glass doors. "That library, right in there?"

"Well, what else do I have to do?" Carrie shook her head. "I don't understand why that's so surprising to you."

Gillian slumped back in her chair, her hands draped limply over the sides. "Well, I'll be damned. Here I was thinking I was going to be the smart one. All this time I've been lecturing you and you just sat there listening politely and never once said, 'Yes, Gills, I know all that already, you big dumb dork.'"

"But, Gills," Carrie said with a laugh, "I didn't know all that. You know far more about my family than I do and more about history than I ever will."

"But if you've read all those books in there then you know more about literature than everyone in this whole town all put together."

Carrie shook her head. "Only if it's American popular literature. I don't know shit about the classics."

"Whew, now that's a relief." Gillian wiped her brow with the back of her hand. "So that means I can talk about Euripides without embarrassing myself?"

"Eur-ribbit-who?"

Gillian laughed and then her face turned serious. "God, Carrie, I think I could fall in love with you."

Carrie's eyes went wide. "Now who's moving fast, country

girl?"

"That's how we do it in the country, love fast and make love slow. But it's a small town thing. I doubt a city girl like you would understand."

"I may not understand it, but I sure do appreciate it."

Gillian leaned over and stroked her knee. "How about if we go inside, get a pad of paper and a pen, and you can tell me what each book is about as I assess its condition?"

Carrie took one last swig from her coffee mug. "Gee, that sounds exciting."

Gillian reached up and pulled a book off the bookshelf. She opened it and flipped through to the title page. "Okay, how about *Pollyanna* by Eleanor H. Porter? List it in excellent condition."

Carrie leaned back against the second floor banister and tapped her pencil against her chin. "I think that was around nineteen ten. A girl survives her misfortunes by always looking at the bright side of things. It was a best seller for a couple of years along with its sequels." She jotted the title and condition on her pad. "It was also a movie with Mary Pickford in the twenties."

Gillian put the book back and pulled down another one. "*The Sheik* by Edith M. Hull. Call this one fair."

"Nineteen twenties." Carrie scribbled on her pad. "That book was just god-awful, but for some reason people ate it up. It was also a silent movie with Rudolph Valentino and the origin of the word 'sheik' used to mean something suave or sexy."

Gillian shelved the book. Her hand hovered over the next one. "Oh, heavens…here's a first edition *Elmer Gantry*, with the Gantry spelled wrong on the spine and everything! It's too bad the cover is missing."

"Poor condition." Carrie made a note on her pad. "I liked that one. I thought it had a good message. That was nineteen twenty-seven, I think, and a film in the early sixties."

Gillian gasped and pulled out another book. She flipped it open to look at the title page. "Oh God, I think I'm going to faint." She sank slowly to the floor and sat down hard.

Carrie looked over Gillian's shoulder at the book she was holding. "Ah, nineteen thirty-six. The best selling novel there ever was, but it was only on the best seller list for two years because by nineteen thirty-eight everyone who could read already owned a copy."

"A first edition *Gone with the Wind*. Oh, Carrie, just look at it!"

"Did you know it took her ten years to write that? In the end, her timing was perfect, post-World War I with the tensions of World War II beginning to build. Right there at the tail end of the Depression, she puts out a book about the fall of the mighty and the proud and then ends it with the hope of a better day. I've always wondered if she knew what she was doing or if she was just following her own feelings."

"Carrie," Gillian's voice was barely a whisper.

"Yes, Gillian?"

"It still has the dust jacket on it."

"Yes, and I remember dusting it too."

"Oh, God," she said and put her head between her knees.

"You're not really going to faint are you?" Carrie knelt on the floor beside her. "I mean, the book can't be all that valuable. It looks like it's been read a million times."

"It is worth a fair bit, but it's not the monetary value of it that gets me all aflutter. It's the history it represents. Layers of history, history on top of history, right here in my hands." Gillian held the book up and fanned through the pages. A small piece of paper fluttered into her lap. She picked it up. The paper was ragged edged and folded in half. Gillian waved it at Carrie. "I really need to teach you to go through things and not just dust the outside of them. You know, one time, I was going through an old cookbook and found a three-dollar bill tucked inside a recipe for braised lamb."

Carrie looked at the paper suspiciously. "I don't think that's a three-dollar bill."

"Nope. It's just a piece of paper, and don't roll your eyes at me, missy," Gillian said sternly before Carrie could roll her eyes.

"This piece of paper could be something important."

"Okay, so what does it say?"

Gillian opened it. She frowned. "How strange. Today is the twenty-second, right?"

"Yes, June twenty-second all day."

"This is dated June twenty-second, nineteen oh-seven."

A chill shivered down Carrie's back as her skin prickled into bumps. "Read it."

Gillian squinted at the paper, turning it this way and that. "It's hard to read. Shaky handwriting, thin ink, bad paper and all that." Gillian tilted the paper into the light. "Let's see. It says, 'To my dearest Celia'...well that's a good beginning, don't you think?"

"Quite lovely." Carrie began to feel a little queasy.

"Okay. Here's what it says." Gillian cleared her throat. "'*Lay me down on your floor, wrapped in the throw your grandmother crocheted, in front of the fire laid with sweet applewood and oak. Sit down beside me on the handwoven rug your mother wrought, my head in your lap, your hands light on my breast and brow. Speak to me, whispering softy, and tell me the stories that live in your mind but have never been written, bound into paper by pen and ink. Watch the fire dance in my eyes.*'" Gillian looked up from the paper, misty-eyed and sniffing. "That was so sweet. I think it's sort of a poem."

Carrie swallowed hard. Her head buzzed with a static hum as bile rose to burn the back of her throat. "What the hell does it mean?" She sat on the floor next to Gillian. Now she was the one who felt faint.

"I'm not sure what it means, but it's lovely. Who do you think it was from? There's the date at the bottom but no signature."

"I don't know. Maybe it was from my grandfather." Carrie knew that was wrong as soon as she said it. It felt wrong before it even came out of her mouth.

Gillian looked back at the paper. "I don't think so. It says nineteen o-seven, but they weren't married until nineteen ten after your grandmother recovered from a prolonged illness."

"I didn't know she was sick. What did she have?"

141

"I don't know, but she was sick enough to be sent away for two years. My assumption is that it was tuberculosis, but that's just a guess. I think the letter probably predates her engagement to your grandfather. Don't forget that he was a doctor and it's entirely possible that he fell in love while tending to her during her illness."

Carrie knew that was wrong, too. Why was she so certain? Something scratched at the back of her mind. It felt like a present waiting for Christmas. It was sitting and waiting but she couldn't touch it. She thought hard. The buzz in her ears turned into a ringing, but whatever it was, it stayed just beyond her reach.

She held out her hand. "Can I see the letter?"

"Sure." Gillian handed her the paper.

Carrie unfolded it carefully. She read it through. Looking at it made her dizzy. The handwriting was so familiar, but she was sure she'd never seen it before. It didn't make sense. "Did you see this?" Carrie pointed to the bottom right-hand corner of the letter. "It's that flower again."

"So it is. Maybe it's a signature of sorts. I bet it stands for somebody's name, like Iris or Rose or Violet or something."

Carrie looked at Gillian. Her skin felt like it was stretching too tight over her bones as a piece of the puzzle struggled to click into place. "But this is a love letter."

"Not necessarily. Women expressed affection more freely and enthusiastically back then. It could be from a very close friend writing to your grandmother." Gillian turned her eyes back to the shelves. "I wonder what book it was in originally? It couldn't have been this one."

"Do you know anything about my grandmother's close friends?"

Gillian shook her head. "No. I've never run across anything to make me think she ever had any friends. She was not the most affectionate of women. Polite but very distant. Very aloof according to the house staff, but that was after her marriage. Anyone who knew her before would be dead and buried by now."

"And yet, someone once loved her enough to write her a poem." Carrie read the paper again.

Gillian frowned at Carrie and carefully closed the book in her lap. "Maybe we shouldn't go through any more books."

Carrie looked at her a little surprised. "Why not?"

"You don't look at all well."

"I feel all right," Carrie lied.

Gillian shook her head. "I so totally don't believe you. You're looking very gray."

Carrie managed a grin. "Terrific, then I'll match your eyes."

"Aren't you a funny girl." Gillian reached out to touch Carrie's cheek. Her hand felt hot and dry.

Carrie's skin felt cold and clammy. "I'm fine, Gills. Really. I just need to take a break or something. Get some coffee maybe or a drink of water."

"How about if I make us something to eat?" Gillian brushed Carrie's hair back away from her face. "It's close enough to dinner time to call it a day."

"I have no idea what's left in the refrigerator besides leftover turkey sandwiches."

"I'll look around. I can be pretty creative."

"Yes, I know." Carrie looked at her with a hopeful grin. "Maybe we could skip dinner."

Gillian looked at her sharply. "I think you need to eat."

"It doesn't have to be dinner."

Gillian leaned over and gave her a kiss. "Silly." She handed her the book, stood and headed for the front stairs.

Carrie folded the paper and slipped it back in between the pages of *Gone with the Wind*. She stood on shaky knees. Her breath was shallow and short, but the nausea was fading along with the buzz in her ears. She put the book back on the shelf and walked slowly down the spiral staircase to the first floor of the library. She caught a glimpse of her reflection as she passed by the mirror. She stopped and stood in front of it. Her face did look gray and haggard, but everything behind her looked as it should. That is, it looked faded and old. It struck her suddenly that while she did feel tired, she didn't feel old anymore, not like she did when she first came here. She thought of Gillian in the kitchen rummaging through the pantry and then of Gillian in the bathtub. She felt herself flush. A very creative woman, that Gillian. She liked her very much and knew that she would, in time, fall head over heels in love. If she wasn't halfway there already. She knew this with certainty. The problem was that a small piece of her felt like it was already in love. And not with Gillian. She touched the mirror. The surface was hard and cold.

Carrie took a sip of her soup as she watch Gillian pick another cracker out of the box, top it with a slice of sharp cheddar and pop it into her mouth. She leaned across the table and wiped a crumb off Gillian's lip. Her fingers lingered over the point of her chin. "Would you like to stay again tonight? I can run you home to pick up a change of clothes and we can stop at the grocery store to get something for breakfast."

Gillian shook her head. "I really shouldn't. Tongues will wag before we're ready for it."

Carrie sat back in her chair. "That doesn't bother me any."

"Then before I'm ready for it." Gillian closed the box of crackers. "I want the chance to break it to my father gently."

Carrie picked up her spoon and stirred it around in her soup. "Your father's a reasonable man. He's not going to stop speaking to you just because you're spending the night with me."

"He is a reasonable man, but he's old and big changes don't come easy at his age. He still has his hopes for me, and I'd like to let him down easily. I don't want him to hear about us as gossip before he hears the truth from me." Gillian wiped her mouth and put her napkin on the table. "Will you be all right if I leave? I'm a little worried about the sleepwalking thing."

"I'll be fine provided I don't sleepwalk into the kitchen and eat this entire wheel of cheese."

Gillian smiled over the table at her. "You better not. I claim half of this cheese as mine and I intend to eat it myself." She pushed her chair back from the table and stood. She yawned and stretched.

Carrie watched her shirt stretch tight over her chest. It made her own chest ache just a little. "When will I see you again?"

"Very soon. I am worried about you. You look better but still a little peaked."

Carrie dropped her spoon into her soup bowl and stood. She walked around the table to Gillian and kissed her on the cheek. "Please don't worry. I'll be fine."

Gillian traced the edge of her face with her fingertips. "See that you are."

She gathered her keys from the kitchen counter. Carrie walked her to the front door, kissed her goodbye and watched her get into her car. It seemed that she had done this all too many times before. She was starting to dislike seeing red taillights disappearing into the trees.

Carrie sighed and closed the door. Without Gillian, the only thing to do was to clean something or read a book. She didn't feel like cleaning and she was running low on books that she hadn't already read at least once. There was still the Pimpernel book even though she had read that one before and wasn't quite sure why she picked it up again. She had put it down days ago and still hadn't finished it.

Carrie went into the library and found the book still sitting on the table under the lamp. She sat, propped her feet on the ottoman and opened it to the page she'd marked with a frayed scrap of ribbon. It was hard going. With only one page turned, she missed Gillian already. The chair, with her feet propped up, was comfortable enough, in a thin cushioned way, but her eyes wouldn't focus on the words. Her mind kept sliding off the page and back to the note they found tucked inside *Gone with the Wind. Lay me down on your floor…Sweet applewood and oak…your hand on my breast…*Carrie's head jerked back up. She blinked at her book. She couldn't see the words at all. The library was dark and still. The sun had set and she could hear night noises drifting in through the windows, the busy whirring and clicking of the cicadas and the crickets.

145

Carrie reached over and switched on the lamp. The air was turning nippy. That was unusual for the day having been so warm, but as Gillian always said, "there was no accounting for the weather." Carrie frowned and tilted her head to one side. Gillian never said that. Somebody else said that, but Carrie couldn't think of who it might have been. She marked her page and put the book down. It didn't matter who said it. It was still chilly. She couldn't turn on the heat because she hadn't had anybody out to look at the furnace yet, but a small fire in the fireplace sounded like a good idea. It would take the chill off the air and look nice glowing and crackling underneath the old mirror.

She carried in two armloads of half rotten logs from the woodpile by the patio and a big bundle of fresh green clippings from the path trimmings. She got the fire going easily enough once she found the matches, though the wood snapped and popped irritably. The smell of smoke was faint but pleasant. Applewood, ash and oak. Carrie dusted the dirt and debris off her hands and stood by the fire watching the flames flitter and flare. Sweet applewood and oak. Carrie breathed in the aroma. It was a delicate smell, the sweet applewood. Maybe too sweet to be just smoke. Carrie breathed in deeper. There was something floral in the air. It was more like perfume than smoke. She stood away from the fire and sniffed around the library trying to figure out where the smell was coming from. A faint whiff hovered over the desk, but it wasn't coming from the flowers, whose petals were curled and brown. She followed the trail of it over to the couch. She knelt and touched the seat. Her hand passed through cold, but the seat was warm to the touch.

Carrie jumped when she heard the first howl, a slow, drawn-out cry that prickled her skin and made her shiver. She heard the horn sound out and the hounds bayed closer than ever, yipping in short staccato bursts. Carrie went over to the patio doors to see if she could see them, but the wings of the house blocked her view. She stepped out into the little garden in between and stood by the picket gate. The chill in the air had grown so sharp it brought smoke to her breath. She wrapped her arms around herself and looked out over the new mown field behind the house. The moon was big and bright, but a fog covered the ground in thick patches, pooling in the hollows and underneath the trees.

A fox ran out of the woods in a swirl of mist. It streaked across the field and ducked under a fence, disappearing into the woods on the other side. Carrie hadn't noticed that fence before, the split rails zigzagging along the line of trees. The baying came even closer. A low moan rose from a soft cry, swelling into a full-throated howl. Others followed in an eerie chorus.

The dogs burst out of the trees with soft fingers of fog clinging to their fur. Some ran with their noses in the air baying and barking, but most ran with their noses to the ground swinging their heads back and forth, jostling each other for the best track. A horse shot out of the woods right behind them. A man in a tall top hat and coat with the tails fluttering behind him sat straight backed in the saddle. He checked the horse to a saunter, paused and blew his horn. The dogs checked their pace but then ran on. The rider slapped the horn against his leg in a frustrated gesture and then urged the horse back into a gallop. A tight pack of horses and riders burst out from underneath the trees, shredding the fog under their galloping hooves. They jumped by ones and twos over the hedge and followed the dogs into the woods.

Carrie blinked at the meadow and rubbed her eyes. Where did that hedge come from? And that bed of flowers? She closed her eyes tight for a second and then opened them again. The chill in the air grew sharper as the hedge, the flowers, the split rail fence disappeared underneath the rising fog.

Carrie shivered and walked quickly back to the house, rubbing briskly at her arms. She shut and locked the doors and closed all the windows. The lamp on the table beside Carrie's chair threw out a dim yellow light. The fire seemed to burn brighter. Thin, jittery shadows quivered against the walls.

She stood in front of the flames to warm her fingers and toes and stared at herself in the mirror. Was she really going crazy? A log shifted and fell. The flames hissed and crackled. Sparks jumped out of the fire and landed on the hearth where they glowed for a second before they darkened and died. Her reflection seemed to waver with the fire's shadows dancing under her chin. The hazy silver made her look different. Her hair looked bigger. Her face looked thinner, younger. Her T-shirt was lacy. The desk was in the wrong place again. A lamp with a stained glass shade sat on the leather blotter, glowing softly. A candlestick telephone sat next to the lamp, its bright green cord running over the edge of the desk.

Carrie heard the music. Not from the music box, but real music, piano, strings and flute, with bursts of laughter and people talking. She couldn't make out what they were saying. The words were muffled and muted, sounding as if they were in another room. How could she be dreaming? She hadn't even closed her eyes. Her heart beat hard against her ribs, making them ache. She felt light-headed and a little queasy. In fact, she felt very queasy, dizzy and short of breath. Her knees wobbled underneath her. She closed her eyes and leaned against the mantel, cradling her head in the crook of her arm. A cold draft blew against the back of her neck. Her stomach twisted and churned.

"Celia, are you all right?"

The broken burr of a voice tickled in Carrie's ear. She lifted her head slowly and raised her eyes to the mirror. Her heart skipped and stuttered. The woman was standing right behind her, red hair shimmering in the firelight. The hat was still lying on the couch. Carrie watched her lift a white-gloved hand and place it on her shoulder. She couldn't feel the weight of the hand, but a coldness crept slowly through her skin, sinking down to touch her bones. The sound of the music grew louder in her ears.

"Celia, can you hear me?" The woman's voice seemed stretched and thin. She lifted her other hand. Gloved fingers curled softly over the slope of Carrie's shoulders and touched her collarbone.

Ice crawled down her spine. "I can hear you." Her voice sounded strange, twangy, faint and far away. She looked at the weightless hands on her shoulders. Real and not real. Carrie desperately wanted the hands to be real. "If I turn around will you still be there?"

The woman laughed. It buzzed and crackled and made Carrie's heart do skittery things. "Of course, you goose. I'm not going to leave you that soon."

Carrie took another breath, her lungs catching against her ribs. Slowly, she turned around. The woman was still there, still hazy and faint. White-gloved hands slid back up onto Carrie's shoulders as the woman leaned forward and kissed her lightly on the cheek.

Cold stabbed through Carrie's face. It sank into her bones, froze her thoughts, iced her blood. Stopped her heart. The room went dark. Carrie's knees buckled and she fell to the floor.

CHAPTER FIFTEEN

Carrie was lying down. A warm hand held on to her cold one, patting it and then rubbing it briskly.

"Celia, can you hear me?" A plaintive voice spoke clearly in her ear. "Wake up, sweetheart. Please, wake up."

Her heart was pounding painfully against her chest. Carrie tried to take a breath. Her ribs pinched and ached. Her head hurt like the day after New Year's and her stomach felt just as unstable. She felt a hand patting her cheek, softly at first and then harder until it was just short of a slap. With an effort, Carrie opened her eyes. The woman with the red hair was bending over her, just as clear and solid as she was. Only, Carrie didn't feel very solid. She felt faded and worn.

The woman saw her eyes open and her body sagged as she pressed her hand to her chest. "Oh, thank the Good Lord, Celia. You gave me such a fright."

The soft cee of the name the woman called her echoed strangely with the hard sound of her name. It sounded right, somehow, even though it was wrong. Carrie lifted a hand and pressed it to her head. Her hand felt cold and weightless. "What happened?"

The woman shook her head. Her hair shimmered, catching the late slanting sunlight in a fascinating way. Copper and gold. Carrie squeezed her eyes shut and then opened them again. Where did the sun come from? Wasn't it night just two seconds ago? The sun was out of place. It hurt her head and made her feel worse than she felt already. Disjointed and shifted.

"I don't know what happened. I was just getting ready to give you your gloves when you turned the most ghastly shade of gray and then fell over in a dead faint. You bumped your head on the mantel when I tried to catch you and then you nearly fell into the fire." The woman's hand fluttered against her chest. "Lord, have mercy, what would your father have said to me if you burned your new dress with the guests already arriving?"

"My father?" Carrie blinked. The images of two very different men drifted into her mind. One was tall and gaunt with a flaming red nose, dead and buried for some years past. The other, tall and robust with a snow-white beard and a hearty laugh. One was her father and the other was...her father. The thought didn't make much sense to her, but her head was still spinning and maybe that was why.

"Yes, your father. It's already a quarter to five." The woman frowned at her. "Where's your watch? I gave it to you so you could be mindful of the time. Did you put it down somewhere? Lord knows, you are always losing that watch." She grabbed Carrie's hand and chafed at the back of it. "What am I going to do with you? Your father will come down any minute now to get you. You must be there at the door to greet Robert when he arrives, and you must be presentable." The woman tugged at her hand. "Can you sit up?"

"Robert?" Carrie thought of a young man with mutton chop whiskers dressed in a coat with sharp pointed tails that buttoned funny in the front. She didn't know why but she was sure that Robert always carried a large black bag with him wherever he went.

"Yes, Robert. How hard did you hit your head? You're not bleeding."

Carrie moved her head from side to side, looking through one eye and then the other. The woman stayed solid no matter which eye she looked out of, but Carrie's brain thought that she shouldn't be solid, that the woman and the sun shouldn't be there at all. She opened both eyes. "I think I'm seeing double."

The woman let go of Carrie's hand and felt gingerly at the back of her head. The press of her fingers was soft and gentle, but the woman's face grew stern and hard. "Celia, there's not even a lump."

Carrie looked up at her, at the rich red hair framing pale skin, at the light dusting of freckles that spread across her nose and cheeks. Eyebrows, two shades lighter than her hair, arched over sharp green eyes. She had a very square face, a generous mouth and a little pug nose. Her features were an unusual combination of things, but all put together she seemed just right. The woman was remarkably handsome. To Carrie, she seemed beautiful in a way that made her heart hurt. She reached out a tentative hand and touched the woman's arm. It was a solid arm. She wrapped her hand around the woman's wrist, and more images crowded into her brain too fast for her to sort them out, but one thing became perfectly clear.

Carrie let go of her wrist. "Your name is Lilly, like the flowers on the music box."

The woman leaned back and raised an eyebrow into an even higher arch. "That's very good, Celia. Can you recall your own name now? You're going to need to know it soon."

"You're being sarcastic." Carrie narrowed her eyes just a little, trying to remember with memories she was quite sure didn't belong to her. "Yes, you are. You've always had a quick tongue, and it's gotten you into trouble before."

Lilly sat back on her heels. Her frown deepened. "I don't see why a woman should be forbidden to speak her mind."

It had the feel of an old argument, a phrase spoken so many

times that it had worn a rut in her tongue. Carrie knew the words to say that would make Lilly's cheeks flame, make her eyes spark with ire. She didn't say them. Carrie didn't want to see her lips thin or her brow crease, the arms fold tightly against her chest. There had been enough of that in the past. There would be too much of that in the times to come. She didn't know how she knew, but she did, as sure as the sun was shining.

Carrie made a move to sit up but found that she couldn't. She tried to bend at the waist, but it felt like her whole torso was stuffed into a toilet paper tube. One size too small. "What is this?" She felt at her waist, at the stiff material and hard rods that pinched and poked her. "Why am I in this contraption? Jesus, it's tight. I can't breathe. I can't even move."

Lilly gave her a tight-lipped look. "The language, Celia. Please. Try to remember how you're supposed to behave when you have guests." She slipped her hands under Carrie's shoulders and lifted her into a sitting position. Carrie's head swam and her vision dimmed. A hand cupped her cheek.

"No, Celia. Stay with me. Don't go to sleep."

Carrie pushed the hand away from her face but it came right back again, a second one following, squeezing her cheeks. "I'm not going to go to sleep, but if you don't let go of me I might puke."

"Oh. And what a horrible word that is." Lilly's hands stayed where they were. "I'm not going to ask where you learned it, though I can gather what it means."

Carrie's head slowly stopped swimming as Lilly's hands rubbed at her cheeks. She grabbed at the hands and held them still. They felt familiar in their shape, in their heat and how they molded themselves to fit into hers. She looked at them closely, flat filed nails, one chipped at the corner, swollen knuckles and work roughened palms. "Your hands are warm. They were cold earlier." She looked up at Lilly who was blushing softly.

"Your hands are cold," Lilly replied. "They always are when you're nervous. Do you want your gloves now?" She pointed her chin to the chair where the wide-brimmed hat sat half on top of a pair of long white gloves.

"I like it better when you wear them."

Lilly almost smiled. "That's not appropriate, Celia. I can wear your clothes when we're alone, but not in front of your guests."

Carrie looked at Lilly's knuckles. She turned one hand over and touched the calluses on her palm. Before she thought about what she was doing, she raised it to her mouth and brushed her lips across them. Lilly jerked her hand away, her pale skin blotching with red. She cradled the kissed hand inside her other, holding it as if Carrie's lips had burned her.

"You mustn't do such things, Celia. Not here. You have guests waiting in the parlor, and your father will come downstairs any moment. Robert will be arriving soon." She looked over her shoulder at the library doors and inched away from Carrie.

It hurt to see her move away and Carrie wondered at the depth of it.

Lilly stood and looked at her. "Will you try and stand?"

Carrie lifted a hand almost as a challenge. "You'll have to help me."

Lilly glanced again at the library doors and then back to Carrie. "You mustn't." Her tone was pleading.

"I won't." Carrie wasn't sure what she was promising not to do, but if she didn't do anything, it should be all right.

Lilly looked at her sharply, but she couldn't keep the expression. Her face melted into an odd mixture of exasperation and fond sadness. She slipped her hands into Carrie's and pulled her gently to her feet. She dropped her hands quickly and knelt with practiced ease to fluff out the skirts Carrie was wearing, tugging on the hem and shaking out the pleats.

Carrie looked down at the crown of her head, the pale skin showing through the red part, and then down at herself. She was wearing a light blue gown with lace trim at the wrists. She felt her chest and neck, at the lace and seed pearls and a collar so high that it nearly touched her chin. She felt her waist. The rods and cords that bound her made her breath come shallow and short.

"I don't think I like this dress." Carrie felt her knees go

154

weak again. Strong hands circled around her waist and held her upright.

"You must hold yourself together now, Celia. Real ladies of quality faint after their engagements are announced, not before." There was a pointed bitterness to Lilly's tone. She shook the hem of Carrie's skirt sharply so that it pooled on the floor around her feet and then she stood. Bright eyes looked at Carrie, pinched with hurt.

It hurt Carrie to see the hurt. "I don't want to be engaged."

The eyes narrowed. "We're a little past that now, Celia."

Carrie couldn't stand to see that expression on Lilly's face, the soft angles thinning into harsh lines. She turned away from her and walked over to the mirror. Her reflection was clearer than it had been before. The tarnish spots were gone. Her face definitely looked thinner than it should have. Her hair was done up in an elaborate braid. She could see Lilly standing behind her, red hair shimmering, gloves dangling from her hands. Carrie turned around, half expecting the room to fade back into dullness, but nothing changed. Lilly was still standing there in her simple dress, looking at her hands, tugging one by one on each finger of the gloves.

"Lilly," Carrie said softly to herself. It felt good on her tongue, like a piece of candy both sharp and sweet. She wanted to say it again, to sigh over it, to hold in her mouth, to let it trickle out between her lips as her tongue caressed her palate. She knew the name so well. Some small growing part of her had known it for years along with half-remembered secrets, like the birthmark on the back of her left knee, the feel of her lips as they brushed across her cheek, the heat of her hands as they buttoned and tied her dresses and stays. Carrie found it hard to catch her breath. Her head still felt dizzy and the pinching at her waist was making her nauseous.

"I have to get out of this dress, Lilly. It's killing me."

Lilly raised her head. "Yes. You always say that. It just takes a while to get use to it. You know that if you stop fighting against the dress it will get better faster." Lilly pursed her lips and looked her over with a critical eye. "The dress is your father's fault, you know."

"Why? Was he drunk when he bought it?" No, Carrie thought. That was the wrong father.

"Shame on you, Celia, for saying such a thing." Lilly scowled as she scolded. "Lord knows it's been nearly impossible to teach you to act like a lady." She looked at the gloves in her hands and shook her head slowly. "If only your father hadn't let you run around in short pants when you were small."

"Could he have stopped me?"

"Perhaps. If your poor mother had lived. If there had been a firm hand to guide you." Lilly slapped the gloves lightly across her palm.

"Isn't that what your hands are for? To torture me to death with whalebones and silk strings to make up for my deficient upbringing?" Carrie tried not to think about Lilly's hands as she inhaled experimentally. If she breathed down instead of out she could take a deeper breath.

Lilly smiled in her direction, but it was slim and unconvincing. "What better use is there for a poor relation? Besides, it's not whalebone but the new steel bands. It's the very latest thing." Her slim smile turned mischievous. "You know that only the very best will do for the torturing of Miss Celia Covington." She snapped the gloves sharply across her palm.

Carrie looked at the gloves and then again at the soft sensual mouth, the corners twitching almost into a grin. "Tell me again… how close a relation?"

Lilly rolled her eyes. "Third cousins four times removed," she said in a tired monotone. "Which was close enough for me to appeal to your father, but not close enough to be family. Ergo, I'm the servant, handmaiden to the heir apparent." Lilly stepped toward Carrie, grabbed her hand and curtsied over it in mock reverence. Her eyes cut to the library doors. She placed a quick hard kiss on the back of Carrie's hand and then dropped it. Carrie looked at her hand. The touch of her lips sent tingles running up her arm, not only for the sake of the kiss, but also for the chance

Lilly took. The same chance she wasn't willing to allow her to take.

Lilly tucked the gloves into the waistband of her skirt and then busied herself brushing invisible specks off Carrie's dress, rearranging the pleats and folds, plucking at the sleeves. "I don't know why you keep making me repeat that. It's not like I've ever forgotten my place."

"You know that's not the reason." Carrie knew it wasn't the reason, but she couldn't remember what the reason was. She thought hard, but her mind still felt jumbled.

They both jumped when the library doors swung open with a bang. A man strode in with quick precise steps. His snow-white beard brushed the front of his gray gold-buttoned coat. Intricate braiding sparkled on his sleeves. A sword hung at his side. He was a tall man, although he had probably been taller once, the slight stoop of his shoulders seemed to take an inch from his height and from his pride. Carrie stared. It was her father, but this man was nothing like her own father. But he was her father and she knew that she should go over to him and kiss him on the cheek. She halfway remembered doing that countless times before. His beard would be scratchy and stiff and he would smile down at her, tolerant and patient, a little patronizing. Carrie was too confused to move.

He looked her over, turned and frowned at Lilly as she fussed with the dress. Lilly saw his frown and stepped back a pace. She ducked her head and bobbed a curtsy.

"Isn't she ready yet? Lord God, what do you women have to do that takes three hours?"

"She had another one of her spells, Colonel Covington. She got a little woozy, but she's fine now. Aren't you, Miss Celia? You feel fine now, don't you?" Lilly poked her in the back. Carrie opened her mouth but couldn't think of what to say.

"Don't you dare, Celia!" Colonel Covington lifted his chin, his beard lifting off his coat. "There will be none of your games today. You will attend to your guests. You will get engaged. You will marry young Robert Burgess, and damn it, you will be happy.

That's an order!"

Carrie stared at this man who was her father and who was not her father as Lilly poked at her back and pulled on her arm. She swayed a little, and Lilly put a steadying hand on her shoulder. She was confused, a little frightened and did not feel at all well. Lilly's grip tightened as the Colonel's beard bristled over reddening cheeks.

"Say, yes, sir," Lilly whispered at her, shaking her shoulder just a little.

"Yes, sir," Carrie said, and tried to stand a little straighter. If she held herself a certain way, almost as if she were falling forward, the dress didn't pinch so much, but she felt the strain of it on her back, and nothing she did made her stomach feel any better.

The Colonel nodded at her gruffly and then his face softened. "I wish your mother could see you now. You look lovely, my dear. Robert's a good man and I know he's very fond of you. You'll be happy, Celia, I know you will."

"Yes, sir." Carrie didn't know what else to say.

The Colonel harrumphed in a wet, misty-eyed way. He came over to her, placed a scratchy kiss on her cheek and threaded her arm through his. Lilly let go of her shoulder, and Carrie felt it as a loss. She wanted Lilly touching her. It steadied her somehow. She leaned heavily on the man's…her father's arm as he led her out of the library.

Musicians were playing in the parlor. Men in white shirts and bow ties sat in a corner playing a badly tuned upright piano, a large violin and something long and flute-like. The music they made was tinny and trilling. The Colonel steered Carrie past the parlor and out the front door where they stood on the porch in the warm summer air. Carriages were arriving, their wheels rumbling down the cobbled drive, circling the fountain that gurgled and splashed. The water flowed cleanly from overflowing urns while the bright stone cherubs spread their wings and smiled as they poured.

Carrie stood next to the Colonel, and Lilly stood just behind her. She felt Lilly's hand pressed against the small of her back. It was a comfort and a prop. People descended from their carriages and walked slowly up the porch steps. Men in long-tailed coats and top hats, women in stiff, pinched dresses of soft muted colors. The Colonel shook the men's hands, pumping heartily, and bowed over the ladies hands with a gallant flourish. Carrie couldn't remember the right words to say. She tried to smile, but it was hard. Her head hurt, her breath came short, her stomach churned. She was still unsteady on her feet.

A young woman stood in front of her chattering, her fan fluttering under her chin. She stopped and looked at Carrie expectantly.

"Say, thank you for coming," Lilly whispered in her ear.

"Thank you for coming. We're so pleased you could join us." Carrie wasn't sure where those words came from, but they sounded all right.

The young woman looked pleased. "Well, of course we wouldn't have missed it for the world. You were so kind to Geoffrey and myself on the occasions of our little wedding. We just had to return the favor." Her fan fluttered faster as she bobbed her head and went inside. A young man bowed to her briefly and went in without saying anything. Carrie turned to greet the next woman standing in line wearing a pinched dress and fluttering her fan.

The last lady in the line pressed her hand and went inside. Carrie was tired and still short of breath. Her legs felt shaky and she wanted to sit, but the Colonel kept a firm hand on her elbow and a sharp eye on the drive. His hand relaxed a little when a young man on horseback came galloping over the cobbles at a reckless pace with one hand on his hat and coattails flying out behind him. He skidded around the fountain, pulled the horse up sharp and jumped down. An old black man came forward and took the reins with an almost disapproving look at the horse's foam-flecked mouth and trembling flanks. The young man didn't look at him as he handed the horse off.

Carrie did. She looked at the old man's wrinkled face and

grizzled hair, the slope of his shoulders and his downcast eyes. His name, she knew, was Samuel. She thought of the name with some affection and a great deal of sadness that she didn't understand. The young man swept his hat off his head and bounded up the stairs without a backward glance, his muttonchop whiskers bristling out the sides of his face. The Colonel shook his hand warmly and thumped him on the back.

"I'm sorry I'm late, Colonel Covington," the young man said with a slight bow. "Agnes Westmore's youngest has the croup. I had to stay until the danger was past."

The Colonel smiled broadly. "A physician's time is never his own. Why, back in the War one of our surgeons missed his own funeral because he was busy setting a leg."

The young man smiled back, shy but proud. "I haven't heard that one, Colonel. You'll have to tell me about it."

"Indeed, my boy. I certainly will." The Colonel pounded a fist against his shoulder. The young man staggered slightly under the blow. He turned to Carrie, covered his heart with his hat and bowed low.

"Thank you for coming," Carrie said to him. "We're so pleased you could join us."

His face broke into a grin and he grabbed Carrie's hand. "I'm sorry I'm late, Celia, my love. Do please forgive me and say that the engagement is still on." He bent his head and touched his lips to the back of her hand. His whiskers tickled her knuckles. Carrie's hand suddenly felt naked under the damp press of his mouth, and she wished for her gloves.

"Of course it is, Robert, my boy. Of course it is." The Colonel slapped a hand against Robert's back. Robert's breath whooshed from his lungs and he dropped Carrie's hand. "And now that you've arrived, we'll go inside and start the festivities." He laid a hand on Robert's shoulder, gave it a hearty shake, turned him around a pointed him toward the front doors.

The young man offered Carrie his elbow. She stared at it until Lilly poked her with a finger. She took his arm and he seemed to stand taller, puff chested and proud. They all walked into the parlor with Lilly one step behind.

There was loud laughter and thick cigar smoke, yellow electric lights behind stained glass shades. The furniture in the parlor was exactly as she remembered it, the couches and chairs, end tables and tea tables, arrayed in the same pattern, though the colors were brighter, the polish shinier. People were talking to her as if they knew her well. Some looked at her strangely and others with eyes full of pity. The older ladies in dark somber colors, in dresses that looked more comfortable than her dress, shook their heads and clucked their tongues.

She felt a familiarity at some of the different faces but couldn't quite recall anyone's name. Someone would shake her hand or kiss her cheek and their name would feel like it was hovering in the back of her mind, but she couldn't break through her own mistiness to lay a finger on it. The rest of the faces flashed by in a hazy stream, as if she were still looking through the wrong side of the library mirror.

"Everyone, your attention, please." The Colonel stood in the middle of the room with Robert at his side, Carrie on his arm, Lilly standing behind them. "We've asked you here today to witness the promising of my dear daughter, Celia Covington, to this fine young man, Doctor Robert Daniel Burgess. Robert, what pledge have you?"

Robert pulled himself up and stood even taller. He reached into his vest pocket and pulled out a ring. He held it up high. "I pledge this ring that was my mother's given to her on the occasion of her marriage to my father. I give it to you, Celia Covington, on your pledge to be my wife."

Carrie's ears buzzed and she felt weak. Her knees trembled as Robert took her hand and slipped the ring onto her pinky finger. It was a small ring of plain gold. Cheers and clapping sounded distant and distorted. The music started again, tinny and trilling, as people moved together to dance or gathered around her and Robert. Men shook Robert's hand and bowed to her. Women bobbed their heads, clasped her hand or touched their cheeks to hers. Carrie looked over her shoulder at Lilly. Her face was pinched and strained with a sick half-smile plastered on her lips. The gloves still dangled from her waistband.

Someone put a glass of something into Carrie's hand. It was warm, sweet and strong. She tilted her head back and drained half the glass. The drink burned its way down her throat. Lilly gave her a disapproving glare and took the glass away from her before she could gulp the rest. Still, it was enough for a slow warmth to begin spreading into her limbs. The warmth would have been pleasant if her stomach hadn't started to churn in an alarming way.

The room grew gray and hazy as cigar smoke filled it faster than the open windows could carry it away. It was getter harder to draw a clear breath. She swayed a little. Her lungs began to burn as the fumes filled her head.

"Celia, my darling, are you all right? Can I get you anything?" Robert's voice sounded solicitously in her ear, his large hand hot against the small of her back.

Lilly stepped in between them. "I think she needs some air. I'll take her out onto the porch." Lilly slipped her arm through Carrie's elbow and turned her toward the foyer.

Robert put his hand on Carrie's other elbow and stopped them. "There's no need for you to get exercised, Miss Lillian. I'll see to her." Robert tugged at Carrie's arm and started to guide her to the door. Lilly didn't let go of her other arm and came with them. Robert frowned at her. "I can take care of my own wife, Miss Lilly."

"She's not your wife yet, Dr. Burgess. I would be remiss in my duties as a companion and a chaperone if I were to let her accompany you alone."

Robert stiffened. "There will come a time when your services will no longer be needed."

"Yes, sir, there will," Lilly said with a short sharp nod. "But that time has not yet come."

They both tugged at Carrie's arms and not exactly in the same direction. Carrie felt pushed and pulled between them. The warmth from her drink turned sour in her stomach and rose to sting the back of her throat. She yanked her arms away from them both and walked quickly out to the porch. She gathered her skirts and sat on the bench, her back forced ramrod straight, the dress pinching at her hips. Robert and Lilly both sat with her, pressing in close on either side. It was too hot for that and she still couldn't breathe. The sour sting in her throat rose higher to touch the back of her tongue.

Robert moved in closer, glaring over her head. "Perhaps Miss Lilly could go get you something cold to drink, Celia, my dear."

Lilly pushed in from the other side. "I rather think a restorative tonic would be just the thing. Miss Celia, would you like Dr. Burgess to go fetch his bag?"

Carrie's head swam. "Please. Both of you. Stop. Really, I don't feel well. I think I need to lie down."

"A short nap might be just what you need." Lilly stood, pulling Carrie up with her.

"The party is just starting, dearest." Robert grabbed her hand and pulled her back down. "Please don't retire so soon."

The heat of the late afternoon, the buzz of the flies, the push and pull of their anger rose in a swirl of red fog. Carrie got up from the bench, leaned over the balustrade and threw up.

CHAPTER SIXTEEN

Carrie's mouth felt puckered. The powder she brushed onto her teeth tasted almost as bad as the bile that burned the back of her throat.

"Here, Celia, wash your mouth out with this."

Lilly handed her a glass of whiskey and poured another for herself. Carrie swished, gargled and spat into the porcelain bowl then rubbed her teeth again with the powder and the silver handled toothbrush. She rinsed, spat again and then drained the rest of the whiskey. Lilly poured her another as she held out her glass. She sipped at it, swishing it slowly around in her mouth before she swallowed.

She made a sour face as the whiskey burned away the bile. "Where did you get that? It's awful."

Lilly smiled as she stoppered the bottle. The mischievous twinkle was back in her eyes. "I've been keeping it by. For medicinal purposes, of course. You know what your Robert says. The worse it tastes the better it is for you." Her smile faded into seriousness. "Are you feeling better?"

"A little bit. Yes, thank you." Music drifted up through the floor of the small washroom, faint and dissonant, as the engagement party moved on without her. She took her glass and followed Lilly into the bedroom of the mistress suite. These rooms had been hers ever since she was old enough to leave the nursery, but it was Lilly who had redecorated them so beautifully. She arranged the furniture, sewed the curtains and picked out the wallpaper, large red flowers with bright green leaves. It was lovely and everything matched so well. Lilly was always better at such things than she was. Carrie blinked at her glass. Those weren't her thoughts, but then…they were.

"That was a truly disgraceful performance," Lilly said reproachfully. The whiskey bottle was nowhere in sight.

Carrie felt her face flush. "I didn't do it on purpose."

"I wonder." Lilly gave her a sharp look and then her mouth began twitching at the corners. "At least you had sense enough not to get any on your dress."

Carrie tugged at her skirts. "I guess that's something. Can I take it off now? Please. I can't breathe."

"Of course." Lilly beckoned with her hand. "Come over here and I'll untie you."

Carrie drank the rest of the whiskey in her glass. The warm brush of it curled in her stomach, making her head even lighter than it already was. She put the glass on the dressing table and walked over to Lilly with legs that were still a little weak and wobbly.

"What am I going to do with you?" Lilly asked as she turned her around. She put her hands on Carrie's shoulders and rubbed.

"The dress, Lilly. Please."

"Yes, Miss Celia."

Lilly began to undo the buttons. Carrie sighed at the sarcasm, but she kept her back turned. Fingers fluttered against her neck as Lilly pushed each button through. The fluttering moved in a slow line down her spine. Too slow, but finally the dress slipped off her shoulders. Carrie stepped out of it and Lilly laid it aside. She began to untie the laces of the corset. As each stay loosened, Carrie's ribs were able to expand a little more. She took a deep breath and almost cried with relief as her internal organs moved back into their right places. Lilly untied the last lace and Carrie shimmied out of the hateful thing.

She held the corset out, feeling its stiff heaviness. She looked at the window and then back at the corset. Lilly tsked at her and grabbed it out of her hands before she could take the first step toward the window. Carrie watched Lilly fold it carefully and put it in the clothes press. She rubbed at the soreness under her breasts.

"I swear to heaven that I'll be damned before I ever wear that thing again."

"Be careful what you wish for."

"That's not a wish. That's a vow."

"You'll have to wear it again if you want to fit into your wedding gown."

"I don't want to fit into my wedding gown. I don't want to fit into any dress that I have to sacrifice a rib to get into."

Lilly laughed softly. "Well, the good news is that fashion is starting to catch up to you. Your letter from Aunt May said that the women in Richmond are now wearing something called a girdle instead of a corset, and their dresses don't always go all the way to the ground but stop a little ways above the ankle. She says it's much more comfortable, but she wouldn't dare wear any such of a thing outside the city."

"And hasn't she come a long way," Carrie muttered under her breath.

"Who's coming?"

"No one that I know of."

Lilly looked at her with a frown and laid a hand on her cheek. "You're not about to have one your spells, are you? Where you get dizzy and say strange things?"

Lilly's hand felt warm. Carrie's cheek felt cold. She laid her hand over Lilly's, softly stroking her fingers. She couldn't help but look into Lilly's bright eyes. "I think we should move to Richmond. Just you and me. We'll rent a small house near Aunt May and keep a little garden outside the kitchen. We'll grow lilies in the spring and I'll give them to you on your birthday."

Lilly's eyes dimmed. She took her hand away from Carrie's face. "That's a child's dream, Celia. You're engaged now." She lifted the hem of Carrie's chemise and rubbed at the red welts the corset left in bold stripes down her stomach. "But someday, I'm going to move to Richmond and you know I'll always keep a room for you." Lilly kissed her lightly on the cheek, her lips lingering against her skin, her fingertip resting just beneath Carrie's ribs. She stepped back, her eyes glittering, pinched and pained.

"You don't like Robert."

"Robert's a fine young man." Lilly tugged at the hem of Carrie's top and straightened out the shoulders.

"Why don't you like him?"

Lilly brushed a fluff of lint off Carrie's arm harder than she needed to. "Why would I like him? I like the way our life is now. In spite of how impossible you are, I don't want it to change." Lilly turned away from her and picked up the dress she had laid aside. She folded it carefully and put it in the clothes press on top of the corset. She closed the door gently and stared, her hand splayed against the wood. "I don't like thinking that soon your affections will be for him and not for me anymore." Lilly dropped her hand. "We've been the best of friends for such a long time, but I know that doesn't give me the right to ask you to become an old maid only to keep me company."

Carrie touched her arm. "Would you have done that for me?"

"What does that matter now?"

"It matters, Lilly. Please."

"Celia." Lilly laid her hand over Carrie's. "I would want to stay with you even if we were dirt poor and had to take in washing for a living."

"Then why am I getting married?" Carrie felt her heart flutter.

Lilly turned away from her. "Because your father says you must. He's been very generous and lenient with you, but he says now is the time for you to put away childish things."

"And you are one those childish things?"

Lilly dipped her head and didn't answer. Carrie put her hand on her shoulder and gently turned her around. Tears shivered in Lilly's eyes. They welled up and spilled over. She turned her head away, but Carrie, with her hand on her chin, turned it back again. She pulled Lilly to her and gently kissed her tears. The right cheek and then the left. Lilly put her arms around her and Carrie held her close as her shoulders shook with silent sobs. She stroked the bare line of skin high up on the back of Lilly's neck.

"I wish I had been born a man," Lilly said softly. "Even a poor man would have had a better chance."

"Chance of what?"

"That someday I might kiss you like a man kisses his wife."

"Oh." Carrie shivered. Her hands clenched, bunching the fabric of Lilly's blouse tight in her fists. "I want you to kiss me like that, Lilly. I do."

"I know you do, Celia, but it isn't right."

"Who says it isn't right?"

"The Bible says it. You know that. You've read it as many times as I have." Lilly raised her head. Her eyes were red-rimmed and sparkling.

Carrie dropped her arms. "I sometimes wonder how different the world would be if Paul had never been born."

Lilly sniffed and took a step back. "But he was, and now it's just the way things are. *For even their women did change the natural use into that which is against nature*...Romans 1:26. You heard the reverend say last Sunday that all women are sinful, and for that reason a woman leaves her father and cleaves to her husband so that someone can have a hand over her." Lilly's face twisted into a bitter grimace. "It's not a wonder that we should feel for each other the way we do, with you running around motherless and in short pants until you were ten and me with the devil's touch on my hair, but if anyone ever caught us kissing like that we'd both be burned for witches."

"No one burns anyone in this day and age, Lilly. With electric lights and motorcars, nickelodeons and the telephone, who believes in witches anymore?"

Lilly took another step back and folded her arms across her chest. "Plenty of people, Celia. This is not the city. Have you ever even seen a motorcar?"

A small, almost fragmented part of Carrie's brain thought of her little compact car and the long, boring drive from Chicago to Virginia. The thought tripped over other thoughts of her favorite horse in the stable, the small carriage she liked to drive. The clash of memories made her dizzy. Her knees began to tremble and she swayed.

"Celia!" Lilly caught her and held her up.

Carrie put her head on Lilly's shoulder and breathed. Soap and powder, sweat and whiskey. She leaned into Lilly molding her body against her. The scratchiness of Lilly's blouse rubbed her bare shoulders. "If we locked the door, who would know?" she whispered.

Lilly's arms tightened across her back. "You must be drunk, Celia. I think I should put you to bed." It was more of a question than anything else with Lilly's voice sounding soft and unsure.

Carrie turned her head to look over at the tall canopied bed. The thin gauzy curtains hung still and unmoving. Lilly's arms across her back felt safe and strong. "Yes. I think that you should. You'll share the bed with me, of course, since I'm not feeling well."

Lilly pushed Carrie away from her. She was blushing deeply. "Celia, you're not to touch me. Promise me you won't."

"Can I help what I do in my sleep?" The memory of a cold night, a warm back, legs twined, soft shoulders underneath the press of her palms made her dizzy again. But it was a different kind of dizzy, one that came with a warm pulse and an ache in all her secret places.

"If you're not truly asleep, then yes, you can help what you do. Promise me, Celia. It's wrong. You know it's wrong."

"If you really don't want me to touch you, then I promise I won't touch you on purpose."

"And that's as good as I'm going to get from you, isn't it?" Lilly nodded and then shook her head angrily. "Of course it is. When have you done anything except exactly what you've wanted to do?" She stepped away from Carrie, turned her back and started struggling with the buttons on the back of her blouse, pulling on them with sharp, angry tugs.

"How about right now?" Carrie felt the spark of her own anger kindle.

Lilly turned back around. "What about right now?"

"I'm engaged to be married to man I hardly know, much less love, and I'm here with a woman that I can't kiss, much less touch. I can't even tell you that I—"

"Don't say it, Celia." Lilly looked at her with fear and alarm. "Please. It only makes it that much worse if you put it into words."

Carrie lifted a hand to her mouth. Her lips hurt with effort not to say the words she felt, her tongue cramped into knots. Lilly turned her back again and began to struggle with her buttons. Carrie watched her twist and bend her arms and wrists.

Carrie stepped behind her. "Do you want me to help you with those?"

Lilly glanced over her shoulder. "You should put your nightgown on."

"I don't know where it is."

"Fine." Lilly sighed and let her arms drop to her sides. "Help me with this and I'll get it for you."

It took forever for Carrie to unhook what seemed like a hundred tiny buttons and then Lilly slipped out of her blouse. The skirt was easier, but Carrie's fingers fumbled as she undid those buttons too. She stood back a step as Lilly shimmied it down and off. Her underthings had laces crisscrossing the back. Carrie started to untie them. As each one came undone, she let her fingers brush against the narrow plain of Lilly's back. The last one fell away and Lilly lifted her chemise over her head. She

170

stood with her back to Carrie, the cloth bunched in her arms held tight across her breasts. It was warm in the room, but Lilly was shivering. Carrie stepped closer and Lilly didn't move away. She reached out a hand and brushed her fingers over her skin, bumping them down her spine and up again, circling the soft places underneath her shoulder blades.

"You promised." Lilly's voice was a low whisper.

"You want me to do this."

"That doesn't make it right. It doesn't make it safe."

That was true, but Carrie couldn't make her hands stop moving over her skin. "Lilly. Please. Give me something of you to carry with me to my marriage bed. Give me some way to live through it." Carrie heard the words her voice was saying without knowing exactly where they came from. It didn't matter. She bent her head and kissed the knobs of Lilly's spine. Her hands slipped around the curve of her waist.

Lilly's shivers turned into trembling. "Is the door locked?"

"You bolted it when we came in."

Lilly's chemise fell to the floor. She turned in Carrie's arms. "You saw me do that?"

Carrie rested her hands on the swell of her hips. "I heard you do that."

"And you knew?"

"I hoped and I guessed and then hoped that I guessed correctly."

Lilly cradled Carrie's face in the palms of her hands. "You're getting sly in your old age, Celia."

"And there's the fox telling the rose it's red."

Lilly pulled Carrie's face to hers and she kissed her. It was an awkward press of mouths, the bumping of noses, a stiff puckering of lips, a bruising crush with a jarring click of teeth. Lilly pulled back, her face fallen in frustration and disappointment. Carrie pulled her back again. She kissed her cheek and rubbed her lips against her skin. She kissed her eyes and her nose, let her mouth slide down the line of her jaw. Her lips brushed across Lilly's and then lightly nibbled at them.

171

Lilly made a small sound in the back of her throat. "Is that how a man kisses his wife?"

"It's how I want to kiss you." Carrie touched Lilly's mouth with her fingertips.

"Do it again," she whispered against her fingers. "Just like that."

Carrie brushed her lips across Lilly's and then leaned into the push of her mouth. Something clicked and fell into place. Lilly's mouth opened slightly. Carrie tilted her head and their lips came together like two pieces of a puzzle. Carrie pulled Lilly against her as a whiskey-like warmth spread through her middle, curled lower and flared into heat. Her hands clutched at Lilly's back. Lilly plucked and pulled at Carrie's chemise, lifting it as high as it would go. She bared Carrie's breasts and pulled her into a tight embrace.

The part of Carrie's mind that was Celia's, the part that had never been touched before, never felt the weight of another body in her arms, the brush of a kiss against her lips, screamed as Lilly's heat poured into her mouth and filled her body to bursting. She held her tight, pushing herself against Lilly in a crush of breasts, a thrust of hips. She ached in way that she never had before, even in her deepest dreams, with a throbbing pain between her legs, a pinching tightness at her breast, a wildfire running over her skin.

Carrie heard herself mew as tears stung her eyes. "Please, Lilly. Oh God, please."

Lilly held her tighter, her hands flat against her back. "Celia, forgive me. I don't know what to do next. Tell me what to do."

Carrie squeezed her hard and then rocked back. "Let go of me."

Lilly's arms tightened. "I don't want to let go of you."

"I need you to, Lilly, because I want to feel all of you pressed against me. With nothing in between."

Lilly made a deep guttural sound as her arms fell to her sides. Carrie knelt in front of her and slipped her drawers down and off. She stared at Lilly's small breasts with light nipples, pale freckled skin, light reddish hair between her legs. It left her stunned and breathless. Lilly pulled her up and slipped her chemise off over her head. She knelt before her, slipping Carrie's drawers down over her hips and legs. Carrie stepped out of them and walked away from Lilly.

"Where are you going?" Lilly held her drawers against her chest.

"Here," Carrie said and slipped into bed. She pulled the sheet up to her thighs. Lilly dropped the drawers onto the floor. She stood and walked over to the bed, oblivious of her own nakedness. She stared at Carrie, her eyes scouring every available inch of her. Her expression was fierce and hungry.

Carrie held out her hand. "Please, Lilly."

Lilly grabbed her hand and held it tight. "I don't know what to do."

"Just come here." Carrie tugged on her hand.

Lilly crawled into the bed and slipped her feet underneath the sheet. She stared at Carrie with wide bright eyes and deeply flushed cheeks. "What do I do?"

"What you've always wanted to do. It doesn't matter, Lilly. Do anything. Do something. Please."

Lilly took Carrie's hand and brought it to her lips. She kissed every finger, lightly licking the tips of each one and then slid Carrie's hand down and placed it over her breast. "I've always wanted this."

Carrie squeezed gently. Lilly's eyes fluttered and closed. "Ah." Her nipple pressed against the center of Carrie's palm and it made her hand tingle. The throbbing between her legs quickened and thickened into sharp pain, a fierce need to touch and be touched. She squeezed, rubbed and kneaded, as Lilly's breath grew ragged and harsh.

Carrie kissed her, a melding of lips and tongue, and reached to touch her between her legs. Lilly rolled onto her back and opened herself, mouth and heart, knees and legs. "Oh." Carrie ran her fingers through the coarse brush of hair, over the soft skin underneath, pressing into her, the warmth and the wet folding

173

softly around her fingers. Lilly arched up into her hand. "Ah." Carrie rubbed harder between her legs, her tongue diving deeper into her mouth as Lilly's hips moved to match the stroking of her fingers.

Lilly's hands were on her breasts, squeezing hard. They slipped down her stomach, over her hips, rubbed clumsily between her legs. "Oh God." It didn't matter. She had wanted this for so long. All touch was good, magnificent, divine. Then, Lilly's fingers rubbed over a spot that made her whole world slip sideways. A deep moan poured from her throat, and Lilly rubbed her there again. Her hips moved to meet her fingers. She couldn't stop them. They had to press into Lilly's hands as Lilly's hands pressed into her, rubbing, stroking, sliding in a rhythm matched in the pounding of her blood. Something began to grow inside her, a trembling delight that filled her body. It grew and filled her so full that it stretched her skin tight. She shimmered on the edge of a glittering brightness, a pounding fullness, a beautiful ache. "Ah." Her body burst open in spasms of lights and stars. "Oh God, Lilly!"

Carrie heard herself whimpering. She buried her face in the crook of Lilly's neck as Lilly murmured soft words, stroked her hair and ran light fingers up and down her spine.

"All these years," Lilly said in a voice that was harsh and rough. "All these years, this is what we've been missing. I never imagined it would be like that." Lilly's fingers traced a circle around Carrie's ear sending shivers racing down her back. "How sad to find it only here at the very end."

Carrie lifted her head and kissed her softly "There will other times, Lilly. Tomorrow night, the night after."

"Tomorrow night is a forever away."

"Then how about right now?"

"Again, now? Can we?"

"We can try. Do you want to try?"

Lilly lifted her head and kissed Carrie's shoulder. "Yes. Right now, yes."

"And tomorrow night?"

"Yes." She kissed the line of her throat. "Tomorrow night, too, and the night after. Every night right up until…"

"No." Carrie laid her fingers across Lilly's lips. "Don't say it."

Lilly kissed her fingers, ran her tongue in between them, took them into her mouth. "Ah." Carrie laid her body on top of Lilly's and felt her legs scissor behind her thighs, the wet of her sliding over her bones, the heat of her soaking into her skin.

"Oh…"

CHAPTER SEVENTEEN

It was too hot a day to be inside, though the ceilings were tall and all the transoms were open. Carrie sat on the front porch, her paper fan clutched in her hand. The air wasn't moving enough to make the transoms worthwhile. She wobbled her fan back and forth half-heartedly. Even the bumblebees seemed lackluster in their buzzing. An increasingly dim part of her mind remembered air conditioning and freezers, but it made her dizzy to think about it. The kitchen had an ice chest full of the ice that had been harvested from the frozen river last winter, stored in large blocks deep underground in the icehouse. But no one thought of chipping it into little pieces and putting it in the lemonade. It was too valuable for that, seeing that it was the only ice to be had in all of Columbia and would barely last until winter. Still, a girl could wish.

Robert shifted on the bench next to her. His jacket was off and his sleeves rolled up past the elbows. Sweat stained the armpits of his shirt. He fanned himself with his hat hard enough that Carrie could smell him, hair grease, horse sweat and iodine. Her own sour body smell mixed with his and stuck in the back of her throat. She waved her fan harder, but that was a mistake. The smell of Lilly on her hands made her shiver. A week's worth of Lilly on her hands and they would never smell the same. She glanced over to the other side of the porch where Lilly sat facing them, far enough away to be almost unobtrusive but close enough to make Carrie wish that it was Lilly sitting next to her on the bench.

Robert followed her gaze and frowned. "Let's walk to the river, Celia. We can sit under a tree and watch the boats go by."

Carrie folded her fan and laid it in her lap. "It's too hot for a walk, Robert. You know Lilly doesn't do well in the heat."

"Fine. She can stay here."

"You know she can't. She's my chaperone. She goes everywhere I go."

Robert lowered his voice to a rumbly whisper. "Does she have to sit on the porch with us?"

Carrie plucked at her skirts. "Of course she does. What would my father say if he came home to find me sitting unaccompanied?"

"I doubt he'd say very much. We're going to be married in three weeks."

"But we're not married yet, so Lilly has to stay."

Robert gave a frustrated sigh and tapped his knee with the brim of his hat. "Sometimes I wonder if you prefer her company to mine."

Carrie tried to keep her face still and neutral. "Lilly has been my companion since I was eight years old. She cares for me and takes her responsibility for guarding my honor quite seriously."

Robert slumped on the bench, pouting. "I want to kiss you, Celia. I rode five miles out of my way just in the hopes that you might say yes."

"Robert, please be patient. That time is coming fast enough."

"Don't you want to kiss me?"

Carrie gripped her fan tight in her fist. "How should I know?"

Robert slapped his hat against his leg. "That's what I love about you, Celia. You have such a wise innocence. How should you know, indeed, if you've never been kissed?" He put his hat back on his head and crossed his legs at the ankles. Dust from his boots fell onto the porch. "I suppose you're right. There will be time enough for that in the years to come." Robert folded his hands across his stomach and looked up at the bright blue sky. "I wonder what our life is going to be like. The world is changing so fast. Yesterday, I saw a motorcar on the Richmond road. The man driving said he had come all the way from Richmond in just four hours and only had to stop twice to change some tires. Can you imagine such a thing? It takes me all day to get to Richmond in a carriage and the horses have to stop all the time. It's not any better on the canal." Robert's gazed dropped to the fountain. "Some day I'm going to have a motorcar."

Carrie snapped her fan open again and shooed a fly away from her head. "Someday everyone will have a motorcar and then there will be too many motorcars and not enough roads. Everyone will have to wait in long lines to get their turn on the road and no one will be able to go very fast after all."

Robert laughed. "I hope I live to see the day."

Carrie didn't answer.

Robert looked at her, his face suddenly grave. "I want you to be happy with me, Celia."

"I know you do, Robert. I believe your affection for me is genuine, but please understand that this is a very frightening time for a woman. It's a big change to leave the place you've always known to go live with people whose habits are strange to you."

Robert tipped his hat back on his head. "Well then, I've good news for you. Your father's asked that we live here with him until the children come. He says we can have over the whole upper east wing until we outgrow it and to heck with the guests. Does that make you less frightened?"

Carrie's eyes cut over to Lilly. "A little less," she said. A light breeze blew a wisp of Lilly's red hair across her face. Carrie watched her tuck it back behind her ear and then turn the page of her book. She thought of Lilly's hands on her body, turning her pages, reading her slowly, line by line, as if she were the most fascinating book ever written. Lilly was as much a fixture of this house as the library was. Surely she would stay.

"May I hold your hand?"

Robert's voice startled her. "I'm sorry. What?"

"I asked if I may hold your hand."

"Oh." With her eyes still on Lilly, Carrie held out her hand. Robert's hand engulfed hers. It was big, broad and rough. Not at all like Lilly's hands, though, her hands were rough, too. His palm felt wrong against hers, its shape and heat, the light sheen of sweat that slicked his skin, the itchy line of dark hair that dribbled over the back. She wanted to take her hand back, to go wash it in the basin with hot water and lye soap. She looked at his hand, an ugly hand, coarse-haired and knobby-knuckled, and then she looked at him to ask for her hand back. Robert's smile stopped her. It was radiant, shining with a joy that she had only just recently seen in Lilly's eyes. She looked back at Lilly. She was frowning at her from over the top of her book, lips pursed into a tight line. With deliberate movement, she turned her back to Carrie and buried her nose back in the pages of her book. Carrie's hand in Robert's felt dirty and unclean. Robert just sat and smiled.

CHAPTER EIGHTEEN

The evening was just as warm as the day had been. Only the light breezes blowing in from the river made it any more bearable. Carrie lay on the top sheet on her back with her arms held out away from her body watching the canopy curtains billow and sway. Her chemise stuck to her skin. The only sound she heard was the loud burring of the cicadas, the croak of a frog and the occasional rustle of leaves shivering in the breeze.

She turned over onto her side and rested her head in the palm of her hand. "Lilly, will you please talk to me?"

"I'm reading."

"No, you're not."

Lilly scowled into her book. "Yes, I am."

Carrie reached over Lilly's lap and tipped the book down. "You haven't turned the page once since early this afternoon."

Lilly slammed the book shut and threw it across the room. It smacked against the wall and fell to the floor in a flutter of pages.

Carrie blinked at her. "Okay. That's something."

"I can't do this, Celia." Lilly's eyes shone in the lamplight.

"Do what, exactly?"

"I can't watch you be with Robert. I can't watch him touch you. I can't watch you look on him with the same eyes that you use to look at me. I can't."

Carrie flopped onto her back and stared into the canopy. The curtains were as clean and white as Lilly could keep them. "Would you prefer that I swap eyes when he comes over? I'll put in a pair of brown ones for him and keep blue ones exclusively for you."

Lilly shifted to look at Carrie, her face angry and outraged. "How can you joke?"

Carrie sat up and wrapped her arms around her knees. "I don't know what else to do, Lilly. If you just tell me what you want, I'll do it."

"Not this." Lilly shook her head, her eyes blinking rapidly. "I don't want this. It isn't right that Robert can hold your hand in front of God and all his saints when I have to sneak up to your room at night to hold you in my arms."

"But I want you to sneak into my room at night. I want you to do it for the rest of our lives."

Lilly gave her an exasperated look. "Three weeks, Celia, and you'll be sleeping in a different room. Or worse, Robert will be sleeping here in this room, our room, with you. I won't be sneaking in at night when he's lying right here in this bed." She slapped the mattress with the flat of her hand. A mote of dust jumped, swirling into the air.

Carrie looked at Lilly's hand. For the last nine years, Lilly had spent more nights in bed beside her than she had in her own room downstairs in the servant's quarters. Her mattress had a Lilly-sized dent on the side closest to the door. Carrie couldn't imagine a Robert-sized dent. She tried to remember if there had been one.

The room skittered and tilted. The red flowers on the wall seemed to fade. Carrie shivered in spite of the heat and reached to touch Lilly's hand. It was still solid and warm, a steadying comfort. The room leveled and the flowers brightened. Lilly was staring at the book on the floor. It had landed facedown and open, its pages bent and creased underneath it. Carrie squinted her eyes to read the title. *The Hound of the Baskervilles* by A. Conan Doyle.

"Nineteen oh-two," she said softly to herself. She had read that one already and hadn't liked it very much. She slid her hand over Lilly's. "It won't be so awful. I only have to spend one night sleeping next to Robert and after that I can keep a room of my own."

Lilly moved her hand away. "Don't be ridiculous. Robert wants children. You're going to have to sleep next to him more than once."

Carrie wrapped her arms back around her shins. "I don't see what children have to do with it."

"Lord, have mercy, Celia." Lilly looked at her with eyebrows raised. "Don't you know where babies come from?"

"Of course I do." Carrie knew full well how babies were made, but Celia's mind was a little fuzzy on the particulars. The room shuddered out of focus again as her disjointed thoughts collided. A small groan trickled up from her throat as her ears began to buzz. She put her head on her knees and closed her eyes.

Carrie felt hands sliding through her hair, gathering it, lifting it up and off her back. Lips pressed against the nape of her neck. "I'm sorry." Warm breath tickled against her skin.

Carrie turned her head a fraction. "Don't be sorry. You're right to talk to me like that. I haven't a mother to tell me these things."

Lilly stroked the base of her neck with gentle fingers. "My mother didn't tell me such things either, but I had brothers and that was almost as good."

Carrie looked at her. The harshness of her tone was at odds with the soft stroke of her fingers. "They didn't hurt you, did they?"

Lilly's fingers stilled and dropped away. "No. Mother sent me here before that could happen."

Carrie sat up straight. "Lilly, you never told me that."

"I wasn't supposed to." Lilly smoothed Carrie's hair back from her face. "You were to think that I came here only to keep you company."

"I did think that." Carrie touched the bend of Lilly's knee. "I never dreamed there might be another reason. Lilly, I'm so sorry."

Lilly shrugged as if it didn't mean anything much. "Mother did the best she could after father died, but she had to work long hours in the mill to keep food on the table." Her eyes narrowed and then saddened again. "At least she cared enough to send me away. I don't know what it cost her to send me here to you and be left with five boys and no one to help her."

Carrie thought of Lilly's mother. Celia had met her once, before she died, and remembered her as a hard-faced woman, stooped and worn. "Oh, Lilly."

Lilly slipped an arm around her shoulders and Carrie laid her head against Lilly's neck. Lilly's other hand brushed at her cheek. "You've got that gray look about you again. Are you feeling all right?"

"No, not really, but I think it's just the heat. It's awfully hot for June."

"There's no accounting for weather," Lilly said tugging at Carrie's shoulders, laying her on the bed. She stretched out next to her, close but not touching. Carrie could feel the heat of her body and it warmed her in a way that had nothing to do with the summer sun. She reached out to touch her.

Lilly stopped her hand. "Tomorrow is Sunday."

An escaped curl of shimmering red lay draped across the pillow. Carrie tugged at it gently, twirling the ends around the tip of her finger. "Yes. That's most unfortunate since it means we can't sleep late. Father will be expecting us up for church." Carrie smiled at her but Lilly looked serious. Almost sad. Carrie's smile faded. "What about Sunday?"

"Your father will be home all day."

"True. And?"

Lilly gently pulled her hair out of Carrie's hand. "I'm going to tell him that I'm leaving."

Carrie sat up. "No, you're not."

"Yes, I am." Lilly rolled over and looked at Carrie. Her face was set. "I'm going to ask him for the carriage on Monday to take me to the train, and if he won't lend me the carriage, I'll walk."

"Lilly, why?"

"I'm going to go live with Aunt May in Richmond. I've already written her. She said I could come."

Carrie stared at her, mouth agape. "Why would you want to go live with Aunt May?"

"She needs someone to keep house for her, and what better use is there for a poor relation?" Lilly said with a sour smile.

"No, Lilly," Carrie said, shaking her head. "You can't leave. I need you here with me."

Lilly didn't look at her. "I've always planned to leave when Robert took you away from me. This is just a little sooner than that."

"But he's not taking me away, Lilly. You heard him. We're going to live here. You can stay."

"And do what? Be a sneak?" Lilly's face was fierce and angry, but she still didn't look at Carrie.

Carrie touched Lilly's stomach. "I like it when you sneak." She slid her hand up to cup the underside of Lilly's breast.

Lilly grabbed her wrist and moved her hand away. "I can't stay with you and Robert. Celia, you must understand. What you're asking me to do is too hard."

Carrie shook her head and cradled her hand. "I don't understand. You can't leave me here by myself. You can't leave me. You just can't." She curled up beside Lilly and laid her head on her middle.

Carrie felt Lilly's fury trembling underneath her cheek. She held herself still for a long count of seconds waiting for Lilly to slap her away. But Lilly took a deep breath and blew her anger away in a sharp stream of air. She reached down a hand and stroked Carrie's hair, twisting the strands and letting them run through her fingers.

"How can you ask me to stay?" Her voice was soft and choked. "Do you think I want to watch you fall in love with your own husband? Do you think I want to lay awake at night in my own little room in my cold narrow bed imagining what he's doing to you, how his hands are touching you? Do you think I could stand that?"

"It won't mean anything when he touches me. I don't love him, Lilly. I don't. I never will."

"Of course you will. Isn't that the way God intended it to be?" The question was sharp and bitter.

Carrie lifted her head. "You don't have to play the martyr for me, Lilly."

"And you don't have to play the simpleton." Lilly tapped her lightly on the nose. "You know what I'm saying. I have to leave here before both of our hearts break or something even worse happens. There's no other choice."

Carrie rubbed her nose against Lilly's chemise. "There's always a choice. I won't sleep next to him at all if you don't want me to."

Lilly laughed, short, sharp and abrupt. "He'll be your husband. You'll have to sleep next to him whether you want to or not."

"I'll say no."

"He'll force you."

Carrie turned her head. "He wouldn't dare." The thought was outrageous.

"Of course he would dare. He'll be your husband. It'll be his right to take anything he wants from your body, your boudoir or from your bank account. You'll belong to him and anything that belongs to you will belong to him."

"And you want to leave me with that?" Carrie sat up again.

Lilly sat up, too, but she didn't look at Carrie. She looked at her lap, her face collapsed into miserable lines. "Once the children come, you'll have something else to love. After a time, you won't think of me anymore."

Carrie reached for her hand and held it in both of hers. "Lilly, I swear, if I live to be a hundred years old, I'll spend my dying breath saying your name."

Lilly's head fell back against the headboard with a thump. "Merciful Lord, Celia, you're making this so hard."

"Don't leave me."

Lilly shook her head, her eyes still pointed up into the canopy. "It's too hot to be arguing like this." She sat up and started to get out of bed. "Let me get a cool cloth for your head."

"No." Carrie held on to her hand and pulled her back again. "Lilly, don't leave. Not now. Not Monday. Not ever. Please."

Lilly looked at Carrie and touched her cheek. "Would you really choose me over Robert?" Lilly asked the question as if she didn't believe the answer could be a good one and then Carrie saw her eyes widen with surprise. "You would, wouldn't you? You really do…" She closed her mouth without finishing her thought. "Oh, Celia." She leaned over Carrie and kissed her. Her mouth was warm. Her breath blew hot against Carrie's cheek.

I would, Carrie thought as she opened herself to Lilly's lips and tongue. Lilly's hands ran lightly over Carrie's skin, down her arms and under her chemise. I do, she thought with the brush of her palms, the stroke of her tongue. Carrie pulled Lilly to her. She lost herself in the warm press of skin, the shushing of sheets, the creak of the bed in rhythm with sweat slicked sliding of hips and breasts. Lilly's hands moved over her, down her belly, between her thighs. She slipped inside her and Carrie lost all track of time and place, where she ended and where Lilly began. The moon slowly arced across a star-studded sky as their soft gasps and groans grew, their motions quickened to an almost frantic pushing and pulling. Lilly cried out against her shoulder, her body convulsing atop her. Her own answering cry came with a shudder that shook her soul.

Sweat pooled and cooled as they lay with their bodies melded together, their limbs twined and tangled. Carrie's eyes drooped and closed as she listened to the soft, even sound of Lilly's breath against her shoulder, the buzz of the cicadas, the rustling night

186

breezes, the soft tap-tapping of footsteps. Carrie opened her eyes. She lifted her head to listen but Lilly stirred, sighing in her sleep, and held her tighter. Carrie kissed her brow, brushing her lips across her skin, tasting the sweet saltiness. She smiled softly to herself, laid her head back down and closed her eyes.

CHAPTER NINETEEN

A door slammed in Carrie's dream with a strange echoing sound, like a thousand doors closing down a mile-long hallway. She opened her eyes to bright daylight streaming outside her window. Lilly was gone, but that was not unusual. She usually rose at first light, although, as Carrie recalled with a sleepy smile, they hadn't gone to sleep until near first light. Carrie wondered if Lilly had slept at all. She brushed her tangled hair back from her face and caught the scent of Lilly on her hands, the deep rich musk, a tang of salt and sweat. It was the smell of the ocean, both bitter and sweet. Carrie touched the dent on Lilly's pillow and wondered where she was, what she was doing.

A light tap-tap-tap sounded on the bedroom door. Carrie rose, slipped on her dressing gown and opened the door. Martha, the cook, stood in the hallway looking uncomfortable and out of place in her food-spotted apron, smelling of mint and peaches. She dropped a clumsy curtsy.

"What is it, Martha?"

"Your father sent me up, miss, to help you with your

dressing."

Carrie looked at the flour on her hands, the shuffling of her feet, the high color staining her cheeks. "Where's Lilly?"

"In her room, miss."

"Is she sick?"

"I'm sure I don't know, miss. The Colonel said he would like to see you as soon as you're dressed." Her restless feet scraped across the floor.

Carrie tightened the belt on her dressing gown with an angry jerk and pushed past Martha into the hallway. She headed for the stairs with Martha bobbing and squeaking behind her, something about dresses, decency and the time of day, but Carrie didn't listen. She was furious, hurt, betrayed. Lilly was going to leave her after all, even after she had promised to stay. It was an underhanded and dishonest trick, to leave her lying there in bed while she made plans behind her back. God only knows what Lilly had said to her father, but she would ask him and he would tell her. She wouldn't let her leave. She couldn't.

She walked quickly down the west wing hallway, losing Martha at the edge of the parlor. She stamped past the billiards room to the heavy oak paneled door of the smoking room. Carrie knocked a sharp rat-a-tat-tat.

"Come."

She opened the door and stepped into the room. The Colonel looked at her from over the top of his newspaper, the smoke from his cigar curling around his head. The image was so familiar, it echoed like the doors slamming in her dream. She could remember seeing him like that, in that same pose, a million times. Now, in his white Sunday suit. A hundred years from now, with a gaunt, clean-shaven face in blue jeans and an old flannel shirt. Carrie's head swam. She staggered and fell against a high-backed chair. The Colonel dropped his paper and rose to catch her by the arms.

"Easy, there, Celia. Sit yourself down, girl, before you fall down." He held her upright and helped her into the chair.

Carrie sat hard, breathing rapid shallow breaths. The cigar

smoke scraped at the back of her throat and made her stomach twist. The Colonel patted her hand awkwardly and then sat back in his own chair. He took his cigar out of his clenched teeth and set it in a dish.

"Shall I ring for Martha and have her help you back to bed?" He ran a hand over his beard, smoothing it against his vest. "Lilly said you were feeling poorly and you do look a little peaked."

"Lilly?" The anger flowed back into Carrie, drowning her dizziness under a wave of furious red. "Lilly's not leaving," she said in a tone sharper than she had ever dared use before.

The Colonel picked up his cigar and looked at it closely. "Yes, she is." His voice was strangely quiet.

"No," Carrie said. "She can't. I need her here to help me." She leaned forward. "I can't go through with the wedding without her. I don't care what she told you. I know she doesn't really want to go live with Aunt May. Please, Father, help me make her stay."

The Colonel put his cigar in his mouth and then took it out again. He tapped a thick circle of ash into the heavy glass bowl and pushed it around with the glowing tip until it broke apart and scattered evenly around the dish.

"Celia," he started but then stopped. The tone was soft. His eyes were hard. The cigar trembled slightly in his hands. "I've buried two wives and I've raised a daughter nearly on my own, but I can't say that I yet understand the workings of the female mind."

Carrie sat back in her chair. "Meaning what, sir?"

Smoke from the Colonel's cigar rose slowly into the air in a thin wavering plume. "Lilly seems to have gotten all sorts of odd notions. Not that she didn't always have odd notions, but she's really rounded the bend this time."

Carrie pulled her dressing gown tighter around her. "What has she been telling you?"

The Colonel's cheeks reddened over his white bristle of beard. "She has somehow gotten the idea that you shouldn't marry Robert and that if you did, you would be miserable for the

190

rest of your life. She thinks your affections lay elsewhere, but that elsewhere doesn't bear too close a scrutiny." The Colonel raised the cigar up to his downturned mouth. His eyes were glittering sharp and hard as iron. "That elsewhere doesn't bear thinking about at all."

Carrie's mouth opened but she didn't know what to say. There wasn't really anything left to say, as Lilly seemed to have said far too much already. She closed her mouth again.

The Colonel gave a disdainful sounding sniff. He shook his head and looked at the ash bowl. It seemed to remind him of something and his eyes softened just a shade. He sighed softly. "With all my heart, Celia, I want and wish for your happiness, but a little gal of seventeen doesn't know enough about the world to know what happiness is. That's why good parents arrange things for their children, so they don't have to spend the rest of their lives living down a very bad mistake."

The Colonel crossed his legs and took a slow puff from his cigar. Smoke streamed from his lips in a thick gray cloud. "I feel that I have been very lenient with you in the past because you are my only surviving child and the hope of my old age. I know that you and Lillian have always been close but, over the years, you have grown too close. She has overstepped her station, and you are in danger of losing your place in yours. I'm going to put a stop to that."

Carrie shook her head. "No." She wanted to put her hands over her ears but she couldn't lift them. "Please. No."

The Colonel ignored her. "I pray that separating you two will be enough to stop this foolishness. Lillian is going to go live in Richmond with Aunt May just as you said, but she's going to go now. Today. Earnest is hooking up the carriage and Lillian is in her room packing her things. And, Celia," the Colonel leaned forward in his chair and grabbed Carrie's chin. He held her head still. "You are not going with her. Is that clear?"

His fingers pinched her face as the smell of fresh cigar clashed with the memory of lemon-scented furniture polish. Carrie's mouth opened again, but the arguments in her head wouldn't roll off her tongue. She heard herself say, "Yes, sir. That's clear."

The Colonel nodded his head slowly. He let go of her chin and sat back in his chair. "Very good. After you're married, of course, you may do as you like and as your husband approves, but while you're still my daughter, living under my roof, you will obey me in this thing."

"Yes, sir." Carrie wanted to scream. Scream anything. Obscenities, insults, her rage and her pain. Her mouth wouldn't form the words though her throat ached with the effort.

"You are not to see or to speak to Lilly again before she leaves. You will go back to your room and stay there until the carriage is gone. We will not speak of this ever again and anything that might have been said, for decency's sake, will never leave this room." The Colonel nodded his head at her once. "That's all. You may go."

Carrie stood. Her hands twitched with the need to throw something, to break and smash, to rend and destroy. She turned and let her hand hit the glass ash bowl. It fell off the table and bounced onto the floor. It didn't break. It only spread fine gray ash over the rug, dimming its colors. Her father picked the bowl up off the floor and set it back on the table. He tapped his cigar on its edge, picked up his paper and opened it with a shake. Carrie opened the heavy oak door and walked out of the room. She shut the door gently behind her.

Her eyes filled with a fog of hurt and pain as she moved down the hallway, through the parlor, into the foyer. She stood in front of the grand staircase, her hand on the railing, her foot resting on the first tread. He father was a man who expected to be obeyed, and she always had. In everything. There had never been a reason not to. He was a good man, a wise man, just and reasonable. But he was wrong about this. He didn't understand. How could he?

Her foot slipped off the tread. She turned slowly and walked through the dining room, through the breakfast nook, into the kitchen past large bubbling pots with their great wreaths of steam. Martha sat at the kitchen table, humming a happy tune while she peeled a mound of peaches. Carrie stepped quietly through the kitchen behind her, through to the butler's pantry and into the east servant's wing.

Lilly's room was the last one at the end of the hallway, larger than the others with a washroom of its own. The door was closed, but Carrie opened it and went inside.

Lilly sat on the narrow cot, a tightly twisted chemise stretched between her hands. A small crudely painted trunk sat open at her feet. It was only half full.

"Lilly?"

She looked at Carrie with unfocused eyes. "A woman shouldn't have to be afraid to speak her mind." Her voice was soft and small.

"Oh, Lilly." Carrie sat next to her on the cot. She slid the chemise out of Lilly's hands and laid it across her knees, pressing the creases out with the palms of her hands. She folded it carefully and put it in the trunk. "You pick the strangest times to be brave."

Lilly bowed her head and pressed the heels of her hands against her eyes. "You don't belong with Robert, Celia. You don't love him. I thought that I could explain it to your father." Lilly dropped her hands into her lap. "I thought I could make him understand."

Carrie touched her cheek. "Thank you for trying."

"He didn't listen."

"No. He couldn't. He doesn't know how."

Lilly took Carrie's hand. She held it tightly in her own. "He sent for Earnest to hook up the carriage. I'm to leave this afternoon. He said I mustn't wait until Monday."

"Yes, he told me that, too." Carrie shifted closer so that they touched at the shoulder, hip and thigh. She laid their hands in her lap. "I wish I could go with you."

Lilly shook her head miserably. "The Colonel's not going to allow that."

"He expressly forbade it."

Lilly shifted suddenly, turning to face her. "Come with me

anyway. Celia, come with me to Richmond." She squeezed her hand tight. "We'll rent that little house with the garden. I'll cook and clean for Aunt May, and we'll find something for you to do."

Carrie smiled sadly. "That's such a wonderful dream, Lilly, but you know we can't. We wouldn't make it halfway before someone would track us down. I'd just get dragged back here and you would be bundled off to Aunt May's in disgrace."

Lilly's hand loosened in hers. "You said you would choose me over Robert."

"If that was my choice to make, I would."

"There's always a choice." Lilly's hand went limp.

"What would you have me do, Lilly? I would change the world for you if I could. Make it flat if you wanted it flat. Turn the sky green and the grass blue. Make cows fly and sing sweet songs." Carrie's own words stung her heart. "Tell me, Lilly, what would you have me do?"

Lilly frowned and let go of Carrie's hand. She turned away from her. Carrie looked at her empty palm. Those words weren't the ones she wanted to say. They were the wrong words, but she couldn't stop them from coming out of her mouth. The right words were in her head, but she couldn't make her tongue work the way she wanted it to. Carrie looked into the open mouth of the trunk, at the small pile of simple homespun dresses and plain underthings. The one pair of shoes. Lilly had only packed her own things and none of the things Carrie had given her.

Carrie's mind was screaming, pounding on the walls of her brain. She felt trapped and bound as she listened to herself say words she didn't want to say. "Lilly, I'm not as brave as you are. I don't think women will ever be free to speak their minds or make their own choices. If you could stay—"

"If I could stay, you would choose me over Robert, but only in secret." Lilly's shoulders sagged as she nodded her head slowly. "I understand, Celia. Really, I do." She reached down and closed the lid of the trunk. She tapped the small wooden peg into the clasp. "When we're allowed to vote then the men will have to listen if they expect us to vote for them. It's something all women should strive for."

Carrie's laugh was hollow and dry. "I don't think they'll listen much even then."

Lilly said nothing for a long while. As she sat, her frown deepened. She looked up suddenly and nodded her head again. "If you can get away, it would be nice for you to visit."

Carrie's mouth moved even as her mind railed against her. "If you still want me to, I'll visit you as often as I can. Every chance I get."

"I have something for you." Lilly unclasped the small silver chain that hung around her neck. A gold locket hung from the end of it.

"Your mother gave that to you."

"Yes, I kept the pictures that were inside. I didn't have a picture of me to replace it, so I put something else in there for you to remember me by." Lilly turned and reached around her neck. She hung the locket so that it lay on the fabric stretched across the hollow of Carrie's breasts. "Think of me when things get too hard for you." She laid her hand over the locket pressing it against Carrie's chest.

Carrie pressed harder into her push, feeling the locket press into her skin. She pulled her face close and kissed her. Lilly made a small sound of protest and tried to pull away, but Carrie held her close. "Lilly, please, just a kiss until I can see you again."

Lilly started to shake her head, but she didn't finish the motion. Carrie kissed her again and Lilly let her. "Oh." Her hands came up to touch Carrie's shoulders and slid slowly down to cover her breasts. Carrie leaned into her hands and pushed her flat onto the cot. She ate at her mouth, stealing every taste she could while Lilly squeezed and kneaded. Their touches grew desperate as they pushed into and pulled each other closer. Carrie's dressing gown twisted and tangled between her legs.

With a sudden heave, Lilly rolled them both over, smashing Carrie up against the wall. Her kiss was hard and deep and bruising. Carrie felt her hands on her face, her breast, tugging at her gown, reaching underneath, yanking her drawers down around her thighs. She clutched at Lilly as a warm solid hand cupped between her legs, holding all of her heat in the palm of her hand. Small groans trickled from her throat as she thrust herself hard up into her.

Lilly screamed as hands tore her away. Carrie saw Earnest the coachman throw Lilly to the ground. The Colonel was standing red-faced by the door. Lilly tried to scramble away, but the toe of Earnest's boot caught her on the chin. Her head snapped back and slammed into the wall. She sank back to the floor with a moan. Carrie rolled off the cot and stumbled toward her. Robert rushed into the room, caught her by the arm and yanked her back. His arms closed around her and he held her tight against his chest. Too tight. He was hurting her and she fought against him, but he just held her tighter, whispering soft absurd coos into her hair as she struggled and scratched and punched. She could hear Lilly screaming and her father's voice booming.

She fought Robert harder as he wrestled her onto the cot. It creaked and groaned under their weight. His body crushed her into the thin mattress, squeezing all the breath from her lungs. It was all wrong. His body was too hot, too heavy, too broad, too scratchy, too hard, swelling in all the wrong places and not in the right ones. Her mouth opened as she gasped for air and Robert shoved something between her teeth. A foul, bitter fluid filled her mouth. She choked and coughed as it burned her tongue and slid down her throat. Robert held her pinned down as she struggled, coughing and crying. Her lips started to burn as her tongue swelled and thickened. A dull gray fog crept into the corners of her eyes. She punched at him and kicked her feet, but her limbs felt wrapped in wool. Her fingers and toes itched and tingled.

He was a crushing weight on her chest, but maybe breathing wasn't so important. Her gasps faded into soft mews as her struggles grew weaker. The weight on her chest lessened as the room grew dimmer. It ceased altogether as the gray fog rolled in to cover her eyes.

CHAPTER TWENTY

She woke in her own bed to the faint light of an early morning sunrise. The cheerful twittering of birds pierced her ears and made her head pound. Her tongue felt heavy and her lips numb. She turned her head away from the light that hurt her eyes. Robert was asleep in the chair beside her. Four red and puckered scratches ran down his cheek. A series of raw half-moon gouges dotted his chin. It looked like he had the beginnings of a black eye, but it was hard to tell in the thin dawn light. Carrie kicked at the sheet and Robert stirred. She tried to sit up and found that she could get nearly upright if she used her arms as props, but her head was buzzing and her stomach roiled. Robert's eyes opened. He got up from his chair without saying a word and stood by the bed, the top of his head lost behind the drape of the canopy.

"Lilly." Carrie's voice was a broken caw.

"Celia, it's all right. You're safe now." Robert bent to touch her hand. Carrie moved it away.

"Where is she?" That was better. Her tongue moved a little

more freely behind her dusty teeth.

"She's at the jailhouse." Robert ran a nervous hand over the front of his chest, smoothing his rumpled waistcoat. "Celia, I'm so sorry. We had no idea she would attack you like that. She won't ever hurt you again. I promise you." Robert's words ended in a quiver.

Carrie sat all the way up, walking her hands behind her until she was more or less vertical. The buzzing in her ears got louder. She took a deep breath and was encouraged when she didn't throw up. "What did you give me?"

Robert averted his eyes and blushed. Carrie looked down at herself. She was only in her underthings. She felt at her throat and her hand closed over the locket. She squeezed it tight in her fist. Its sharp edges cut into her palm and her head cleared a little.

"I gave you laudanum. Your father phoned the central exchange and they put out a message. I got it at the Westmore's. He said that he had overheard some disturbance the night before between you and Lilly. He was going to send her away and thought you might be upset. I was to come help him calm you." Robert raised a hand to his scratches. "It seems I arrived just in time."

"Dear God." Carrie looked over at her bedroom door. She felt sick.

Robert shifted his feet uncomfortably. "Please don't fret, now, Celia. No one blames you for being hysterical after an attack like that. It was a horrible thing to see, like a dog turning on its owner. And after you and your father had been so kind." Robert stole a quick appraising glance at her. "At least you're looking better now. I was afraid I'd given you too much from the way you slept."

"How long have I slept?"

"Through the day yesterday and then through the night."

Carrie looked around the room for her clothes. "Where's my dressing gown?"

Robert's blush deepened. "It was ripped. Martha took it to

be mended."

Then she would have to do this without clothes. "Where's the jail from here?"

Robert reached for her hand again. "Please don't worry, Celia. She can't get out. She can't hurt you anymore."

Carrie raised the sheet to cover her chest. She didn't really care what he saw, but she needed to keep him away from her and off balance. "Where's the jail, Robert?"

Robert sat back in the chair and looked to the floor. "It's on the near edge of town just on the other side of the river."

"On the main road?"

"Yes. You've driven past it before, if you didn't know what it was."

"Shit." She wouldn't be able to cross the river. If the central telephone exchange was involved, everyone would know everything by now. Someone would stop her.

Robert blinked, looked at her and then away again. "Celia?"

Carrie fought to calm herself, to still the dark panicked place inside that threatened to unravel and overwhelm her. She hid her face behind her hands and breathed deeply. "Robert. My dear. Forgive me. I'm still a bit muddled. I'm sick and I'm thirsty and I hardly know what I'm saying."

"Oh, Celia. I'm sorry. Let me get you some water." Robert got up quickly and fetched the water jug and a small glass from the nightstand. He poured some water into the glass and handed it to her. She drank it all in big fast gulps and her head started to feel much clearer, if her stomach protested. She motioned for Robert to hand her the jug. He turned it around and gave it to her handle first with his eyes still fixed firmly on the floor. She took the jug, poured herself another glass and put the glass on her bedside table. She braced herself.

She swung up and out, smashing the jug against the side of Robert's head. He went down in a pool of water and shards. Carrie hauled herself out of bed. She knelt on the floor beside him and started stripping off his clothes. Robert was heavy and she was still weak. His arms flipped and flailed as she struggled to get him out of his jacket and shirt. His legs felt like thousand pound weights as she struggled with the pants.

The whole process took longer than she wanted it to and she had to rest after she had everything she needed. She drank the water in the glass and sat on the floor until her muscles stopped trembling. Robert lay in his undershirt and drawers where Carrie had rolled him, a pool of pink water spread in a halo around his head. The rise and fall of his chest was the only thing moving. She looked at the jacket, the waistcoat and shirt. They were wet, but that was all.

She stood slowly. Her head was clear and her stomach had more or less settled. She started putting on Robert's clothes. The shirt and the pants were too big. Her fingers fumbled clumsily with the cufflinks and the tie. The jacket was hot and heavy. His socks stank and her feet swam inside the boots, but it would have to do. She piled her hair on top of her head and pinned it down as flat as she could. It wouldn't look right up close, but from a distance, it might get her by. According to Robert, she had slept through Sunday. That meant it was Monday. Her father would be at his mill. Martha would be in the kitchen with all the rest of the help polishing the silver. The groundsman would be in the garden, the stableman with the horses, the kennelman with the dogs. She would have a clear path to the road if she cut through the northwest field.

She ran out of the mistress suite and down the front stairs two at a time, her feet sliding around inside the boots. She grabbed Robert's hat off the hat stand and smashed it on her head as far as it would go. She opened the door and stepped out onto the porch. Robert's horse was tied to the rail, waiting patiently, plucking at the grass within its reach. She couldn't take Robert's horse. People recognized horses even before they recognized other people. She would have to run. It would take her not quite an hour to jog to the river if she went along the road, maybe even more with poorly fitting boots on, but she couldn't hurry. She had to move at a reasonable pace or she wouldn't make it at all. She hadn't run in many years, not since she was a girl in short pants racing the boys to the river and back. Carrie stepped off the porch and started across the drive. It had been a very long time, but her body remembered the easy loping stride, the rhythmic pumping of her arms and legs, the whistle of the wind past her ears. She turned off the drive and ran across the field, through the fresh green growth of summer rye, the young blades whipping against her calves.

Her feet broke through the rye and stumbled onto the road. The earth wobbled under her boots as the world skittered across her eyes. Brown dirt and deep ruts flashed into black pavement and yellow lines. Carrie staggered and fell, her hands splayed against the dirt. She squeezed her eyes shut and then opened them again. A pebble poked into her palm. A beetle crawled past her finger. It was just dirt under her hands, hard-packed and solid, but it was brown and not black. She sat back on her heels and then staggered to her feet. She slapped her hands together and brushed the dirt off her knees, scrubbed at her eyes. The road stayed dirt. She took a few tentative steps, walked a bit faster and then broke into a jog.

Carrie tried not to think about anything. She couldn't think about anything. She listened to the slap of her feet, to the rush of her breath, the shushing of her elbows as they rubbed against the jacket. Her mind tried to stay focused on the road in front of her, on moving her feet, on breathing. She tried to think only of the running and not on what she might find when she got to town. Her feet stumbled, scuffing in the dirt, scattering little rocks, but she recovered her balance and she ran.

She knew she was nearing the river by the change in the air, the smell of fresh water and green growing things on top of the fishy stench of new death and old rot. She slowed to a purposeful walk. A man in a cart passed her from behind. He tipped his hat without looking in her direction. She touched the brim of hers and kept walking. He passed by her without a pause. She buttoned up the jacket, put her hands in her pockets and kept her head down as more people passed her on the road, a man on a horse, one leading a donkey, a woman with a basket. Carrie walked as if she knew where she was going and didn't have time to stop. The woman looked at her curiously but no one tried to talk to her.

She rounded a bend in the road and saw the river, a wide blue-brown ribbon of water that flowed in a slow arc, pushing against one bank, pulling at the other. It was a quiet stretch of river, deep and deceptively still. Carrie knew it was stronger than it looked. The ferryman was holding the boat steady while its passengers climbed aboard, the woman with the basket, the man with the donkey, a small black boy with a gunnysack huddled in the far back corner as far away from the white people as he could get, and a few others, mostly men in straw hats and sagging trousers. The boat was full of people. Too many people. It only cost a penny to cross on the ferry and she did have one. There was money in Robert's pocket, quite a few bills, a pocket watch and some small change. She had pennies, but she didn't dare get too close to anyone, much less get stuck in the middle of a crush of people.

She couldn't take the ferry, but maybe she didn't have to. Lots of people kept small boats tied up along the shore. Her father kept more than one on his stretch of the riverbank for sending someone to fish the shallows or to take her picnicking on the west peninsula. The boats weren't made for crossing the whole wide width of the river, but people did cross in them all the time. People with secrets to keep or without a penny to spare. If they could do it, so could she.

Carrie stepped off the road and onto a side path that wandered along the slope of the riverbank. She followed the trail as it turned and twisted beside the river. Not too far along, she spotted a flat-bottomed rowboat tied underneath an overhanging tree. She scrambled down the bank and stepped into it, untied the rope from the limb overhead and crabbed her way to the middle seat. She pushed off with the oars digging into the silt and began rowing.

Four strokes away from the bank, the current was much stronger than she had even imagined. The boat spun around in

202

a circle before pointing its nose downstream. She didn't want to go that way. Downstream would take her farther from town, closer to Richmond, to the east and to the sea. Farther from Lilly. Carrie struggled with the oars, with the unfamiliar motion, until she found a method and a rhythm that carried her almost in the direction she wanted to go, though the river still pushed her relentlessly downstream.

She pulled and strained and pulled again until the swish and plop of the oars started to sound like an echo that would never end. Her legs started shaking with fatigue. Her hands burned where the rough wood scoured her palms, but it wasn't as sharp as the burning muscles of her back, the bite of pain just below her shoulder blades. She was beyond what she had ever tasked her body with before. She had done more than she knew she could do, but she couldn't think about her body's hurts. She couldn't think about Lilly. She couldn't think about anything but the stroke. Lean forward, dip the oars. Plop. Pull back, lift the oars. Swish. Lean forward, dip the oars. Plop. Pull back, lift the oars. Swish.

The boat jolted and ran aground. Carrie jumped up and the boat tilted dangerously to one side, almost spilling her out. She fell back into the bottom. She tried again a little slower and managed to get out without getting her boots wet. She scrambled up the side of the bank and stopped at the top to rest her legs and look around. There was a field with a board fence and a red barn with a tin roof. White-splotched cows were grazing on the green summer grass.

It was the riverside field of the Westmore's farm. She knew the place. She had picnicked there, played with their children, picked wildflowers, chased butterflies. That wasn't what she thought about, though. She only thought that seeing the farm now meant that the river had carried her almost two miles from the main road. Two miles farther from Lilly than she wanted to be. She walked in a little ways from the bank and stepped out of the weeds onto a cow path. It ran beside the river for as far as she could see, heading back toward town. Carrie settled her hat more firmly on her head. Her blistered feet ached and throbbed, the muscles in her thighs burned and pulled, but she wasn't going to think about it. She was just going to do what she had to do. She bent her knees and started running again.

CHAPTER TWENTY-ONE

Her feet stumbled over nothing as the cow path dumped Carrie back out onto the main road sooner than she expected. She staggered to a stop and bent over double with her hands on her thighs, her breath burning in her lungs, her legs...No. She couldn't think about her legs. With some effort, Carrie straightened herself up again and looked around her. The ferry was already halfway back across the river and the road was empty of its previous passengers for as far as she could see. She started walking again.

She kept to a fast walk instead of a jog, just in case someone came around the corner, but the jail wasn't far. Around the bend and she could see it just down the road. It had to be the jail, she knew, from the bars on the windows and the dilapidated state of the building, its sagging roof and unpainted clapboard. Carrie looked all around her, but the road was still empty. She stepped off the road and into the high brush so she could circle around and approach the jail from the back. There were woods not too far away, but they were farther than she would wish them to be if she and Lilly had to run. She crept through the weeds until the jail itself hid her from the road.

The brush ended in a wide empty space around the building. The ground all around it was dirt and rocks as if no green growing thing wanted to live so close to such a place. Carrie ran across the bare ground at a low crouch and pressed herself flat against the back wall. She waited and listened. All was quiet. No one was shouting. No one was sounding an alarm. She turned around and stood on her toes to peek inside a barred window. That cell was empty. She crept up to the next window, got up on her toes and looked inside. That cell was empty too. Her heart started to beat hard inside her chest. She looked into the third cell. It held a narrow bed and a chamber pot but, otherwise, it was empty. There weren't any more cells. They were all empty. Lilly wasn't there.

Carrie leaned against the side of the building. Her body's aches and pains began to overwhelm her, feet and legs, shoulders and arms. She wanted to lie down right there, cover her head with dirt and ashes, scream her throat raw, howl at the sun. She slid down the side of the building and sat on the ground. What was she supposed to do now? Where was Lilly and why had Robert lied? Carrie's head dropped into her hands. The dark, panicked place inside her mind began to unfold, to open into a bloom of madness. The wind blew a little dust storm across the toes of her boots as she tried to choke the panic back. She sat as quiet and still as she could, listening to the wind flutter through the trees, to the soft whisper of leaves as they rubbed against each other. To the soft jangle of a chain.

She lifted her head and she heard it again, a soft jingling, a light clinking. The sound came from the shed near the woods. Carrie eased herself off the ground and limped over to it, stumbling slightly as she bent over low. She moved around to the back of the shed and put her eye close to a chink in the boards. Lilly was sitting in the dirt, disheveled and dirty, one ankle manacled and chained to a bolt in the wall. Carrie pressed her forehead against the boards. She wanted to cry out, to shout with joy, to scream her relief. She wanted to tell Lilly that she was there and everything would be all right. But she wasn't sure that it would be, not just yet, so she said nothing.

Carrie stood and stepped quietly back to the jail. She walked around to the side and peered into a window with real panes of glass and no bars. A man with an unkempt beard sat at a rough-hewn table drinking from a tall jug, something that left a foamy trail across his moustache. He wiped at it with a sleeve. Carrie thought for a moment as she looked around for something she could use. The man inside had hurt Lilly. She spotted an ax stuck into a stump over by the woodpile. A lot of people had hurt Lilly. Carrie walked quietly over to the stump and pried the ax out. She wanted to hurt everyone who had ever hurt Lilly. Starting with herself.

Carrie peered into the window. The man was drinking deeply. She walked around to the front of the jail and looked both ways down the road to make sure it was empty. It was. She stepped quietly around to the front door, knocked hard and then ducked back around the corner. The door opened. There was a moment of silence and then the scraping of footsteps, but they were headed in the wrong direction. Carrie beat on the side of the building with the handle of the ax. The steps turned around and the man came shuffling around the corner. Carrie swung the ax. She hit him upside the head with the flat of it. He slammed into the side of the building and slid to the ground without a sound. She stooped to get his keys. The man's belt was made of old cracked leather that split easily when Carrie yanked. The man groaned and rolled onto his back. She raised the ax to hit him again, but his eyes remained closed.

She ran back to the shed. Carrie threw down the wooden crossbar and opened the door. Sunlight fell in on Lilly, who cringed deeper into the corner, her arms covering her chest. Her hair fell loose across her shoulders. The bruise on her chin had turned a dark purple. Her feet were bare.

"Lilly, it's me."

"Celia?" Lilly blinked up into sunlight.

Carrie bent to unlock the manacle. She guessed right on the first key and the cuff fell off Lilly's ankle with a clank. "Can you stand?" Carrie looked at the red ring of scraped skin that circled just above her foot.

"I can stand." Lilly lifted her hands. "If you'll help me."

Carrie grabbed her hands and pulled Lilly to her feet. She stood solidly and looked more stable than Carrie felt, but her face was pale and her hands were shaking. "Can you walk?"

"I think...yes. I can try, but my feet..." Lilly looked at her feet. "They took away my shoes and all the pins for my hair." She raised a hand to touch her head and then slowly lowered it again.

Carrie reached out and touched a tangled strand. She tucked it gently behind Lilly's ear. It wasn't much but it was a start. "Stay here. I'll be right back."

"No, Celia." Lilly grabbed at her, clutching her arm, her eyes wide with fear. "Don't leave me inside here."

Carrie squeezed her hand. She wanted to wrap her arms around her, hold her tight, kiss the fear away, but there wasn't time. She didn't know how long the jailer would stay unconscious and they had to move. She pulled Lilly out of the shed and led her a little ways into the woods. Lilly stepped gingerly through the brush and then leaned her back against a large tree.

"Can you wait here?"

Lilly sank to the ground and hugged her arms around her knees. "Robert thought I was attacking you. Your father..." She looked at Carrie with frightened eyes. "They were going to send me to a crazy house. I don't want to go to a place like that, Celia. I'm not crazy. We're not."

Carrie bent and touched her face with the tips of her fingers. "No one is going to send you anywhere. I won't let them." Robert might have thought Lilly was attacking her, but her father sure didn't. She wondered if Lilly knew that, too. From the fear in her eyes, Carrie guessed that she did. "Wait here. I'll be just a minute."

Lilly shrank down even further, her brown skirts blending with last year's fallen leaves. Carrie ran back to the jail. The guard was still lying by the side of the building. His head was bleeding, but he was groaning steadily now, his hands twitching. Carrie thought about hitting him again, but she had left the ax by the shed and she couldn't bring herself to kick him in the head. They would have to trust that it would be a while before he would wake up enough to holler for help. He wouldn't know which way they had gone, anyway. Carrie stripped his boots off his feet. They were old, the soles worn thin. Their rank smell nearly gagged her as she pulled them off. The man's feet were wrapped in filthy rags. She didn't like to think about Lilly putting those on her feet so she left them. The boots were bad, but it would be better than trying to run through the woods in bare feet. She ran back to Lilly who hadn't moved an inch.

Carrie handed her the boots. "Put these on."

Lilly looked at the boots like Carrie was trying to hand her a slug and made no move to take them. Carrie knelt beside her and held out her hand. Lilly lifted her foot slowly and put it in Carrie's hand. Carrie slipped the boot onto Lilly's foot. Lilly looked sick, but she held out her other foot and let Carrie put that one on her too. Carrie stood and pulled Lilly up with her. Lilly's face was still pale and her body was trembling.

Carrie took her hand and spoke to her gently. "We have to go now."

Lilly took a few tentative steps, lifting her feet as if she were wading through muck. "Where? Where is there to go?"

"I've been thinking about that. They'll be expecting you to move east, downstream, toward Richmond, so we should probably follow the river west, upstream."

"The river goes south from here and then west." A thoughtful look came to Lilly's eyes. A little color flowed back into her cheeks. "The railroad follows the river all the way to Lynchburg mainly on the north bank. We should head for Lynchburg but on the south bank so we don't have to hide from the trains."

"I crossed the river in a rowboat. It's about two miles

downstream from here."

Lilly shook her head and her hair fell into her face. She pushed it back with a jerk of her hand. "We should head south now. There's a bridge at Bremo's Bluff about ten miles up the river. We should head for that."

Carrie studied her closely. She was still very pale and she was breathing too fast. "Are you ready?"

Lilly gave a short, abrupt nod. "I'm ready to get away from this place."

"Let me make sure the road is clear and then we'll cross it and get to the woods on the other side. I think that if we stay between the railroad and the river, we won't get lost."

Lilly's chin began to tremble. She shut her eyes and then opened them again. "I don't care if we get lost. Provided we stay lost."

Carrie squeezed her hand. "You're a very brave woman, Lilly."

Lilly looked at Carrie's hat and clothes and then at the boots she was wearing. Carrie grinned for the both of them, gave her a little sketch of a bow as she lifted her hand and kissed her fingers.

CHAPTER TWENTY-TWO

They traveled all day through the woods. They didn't go very fast or get very far. The cow path they found soon turned in the wrong direction and instead of following it, they kept to the trees. Carrie's stolen jacket was hot and snagged on brambles and briars but not as bad as Lilly's skirts. By the end of the day, her skirts were almost in rags. When they got to where they were going, they would both have to buy new clothes. Or steal them. Not any part of Carrie's mind was sure how much the money in her pocket was worth, how far it would go or how long it would last.

They walked through the woods until the sun sank low behind the treetops and they were both stumbling tired. Carrie's feet were on fire and Lilly was leaning on a stick limping badly. They stopped when they crossed a small stream, its light clear water bubbled down from the hills with chirpy giggles as it ran toward the river. They stopped to drink and to bathe the sweat off their faces. Lilly sat on the bank and took off her boots. Her right foot was swollen, red and blistered. Her left foot was bleeding. Carrie took her boots off, too and then her socks. The boots she was wearing were a better make, and while her feet were blistered and sore, they didn't look as bad as Lilly's feet. Carrie rolled up her pants and stuck her feet in the stream's cold water. After a moment, Lilly did the same. Carrie thought it was a shame that the stream wasn't deep enough for a swim. A bath and then a nap would be a wonderful thing. Or maybe a nap and then a bath. Lord, she was tired.

Carrie leaned back on her elbows as the water swirled around her ankles. "I think we should stop here for a while."

Lilly's feet were in the stream beside hers, her skirts tucked in around her knees. She put her hand through one of the tears and rubbed at the back of her thigh. "I'm not sure I could go much farther."

"It's still pretty warm and the sky looks clear. I doubt it'll rain on us if we sleep in the woods."

Lilly smiled. Thin as it was, it was the first one Carrie had seen all day. "You can't make predictions like that. A big, bad-tempered storm cloud could be hovering right over the horizon just waiting for someone to say 'it won't rain tonight.' I keep telling you that there's just no accounting for weather."

Carrie chuckled and let it turn into a laugh. It was a good laugh. It lightened her heart and eased her mind. But then she couldn't stop. She kept laughing even after the funny was gone. It shook through her in spastic convulsions and she couldn't shut it off. The laugh reached down inside her and touched her panic. It spread through her brain and rose to the surface in waves of high-pitched giggles and snorts, her face twisting and grimacing, her sides aching.

Lilly slapped her cheek hard with a palm full of water. Carrie gasped and sat still, her breath ragged and harsh as the water ran down her face and dripped off her jaw. Her eyes were wide and staring. Something was screaming, pounding on the walls of her mind. A confusion of images swirled and boiled. The fountain in the drive, bright and bubbling, a cherub chipped and pitted with age, missing a wing, the library with a stack of new books, a book in her hand with its pages yellowed and cracking, the mirror, bright, then dull...her face, young, older, thinner, fatter.

Carrie felt hands on her cheeks. Rough hands. Strong hands. Her eyes slowly focused on the bright green of Lilly's eyes. Lilly was still there, still solid and warm, a vibrant presence even in her exhaustion. Carrie could see the sag of her shoulders, the limp droop of her curls, the purple swelling of the bruise on her chin just starting to yellow at the edges.

"Lilly." The name tasted good on her tongue. It always had. "Lilly." Like a sweet-tasting medicine, it calmed her mind. "Lilly, I'm sorry."

Lilly breathed in deeply. She let it out and her body sagged even more. "It's all right. I feel the same way." Lilly swayed and Carrie rose to catch her.

She stood, pulling Lilly up with her. "We need to find a place to rest." Carrie picked up their boots but Lilly shook her head. She wouldn't put hers back on. Carrie tucked both pairs under her arm and put her other arm around Lilly. In the state they both were in, they wouldn't have gotten very much farther anyway.

Carrie steered them deeper into the woods. They walked gingerly on their sore feet, stepping carefully until Lilly spotted a tree with thick brush on three sides that could, if they were sitting, hide them from casual eyes.

Carrie sat with her back against the tree and Lilly rested against her, tucking her head in the hollow of her neck. Carrie put her arm around her shoulders and draped the jacket over them both. She rested her cheek on Lilly's hair. Lilly tucked the jacket in tighter around them. Loose change jingled in the pocket.

"Lilly?"

"Hmm?"

"Is a hundred dollars a lot of money?"

Lilly stirred slightly. "It is to me, but it might not be to some."

"Why do you think Robert would have a hundred dollars in his pocket? Doesn't he usually get paid in chickens or something?"

Lilly lifted her head. "You have a hundred dollars in your pocket right now?"

Carrie thought about the bills and coins. "Around that. I didn't count it exactly. There's a nice pocket watch, too, if you want to know what time it is."

Lilly closed her eyes and put her head back on Carrie's shoulder. "I don't want to know what time it is, but I wish you had told me about the money sooner. With a hundred dollars, we could have taken the train to Lynchburg. We could have been riding in a first-class carriage, eating a supper of lamb chops and mint jelly, with fresh warm bread dripping with butter and honey and a big bowl of fat red strawberries for dessert."

Carrie's stomach gurgled. "That's cruel, Lilly." It made Carrie realize how hungry she was. Hungrier than she'd ever been before in her life. She hadn't ever missed a meal when she wasn't sick or sleeping. She never dreamed of missing six. It was a hard feeling, not painful, not yet, but uncomfortable and disturbing. "What do you think Robert had the money for?"

"Oh, I don't know. Maybe your father gave it to him as an advance on your dowry."

Carrie had forgotten about the dowry, her purchase price, the money a family paid to have some man take a daughter off their hands. The thought made her angry and the anger cleared the last of the fog from her head. She felt a lot less guilty about smacking Robert with the water jug.

Damn the patriarchy, she thought with a dim part of her brain, though she didn't really know what she meant. "Is a hundred dollars enough to rent a room somewhere, not too ugly and not too nice?"

"Yes. Quite enough, but we'll both have to get new clothes before we get to where we're going. Mine are a mess, and you don't look anything like a real boy. Even if you cut your hair short you wouldn't."

"So, I need a dress and you need a new one."

"Yes, but not like the dresses you're used to. We need working clothes, simple and plain woven."

"Do we have enough money to buy clothes and rent a room?"

"Yes. It's enough to keep us for about half a year if we're frugal and if you don't mind eating porridge and tripe."

"I don't mind eating porridge." She would have to think hard about the tripe. Carrie tightened her arm around Lilly's shoulder. "Lilly."

"What?"

"I'm sorry I didn't say the right things to begin with. I didn't know I could do this. I thought it would be too hard."

Lilly slipped her hand across Carrie's stomach and gave her a squeeze. "It still might be too hard. If you want to go back to your father after a while, I won't try to stop you."

Carrie stared at the woods in front of her, at the shadows growing under the trees. "He won't want me back."

Lilly's body stiffened. "Your father loves you very much. He just wants you to be happy in a way that he can be happy for you. I know he'll want you back." She paused and the hard set of her shoulder dug into Carrie's ribs. "You can go back now if you want to."

Carrie shook her head, rolling it against the rough bark of the tree. "I don't want to go back if you can't go with me."

Lilly's shoulders relaxed a little. "If you stay with me, your life is going to be a hard one. We'll have to do a lot of pretending and then we'll have to pick up and move when people start asking us the wrong questions."

"If we end up living in a hole and scurrying between the walls like little mice, I'll still want to be with you. I'm only sorry that it had to take all this to make me realize that. If I had known better, we could have planned and spared us both a lot of bother." Carrie kissed the top of Lilly's head. "I'm sorry you're missing out on the lamb chops."

Lilly squeezed her waist again and settled against her more comfortably. "When we get to Lynchburg, we can take some of Robert's money and treat ourselves to a really good meal. I don't know that we'll get a chance to eat before then."

Carrie frowned at the shadows. "How long will that be?"

"If we don't walk any faster than we did today, about seven more days."

She didn't sound very confident about that. Still. If she was right. Seven more days. Twenty-one meals. Carrie's stomach rumbled. "Can we really take the train?"

"Is the money you have in small bills or large ones?"

"A few large ones but mostly small."

"That's good. If we get new clothes and wash up a bit, we could get a third-class seat without attracting too much attention. But if we do get on a train we should go farther than Lynchburg."

"Where do you want to go?"

Lilly didn't answer at first. Her pause seemed hesitant and unsure. Then she shifted a little and touched Carrie's foot with her own. "I've always dreamed of seeing a real city, like New York or Chicago. I want to go somewhere we can get lost in the crowd and no one will care who we are."

Chicago. To Carrie, the idea of going to Chicago seemed both comfortingly familiar and frighteningly strange. "What about Lynchburg? Why don't you want to stay there?"

"Lynchburg's pretty, but it's not a real city. I want to see tall buildings, eighteen, nineteen, twenty stories high. I imagine you could see the whole world from the top of a building like that."

"What if the building was a hundred and ten stories tall?"

"Don't be silly, Celia. No one will ever build a building that tall. What would be the point? The top would be lost inside the clouds and then you couldn't see anything."

Carrie smiled and rubbed the arm Lilly had draped across her lap. "Chicago." The word sounded funny the way it came out of her mouth. "It gets really cold there in the winter. Colder than anything you've ever known before."

"And how would you know that, Miss Smarty?"

"I...read about it somewhere. In a book. Upton Sinclair, I think."

"Oh, yes. *The Jungle*. We just got that one. You've read it already?"

"Enough to know we shouldn't eat the sausages." Carrie leaned her head back against the trunk of the tree and settled her cheek against Lilly's hair. "Let's do it, Lilly. Let's go to Chicago."

Lilly snuggled in closer to Carrie. "There's a whistle-stop at Bremo's Bluff. We're not that far from it now. If you're serious, we'll have to come up with a good story about why we're traveling so far alone."

"I'm sure we can think of something."

"You're serious then," Lilly said against her shoulder. "You'll take me to see a real city?"

Carrie's arms tightened around her. "Anywhere you want to go, Lilly. I'll take you there."

"It'll be harder for you to change your mind and come back here if we go that far."

"I'm not going to change my mind." Those weren't all the words she wanted to say, but Lilly had never let her say the words that sat in her heart. She could say them now. They were going to be together forever. She could tell Lilly exactly how she felt. The words fluttered around the back of her throat. Her lips moved but she didn't say them out loud. She turned her head and kissed Lilly's hair. "I know it will be hard, but we'll find a way to make it work."

Lilly patted her sleepily on the hip. Carrie sat still and listened to the night sounds, the rustling, the whirring, the croaking and the clicks that seemed almost timed to the rhythmic sound of Lilly's soft snores before she closed her eyes and fell into an uncomfortable sleep.

CHAPTER TWENTY-THREE

They woke in the half-light of dawn to a sudden burst of birdsong. Carrie's neck was stiff, her back and legs were sore. They both groaned as they stood to stretch the kinks out of their muscles and to take the chill from their bones. Lilly's feet still looked red and swollen but not as bad as the day before. Carrie took her hand and they picked their way out of the woods back to the clearing by the stream.

The water seemed almost warm against the chilled morning air. Carrie splashed her face and drank as much as she could hold. It made her stomach hurt less, but she doubted it would last. Lilly sat on the bank struggling to put her boots on. Carrie had given her the socks she had taken from Robert, but she didn't know how much that would help. Her own feet were blistered and raw even with the socks. The blisters would be worse after today.

Lilly stood, leaning heavily on her stick, her shoulder bowed and her face pinched.

Carrie watched her take a few tentative steps. "How far do

you think it is to Bremo's Bluff from here?"

Lilly looked at the woods around her as if the trees might offer up a clue. She shook her head a little ruefully. "Only a mile, I guess, maybe two."

"Do you think you can make it that far?"

Lilly gave her a tired look. "Is there a choice?"

"There's always a choice." That earned her the ghost of a smile. "You can lend me your dress and I'll go get clothes for us, better shoes, buy our train tickets and come back to get you."

Lilly shook her head. "No, Celia. Thank you for the offer, but I don't think I could stand to wait here alone. It's better to be moving forward together even if it's slow." Lilly held her stick tighter and took a few more steps. She dug the stick into the middle of the stream and made the short hop across the water. Her face paled when her feet hit the bank on the other side. She tottered but she didn't fall. Carrie hopped the steam with an easy jump, took Lilly's free arm and draped it across her shoulder. She slipped her own arm around Lilly's waist and they took their next few steps together. It would be slow, but it would work.

They started weaving their way through the woods, one short step at a time, through brambles and bracken, over fallen logs, skirting around meadows, moving as west as they knew how to go. The leaves on the trees above their heads turned a pale green as the sun rose above the horizon. The light in the woods began to shine with an emerald glow as the sun rose higher overhead. They kept moving forward at a slow, shuffling pace, their feet scraping through the leaf litter, stumbling over rocks, their toes tangling in the brush. The birds twittered and called as the squirrels fussed at them from the branches overhead.

The sun had risen high when they came across another small stream. Carrie helped Lilly kneel to scoop some water. Carrie knelt beside her and bathed her face and neck, took her hair down, shook it out and pinned it back up. She stood and fanned herself with the hat. Lilly stayed on her knees by the bank of the stream, her face scrunched, looking as if she were trying hard not to cry.

"We can rest here if you want to, Lilly. It can't be far now."

Lilly shook her head. "It doesn't take all day to go two miles." She dipped her hand into the water. It trickled over her palm with a light burbling sound. She scooped the water up, splashed her face and blew out a wet breath. "This looks like the same creek we crossed two hours ago and that one looked like the same creek we crossed this morning." Water dripped off her chin. "Celia, I think we're going around in circles."

Carrie looked at the water gurgling over the stones. "It can't be same stream. If we drifted too far north, we'd see the railroad tracks, too far south and we'd see the river."

"We should have seen something by now, farms, fields, cows. Something."

"Maybe we should head for the river and get our bearings from that." Carrie hoped that Lilly would know which way to go. Not all streams flowed to the river, and with the sun so high above their heads, she couldn't even guess which direction was south.

Lilly dried her face with her sleeve. "Yes. That's probably what we should do." She lifted her hands and held them out to Carrie. "Help me stand, please."

Carrie helped her to her feet. Lilly just stood for a moment with her shoulders hunched. Then, with an effort, she pulled herself up straighter. She looked Carrie over carefully. Her mouth turned down slightly in a disapproving frown. She reached out to straighten her tie and then smoothed the lapels of her jacket. Lilly took the hat from Carrie's hand, brushed the dust off the bowl and brim and put it back on her head. She straightened it, licked her thumb and scrubbed a smear of dirt off her cheek. Carrie stood still as Lilly stared at her with an odd expression.

"You look nice with the hat on, Celia. It's odd, I know, but it almost seems like trousers suit you better than skirts."

Carrie felt a blush rise to her face. "You said I don't look anything like a boy."

"You don't. You look like a girl in trousers, but it suits you somehow." Lilly stepped into her and put her hand on Carrie's chest. She felt the locket underneath her shirt and smiled. Carrie pulled her in and kissed her, soft and slow. They both had foul breath and their clothes stank worse than swamp rot, but Carrie didn't care and Lilly didn't seem to either.

Lilly pulled away first, her breath short and shallow. "We can't."

Carrie nodded. "I know."

Lilly frowned sharply, looked around at the woods and then at the sky.

"What is it?"

"The birds have stopped singing."

Carrie listened. The woods was quieter than it had been all morning. "You think a storm is coming?"

Lilly waved a hand at her. "Wait. Listen."

Carrie listened to the sound of Lilly breathing, the rustle of her skirt, the light burble of the stream and heard nothing else. A small breeze blew through the leaves with a soft rustle of shimmering applause. A dog barked. A short yip followed by a slow, mournful howl. There was an answering cry and then she heard the whole pack baying. Carrie looked at Lilly who was looking at the trees, her eyes wide and white.

Lilly grabbed her sleeve and pulled her into the stream. "In the water. Quick. Keep to the creek. Head for the deeper woods. They might lose our scent."

They ran upstream as fast as they could with their boots splashing, feet slipping and the shreds of Lilly's skirts catching between her legs. She hiked her skirts up, held them in a bundle around her waist and kept running. Her drawers were soon soaked to her knees. The water got shallower, the rocks looser as the stream thinned and started to run out. A narrow deer path ran across it, dipping down one bank and rising into the dense wood on the other side. Carrie pulled Lilly up onto the path and they ran as fast as Lilly could go.

The deep howl of a hound sounded from close behind them. They ran even faster as the rest of the pack answered from both sides. Lilly stumbled. Carrie caught her before she fell and dragged her onward. They were both gasping. Carrie could feel the air burning in her throat. Lilly stumbled again, and this time Carrie couldn't catch her. She went down in a heap. Carrie pulled her up again, but Lilly could barely put her right foot on the ground. They left the path and stumbled through the trees with Lilly's leg half collapsing under her with every step, Carrie doing what she could to hold her up and urge her on.

The trees ended abruptly at the edge of small clearing. The clearing ended at the edge of a deep ravine. Carrie skidded to a stop, teetering on the brink, arms pinwheeling wildly. She felt Lilly grab a handful of jacket and pull her back from the edge. They both turned at the same time.

A dog burst through the underbrush. It lifted its head and howled a long, deep note. The answering cries came from every direction. The dog lowered its head and snarled. Other dogs crept out of the woods. These were not the friendly faces and floppy ears of the foxhounds that Carrie knew, but snapping teeth, raised hackles and menacing growls of angry wolves. The lead dog lunged forward snapping at Lilly's skirts. Carrie kicked at it, her foot landing a solid blow against its ribs. The dog skittered back, its growl deeper and more threatening. The other dogs moved in, tightening the circle. Lilly shoved her walking stick into Carrie's hands and Carrie swung it at the closest nose. A rock flew past her and hit a dog who jumped with a yelp and backed away. Carrie glanced over her shoulder to see Lilly stooping for another one. A dog lunged for her stick. She swung again. The blow landed on the side of its head with a horrible thwack. It fell over and lay still. The dogs in the front growled and barked while the ones to the back barked and howled. Another rock flew past Carrie and she swung her stick at the next snarling dog.

A horse stepped through the trees, its rider stooping low over its arched neck. The man looked at them with narrow eyes. He sat straighter, raised a horn to his lips and blew. The dogs backed up as the horse advanced. Four more horses stepped out of the woods, the riders looked at them with cold, angry faces. One of the horses sidled closer to Carrie. She raised her stick. A man

222

with a bristling mustache spoke down at her with his eyes still fixed on Lilly.

"This doesn't concern you, boy. Go home and leave it be."

Carrie swung the stick at the rider's knee. She missed and the horse reared, whinnying with pain. A boot smashed into the side of her face. Stars exploded in her eyes. She staggered backward, seesawing on the edge of the ravine, arms flailing. The edge crumbled under her boots and she fell. She tumbled down the steep bank, slipping and rolling, her hands clawing at weeds, her toes scrambling for purchase. Halfway down, she hit a tree with an oomph that knocked the air out of her.

She hung there trying to remember how to breathe. There was a sharp pain in her side. She took a series of short, shallow breaths and untangled herself from the lower branches. Gasping around the pain in her ribs, she scrambled back up the bank grabbing at saplings, handfuls of grass and weeds, digging her toes into the dirt.

Her head cleared the top. A horse shied and danced away as a rock hit it on the haunch. Its rider cursed savagely and sawed at the reins. Lilly stooped for another rock. A different rider circled behind her and grabbed her by the scruff of her dress as she stood. Lilly screamed. Carrie scrambled to get her knee over the edge, but there was nothing to grab. The rider hauled Lilly onto the horse and threw her across his lap. She struggled and yelled, kicked and punched at him. Carrie dug her fingers into the dirt. The horse pranced and jumped under Lilly's flailing. The man held her down by the cloth of her dress bunched in his fist. Carrie hauled herself over the bank groaning as the edge pressed against her ribs. The man raised his fist high into the air and brought it down with a loud crack. Lilly went limp. Carrie struggled to get to her feet. The riders wheeled their horses and disappeared back into the woods, the dogs following close behind.

Carrie stood doubled over trying to breathe past the pain in her side. Her eyes fell on her hat that was lying dented and dusty on the ground. Anger surged through her. It mixed with her panic and exploded through her brain with a furious roar.

She snatched up her hat and smashed it on her head. She ran after the horsemen. Her aches forgotten, her pain ignored, she ran through the woods as fast as she could go, dodging branches, leaping over logs, bulling her way through the undergrowth. She made it back to the path in time to see the horsemen disappearing around a bend, back the way they came.

She didn't think about it. She just ran. Even after the horses left her far behind, she still ran after them, coughing on the lingering dust thrown up by their hooves. She reached the stream and saw by the gouges in the bank where the riders had crossed it and kept going straight down the deer path. She wasn't sure where that path went. There were any number of farms north of the railroad tracks between Bremo and Columbia but no towns that she knew of. She crossed the stream, skidding over the loose stones and scrambled up the other side. She ran again, as hard she could, and then she just kept running.

The path hit the railroad line and the wagon trail that ran alongside it. Carrie slowed but didn't stop. There were fresh tracks in the dirt heading back to Columbia. She was pretty sure that direction headed back to Columbia. The riders were probably taking Lilly back to the jailhouse. Carrie shrugged the jacket off as she ran and tied it around her waist. She ran faster.

She ran along the wagon trail until sweat soaked her clothes and her tongue felt swollen inside her mouth. A train came roaring down the eastbound tracks, a large black engine belching a plume of black smoke. It whistled at her. The conductor leaned out the window and waved, but she paid it no mind. She just kept running. The engine passed her, its thick plume swirling in the wind of its own passage. The passenger cars with their tiny windows, the flatbed cargo cars stacked with crates, a shiny red caboose rounded the bend and then it was gone. She heard the whistle sound again from a distance. She could feel her heart pounding in her chest, her ragged breath tearing at her throat, the blood squelching in her boots as she ran. She couldn't think about her feet or her legs or her lungs. She rounded the bend that the train had gone around and stumbled out onto a road she knew. It was the Richmond road that went through Columbia. She was very close to town. She felt like crying with relief and then she just felt like crying. They must have been going around in circles after all.

Carrie slowed to a walk. She untied her jacket from around her waist and put it on. She put her hat back on and pulled the brim low over her eyes. They had never gotten very far from town. They never really knew where they were. They wouldn't have made it to Lynchburg. Carrie wiped at her face with her sleeve. She couldn't think about that or the things she should have done, the words she should have said. She was close to town and the road she was on was the fastest way she knew to get back to the jail. She would get Lilly out again, and this time they would head north and not stop for anything. They'd steal a horse or jump a train or something. Anything.

A wagon rumbled down the road coming from town. The dust from its wheels rose in a cloud behind it. Carrie squashed her hat down further, hunched her shoulders and pulled the jacket close in around her. She kept her walk purposeful and determined. The wagon started to pass her. She glanced up out of the corner of her eye. The driver was an old black man with silvered hair and a face that had seen too much sun or too much hurt. Carrie knew him well. It was Samuel. He turned his head to look at her. His hand froze halfway to the brim of his hat and his eyes widened. She looked away, but it was too late.

"Whoa, there, mule." Samuel clucked his tongue and pulled on the reins. He drew the wagon alongside her. Carrie thought about running across the railroad tracks and back into the woods, but he had seen her and recognized her face. There wasn't any point.

"Miss Celia." Samuel lowered his eyes, tipped his battered old hat and then settled it back on his head. He looked up and down the road. It was empty, but he still looked nervous. "Everybody out lookin' for you." He didn't look directly at her but kept his eyes on the mule's hindquarters. "There's been quite a to-do these last two days with young Robert lying prostrate and the

Colonel in a sweat of worry."

"Drive on, Samuel. Don't tell anyone you've seen me."

Samuel shook his head slowly from side to side. "I'm sorry, Miss Celia. I don't reckon I can do that, being in the Colonel's hire and all that. Anyhow, it's best if you let me see you first."

"Why?"

"Meanin' no disrespect, Miss, but your hair's all spilling down and you is leavin' tracks that's easy to follow."

Carrie looked at her feet and the red stained dirt around them. Fire and pain bloomed through her body. She slumped against the side of the wagon. "I have to get to the jail, Samuel. They took my Lilly. Men on horses. Bad men. I saw them hit her."

Samuel scratched at the stubble on his chin. "It's hard to reckon some of the things I been hearin' about Miss Lillian, she always havin' a kind word for us folk an' all. They sayin' she gone crazy, running about attacking people with hatchets and such."

Carrie's hands clutched at the rough wood. "She's not like that, Samuel, you know she's not."

Samuel shook his head slowly. "The man at the jail. He's dead. Got his head bashed in and left to bleed to death on the cold ground. The men that catched her say she had his boots on."

Carrie's heart jittered and skipped painfully inside her chest. "Samuel, please. Please, I have to get to her."

"She ain't at the jail no more. They give her a speedy two-minute trial, charged with witchcraft and murder."

"She didn't do it, Sam. I swear by all that's holy, she never hit that man."

"Hmm." Samuel slid the old leather reins back and forth between his thick fingers. "That's mighty curious."

Carrie pushed herself upright with a hiss of pain and stood as best she could on her burning feet. "Sam, I…I hit the man. With the flat end of an ax. From the woodpile. I never meant to hurt him. I only wanted the keys. Sam, please. Don't let them hurt her. Anymore. For something I did."

Samuel turned his head slightly and looked at her. His eyes

widened. "Lord God, Miss Celia, what happened to your face?"

She touched her cheek. It was hot and swollen. It started to hurt. She couldn't think about that either. "The men that took Lilly. I tried to stop them. It was his boot. That's the truth, Samuel. I swear it."

Samuel's eyes, in his wrinkled, sun-scarred face, were piercing. Carrie returned his gaze as squarely as she could. Her hands gripping the side of the wagon, white-knuckle tight. He nodded slowly and then looked away again. "We better get a move on, Miss Celia, if we're to stop what needs stopping. If we can get over the river quick, we can reach the old oak before they finish saying all the prayers. You'd better get on in the back and hunker down low. No time to stop and answer questions about why you dressed like that or whose boots it is that you have on."

Carrie looked at the high sides of the wagon. Then she looked up at Samuel who was waiting patiently. She held her hand up to him. He looked surprised and a little scared. He looked over his shoulder at the empty road behind him and then back at her hand. He hesitated a moment more, but then grabbed her hand in both of his and hauled her into the wagon. Carrie half climbed, half fell into the back. She lay flat and pulled an old tarp over her head. It smelled like rope and stale oats.

"Heeyah, get on there, mule." She heard the reins slap and the cart jerked forward. It lurched and bounced as Samuel turned it around and started back the other way.

Carrie knew the oak tree Samuel was talking about. The colored folk called it The Oak and sang sad songs about it. It was a beautiful old tree that stood in the middle of a meadow between her house and the river, almost in her own backyard, with large spreading limbs, full of birds in the spring and squirrels in the fall. But no one ever picnicked under it or sat under its leaves to enjoy the shade. The white folk called it Corbin's Oak after the first man they ever hung there. The well-to-do white folk never mentioned it at all.

It was hot under the tarp, and Carrie wished she had thought to take the jacket off. She jolted around against the rough planks

227

of the wagon bed as she heard Samuel cry out, "Make way! Make way! I'm late to see the Colonel. Have mercy, please, sir, and pray that he don't take it out of my hide or my pay. Thank you kindly, sir. Bless you, ma'am." Carrie felt the wagon roll onto the deck of the boat and then sway slightly back and forth as it made its way across the river. Sooner than she would have expected, they bumped against the south bank. The wagon rolled off and started bouncing along the road again as Samuel goaded the mules into going faster than they wanted to with a "Heeyah" and a "Get on up there, you ol' cuss."

Exhaustion spread through all her limbs, dulling her aches and pains. The jolt and sway of the wagon became almost soothing in its rhythms. Carrie was half in a daze when the wagon stopped. She felt a tap on the top of her head and the tarp pulled away.

Samuel looked at her from his seat. "This is your stop, Miss Celia. You got to run as fast as you can 'cross that field, straight through that line of trees and you'll be there faster than I will. I got to go 'round the far way on account of the wagon."

Carrie clambered over the side of the wagon. Her feet hit the road and her knees gave out from under her. She fell to the ground with pains shooting through her legs, stabbing into her body. She clutched at her ribs, gasping. Strong hands lifted her and gently leaned her against the wagon. She caught a hold of the sides, breathing deeply, trying desperately to push her pain aside. Slowly, she straightened herself up. Samuel stood beside her with his eyes cast down. The white men of the town would hang him from the highest branch for touching her even once, much less twice. He knew it. They both knew it.'

"Samuel, don't come to the oak. It won't be safe for you."

"I got to back you, Miss Celia."

"They won't listen to you. Go to the house. Get my father."

Samuel gave her a look with eyes full of pity. "You think he don't know already?"

Carrie's legs wobbled. "What are saying, Sam?"

"Your young Robert's the only one who raised an objection, but he can't help you 'cause he can't get out of bed on account of his head."

"Oh, dear God." Carrie bent over. A wave of nausea rose up through her. Everything she had done was wrong. Every action she took, every turn she made only made things worse. She pressed the heels of her hands hard against her eyes to keep the dark panic from unfolding. No. It was too late. It had already bloomed and what lay at its center was despair, oily and black, darker than night. It bubbled up into her throat in a soft, low moan. She felt a heavy hand on her shoulder shaking her.

"There ain't no time for regrets, Miss Celia. You need to go now. Run. Run fast and I'll be there as soon as I can get there."

Samuel was touching her again. For the third time. She looked into his face and drank in his courage. It had to be his courage that helped her stand upright, because she didn't have any more of her own. She pushed away from the wagon and Samuel's hand dropped from her shoulder. "God bless you, Samuel."

He tipped his hat to her. "He does, Miss Celia. He does. Now go."

Carrie turned and ran across the field, leaping the furrows of earth in graceless bounds. One footfall at a time, in a limping, loping stride, the earth pounding up through her feet, filling her body with hurt. It took her longer to reach the trees than she thought it would. Either the trees were farther away than they looked or she was running slower than she thought she was, but she still ran. She ran even as her breath rubbed her throat raw, the catch in her ribs became a stabbing lance, her feet went beyond pain and dulled into a throbbing mess of numbness.

She reached the trees and ran into them, not slowing down. Branches whipped at her face, briars pulled at her coat. She shrugged the jacket off and threw it from her and she ran, around trees, over logs, through bushes and brambles. Nothing slowed her pace until she burst into the clearing.

She skidded wildly over the grass and came to a stop.

Her breathing was hoarse and harsh, her chest heaving, but her muscles froze. The clearing was empty of men and horses. It was silent of the voices she expected to hear. The tree stood in the center of the small meadow with slanted sunlight shining through its boughs, its limbs swaying gently, leaves fluttering lightly. The only sound she heard was the cooing of doves, the rasp of her breath and the creak of the rope as Lilly's body swayed back and forth.

Carrie stumbled forward, legs moving in an awkward, wooden shuffle. She stared at the bare and bleeding feet swaying gently in front of her and she reached up to still them. They were cold. She cupped the feet in her hands. They were ice-cold. Carrie tried to say Lilly's name, but her tongue wouldn't move. Small choking sounds trickled up from her throat. She held the feet and rubbed them as if she could warm them again with her touch, but the cold from the feet seeped into her hands, crept up her arms. She pressed her face against them, held them to her cheek. Kissed them.

Cold pierced through her brain and stabbed down her spine. She tried to scream, but the sound was too big and stopped up her throat. Her blood turned to ice and froze inside her heart. Her head spun as the darkness bloomed. The world tilted, jittered and skipped. She swayed, stumbled and fell.

The earth pressed hard against her swollen cheek, the grass tickled, a small pebble scratched. The rope still creaked...and creaked...and creaked. She curled into a ball and pressed her hands tight over her ears, breathing in shallow, gasping breaths until her heart froze solid and stopped its beating.

The world unraveled.

CHAPTER TWENTY-FOUR

A warm hand touched her frozen shoulder.

"Carrie? Wake up, baby. Please wake up."

Someone was shaking her, patting at her cheek. It hurt. Everything hurt. Her arms. Her legs. Her feet. Her soul. Carrie rolled onto her back and opened her eyes. She looked up at Gillian who was bending over her. A swollen moon hung sullen in the night sky just over the top of Gillian's shoulder. Carrie lifted her head and looked around. She was in a wide meadow, the house visible just over the rise of the next hill. A badly hacked stump of an old tree sat in the middle of the field. Carrie sat up and something cold touched her chest. She wrapped her hands around the locket. The braid of hair inside it. It was Lilly's hair, the vibrant red faded and brittle with time.

The darkness in her mind shred into ribbons of light. Carrie started to cry. Gillian wrapped her arms around her and held her close as Carrie cried for Lilly and for Celia, for Robert and the Colonel, for all their dying dreams and for Samuel, who never had the chance to have any.

Gillian held and rocked her, whispered soft words into her hair. Her hands, solid and warm, pressed tight against Carrie's back. When the sobs subsided, she stroked Carrie's face and brushed the dirt out of her hair. She touched Carrie's bruised and swollen cheek.

"You're hurt."

Carrie took her hand away. Her cheek did still hurt, along with her ribs and her feet, but the pains were fading like the morning after a bad dream. She didn't want them to fade. They were all she had left. She looked at Gillian. Her hair wasn't red, and for the briefest moment, Carrie hated her for that. But it wasn't supposed to be red and this was Gillian who was beautiful to her in a way that made her heart ache. And her heart did ache.

"Gillian." Carrie said her name slowly, savoring the feel of it on her tongue. "Gillian." It was a sweet-tasting name. "What are you doing here?"

Gillian cocked her head to the side. "I might ask you the same."

"I…" Carrie stopped because she couldn't think of words to explain it. She wasn't sure she wanted to right now. "I asked first."

Gillian sat back on her heels and looked at her with slightly narrowed eyes. Then she nodded her head. "I went home and as I was sitting on the couch watching TV, it occurred to me that watching TV wasn't really what I wanted to be doing. So, I drove back here to ask if I could borrow a book."

"A book?"

"Right. A book. I thought, maybe, I could read it to you. You know, out loud. And maybe I could spend the night if we stayed up too late." Gillian reached out a hand toward Carrie's cheek, but she dropped it before her fingers touched. "When I got here, the front door was open and the lights were on in the library, but you weren't in the house. I walked all around outside the house calling for you. I came around the corner of the west wing and saw you running across the north field like a frightened jackrabbit. So, I ran after you." Gillian looked at the old tree stump and frowned. "I saw…well, I don't know what I saw. Shadows or something moving around the stump. For a second, I thought it was a tree. Then you ran into the clearing. I saw you reach up into the air and then you collapsed."

Carrie took Gillian's hand and placed it on her bruised cheek. It hurt less than it had a minute ago, but it still hurt. Carrie was grateful for that. "Do you love me, Gillian?"

Gillian slid her hand into Carrie's hair, leaned forward and kissed her mouth. "I think it's too soon to know for sure."

"Okay." Carrie nodded. "But do you think you could someday? Maybe someday soon?"

Gillian looked at Carrie with a quizzical half smile. "You're a very strange woman, Carrie Jane, but yes, I think I could."

"And you won't let anyone stop you or tell you it's wrong?"

Gillian thought about that. "Well, I won't be able to stop people from telling me it's wrong, but I won't let anyone keep me from loving those that I love."

"Will you tell me you love me when you're sure that you do?" Carrie's eyes welled. "Out loud, I mean? In words?"

Gillian smoothed Carrie's hair back and tucked the strands behind her ear. "I will look you straight in the eyes and say, 'Carrie, I love you.'"

Carrie tugged at her ear. "I didn't quite catch that last part. How are you going to say it?"

Gillian grinned at her. "I'll let you know when the time comes. You'll have to be satisfied with that." Gillian's smiled dimmed. "Carrie, I want you to tell me what's going on here. Why were you running across the field in the dark and why did you fall down like that and how did you get that bruise on your face?"

Carrie touched her cheek. The pain was still there. Her other pains had faded almost to nothing, but the bruise remained. She touched the locket. That remained too.

"It was a dream, I think. Maybe. It was about Celia, my grandmother, and a girl named Lilly that she loved."

Gillian raised an eyebrow. "Lilly, like the flowers on the ring and on the music box?"

"Yes. Lilly, as in short for Lillian."

"Lillian. What an odd coincidence."

"If it is one." Carrie looked closely at Gillian. "I'm not sure I believe in coincidences anymore. The poem, I think Celia wrote that for Lilly. And the letter, I think Lilly wrote that just before…" Carrie's throat closed and she choked on the words. She shook her head and wiped at her eyes. "Lilly died. I think Celia was never happy with Robert, with my grandfather, because she always loved Lilly. The trunk, in the attic, those were Lilly's things. The little grave marker in the cemetery is where Lilly is buried."

"What about the ring with the flowers? Was that Lilly's?"

"No. That was what Robert gave Celia on their engagement day, only it was a plain band then. I think Celia had the flowers etched on it after she and Robert married. So she wouldn't forget." Carrie touched the locket and pressed it against her skin. "She never did."

"That would explain a lot of things if it were not just a dream."

Carrie looked over at the old tree stump. A fresh wave of pain rolled over her heart. "I don't think it was just a dream. I don't know what it all was, but I do know there's still something that I need to put right."

"Then by all means you should go put it right."

Gillian stood and helped Carrie to her feet. A phantom twinge of pain shot through her heels and she looked down. Her legs were in blue jeans and her feet were in sneakers. She took a step and the twinge was less, then another and her feet felt fine. Gillian reached for Carrie, and Carrie slipped her hand in hers. They walked over the rise and up the hill to the house.

In the library, Carrie went straight to the old desk and opened the bottom left drawer. She pulled out Robert's letters and put them on the desktop. Underneath the letters was a Bible. Carrie took it out of the drawer. It was thick and heavy, its paper a brittle yellow, the binding cracked with age. She laid it on the desk and carefully opened it to the very back, to the pages of births and deaths written in so many different hands. She found the pages of marriages and the entry that said, Celia Covington Burgess, married to Robert Daniel Burgess. She took the fountain pen from the desk, dipped it into the inkwell and drew a line from Celia's name into the margin.

She wrote, *Lilly, beloved partner and companion.*

Epilogue

"There you go, Ms. Bowden. Just like you ordered it." The man wiped the dirt off his hands and onto his jeans. He took a small brush from his back pocket and dusted the dirt off the new grave marker. He stood straight and scratched an eyebrow with the back of his thumb. "None of us are quite sure why you want it, though. Even the old-timers aren't sure who this Lilly person was, but there are a couple of betting pools going. Care to give me a hint to help me out with my Christmas shopping?"

"Not on your life, Roger," Gillian answered before Carrie could say anything. "If you were a smart man, you'd have Evelyn's new washer on layaway already."

"I am a very smart man, Gills. I got the matching dryer, too." He tipped his cap at them. "Well, you ladies have a good day. Let us know if you want any of the other stones replaced. We're always happy to help out for a not-so-sad occasion. I'll see y'all this evening."

Carrie watched him get into his truck and drive it carefully down the path. He turned into the driveway and out of their sight. Gillian reached for her hand and their fingers twined.

Carrie stared at the new stone. "It's pretty. I think she would like it." She regretted that there was no last name on it. Carrie felt like she knew it well, once upon a time, but she couldn't remember what it was now no matter how hard she tried.

Gillian squeezed her fingers. "I'm glad they were able to get someone to do the flowers. It looks right like that."

"Yeah, it does." Carrie scuffed her toe in the grass. "The only thing missing is Celia."

"Any luck with the rezoning?"

"No, but I haven't given up yet." Carrie looked at Gillian who was looking at her with a mix of amusement and concern. She tugged on her hand. "Shall we go back to the house? They should be done with the floors by now and I think the caterers will be here soon."

Gillian grinned and gave an excited little hop. "I can't wait to try on my dress."

Carrie laughed. "I can't believe you actually want to wear it."

"You'll have to help me get in it, you know."

Carrie nodded. She knew. "I'll have to help you get out of it, too."

Gillian pulled her closer and slipped an arm around her waist. "I'm looking forward to that. Are you sure you don't want to wear the one in the attic?"

Carrie's smile dimmed as she looked at the new stone. A cold shiver shimmied up her spine. "Not in a hundred years," she said. "Not in a thousand."

Music and laughter drifted in through the library doors. The overhead lights were dim as Carrie stood in front of the mirror. The frame had been polished to a high shine, but the inside was still hazy and spotted. She looked at herself critically. The dress she had on was wrong in subtle ways, the neckline too low, the waist too high, her arms too bare and her gloves too long. Her hair was too short to do authentically, so she had only tied it back with a ribbon. There wasn't anyone to dress it properly, anyway. It was all wrong in a way that felt all right.

The party had been going on for hours. The parlor had been cleared and made into a ballroom where a quartet played, and Mr. Dumfries was busy spinning all the older ladies around the room in his rendition of a fox trot. He had brought a van full of people from the old folks home, people who remembered this house as it had been and tittered delightedly over how it was now. Amy-Lee and Chuck showed up together, and they hadn't exchanged a cross word all night.

Gillian danced with her, a Virginia reel, not that she knew what she was doing, but she did what Gillian told her to do and it worked out fine with no broken toes. They danced a slow waltz, got a few scowls and frowns but mostly winks and nods and an "*I knew it all along*" look from Jo and her girlfriend. A huge smile came from Mr. Dumfries. It was overwhelming. Gillian had been shocked to her core.

Mr. Dumfries, a little tipsy from the wine and the dancing, wrapped them both in a big bear hug. "I love you girls. Be happy."

Gillian burst into tears and went off with her father to have an overdue heart-to-heart. Carrie came in to the library for a moment of rest, but she didn't feel very restful. She stared into the mirror expectantly, looked over her shoulder at the empty room and then back into the mirror. Nothing happened. The locket around her neck glittered as her chest rose and fell, but the room reflected behind her remained as it was, dim and dull-colored. And empty. The mirror was only a mirror. She touched it lightly with the tips of her fingers, tracing the outline of her face, the glitter of gold between her breasts.

"I love you, Lilly." She spoke to the mirror, to the room, to the past and maybe to herself.

"I love you," she said again. Nothing changed, but her heart felt lighter. She smiled at her reflection, a quirky, mischievous smile. Carrie straightened the shoulders of her dress a little and walked over to the doors. She opened them with a flourish. The music and laughter poured through. Gillian waved at her from inside the parlor and beckoned as a new waltz started. A smile spread across her face as she turned off the overhead lights and shut the doors behind her.

Publications from
Bella Books, Inc.
The best in contemporary lesbian fiction

P.O. Box 10543, Tallahassee, FL 32302
Phone: 800-729-4992
www.bellabooks.com

WITHOUT WARNING: Book one in the Shaken series by KG MacGregor. *Without Warning* is the story of their courageous journey through adversity, and their promise of steadfast love.
ISBN: 978-1-59493-120-8
$13.95

THE CANDIDATE by Tracey Richardson. Presidential candidate Jane Kincaid had always expected the road to the White House would exact a high personal toll. She just never knew how high until forced to choose between her heart and her political destiny.
ISBN: 978-1-59493-133-8
$13.95

TALL IN THE SADDLE by Karin Kallmaker, Barbara Johnson, Therese Szymanski and Julia Watts. The playful quartet that penned the acclaimed *Once Upon A Dyke* and *Stake Through the Heart* are back and now turning to the Wild (and Very Hot) West to bring you another collection of erotically charged, action-packed tales.
ISBN: 978-1-59493-106-2
$15.95

IN THE NAME OF THE FATHER by Gerri Hill. In this highly anticipated sequel to *Hunter's Way*, Dallas Homicide Detectives Tori Hunter and Samantha Kennedy investigate the murder of a Catholic priest who is found naked and strangled to death.
ISBN: 978-1-59493-108-6
$13.95